"Fountain spins metaphorical gold . . . a fine stylist, he gets his message across without forsaking characterization and vivid descriptiveness. . . . Fountain should be read for his metaphors and similes. . . . This is why we turn to quality fiction, not for information or ideology, but for a revealing view of the human condition."   —*Miami Herald*

"Wonderful . . . lush, sophisticated, often very funny . . . Fountain is an original, a wry and earnest voice . . . and like Fountain himself, [his characters] are all observers passionately in love with observation. . . . Tragic, self-defeating missions—they're a dime a dozen these days. But true observers—lyrical, playful, alive to the hidden wit and subversion of disaster—well, they're rare."   —*Boston Herald*

"[Fountain's] really a bright light on character in extreme conditions, doing good or bad, that uncomfortable divide between right and wrong."   —Will Blythe, *The News and Observer*

"[A] wonderfully realized collection. . . . The best reason to read *Brief Encounters with Che Guevara* is for its spectacularly precise writing. Line by line, word by word, Fountain chooses just the right details, metaphors, similes, and descriptions, so that the reader says, Yes, that's right, that's how it is. Fountain's language reveals his ability to depict the subtlest of feeling and to appreciate detail that makes life rendered in sentences seem as life lived."   —*San Francisco Chronicle*

"In this first collection the author brings the virtuosity of Greene and le Carré to tales of foreign adventures."   —*Boston Globe*

"Superb debut story collection. . . . These stories display a fluency with what's going on in our world that's sure to elevate Fountain to the lofty realm of Douglas Unger (*Looking for War*), P. F. Kluge (*Biggest Elvis*), and the current titleholder, Bob Shacochis (*The Immaculate Invasion, Easy in the Islands*), with their literary antecedents being, most notably, Hunter S. Thompson, Evelyn Waugh, and Katherine Anne Porter. However he's attained his material, Fountain knows the Third World; he captures Myanmar, for example, with a precision that suggests firsthand knowledge. Ultimately, these are stories about people, mostly American innocents abroad, who want the world to be other than it is, who pay the price for that hopeless desire. One would love to think that anyone in contemporary government, especially the Foreign Service, would chance to happen upon this book. But those who really need to learn its lessons are the ones who will pick it up for their attraction to that name in its masterly title: Che Guevara, the romanticized philosopher-warrior who so many of us wish in the depths of our nights hadn't been the killer that he was." —Salon.com

"Finely crafted . . . irony abounds in Fountain's mini-theaters of the absurd, where Kafka would feel right at home." —*Texas Monthly*

"An impeccable debut collection; if Fountain can keep it up, he's an heir to Paul Theroux." —*Kirkus Reviews*

"While Fountain undoubtedly knows his Graham Greene and Paul Theroux, his excursions into foreign infernos have an innocence all their own. In between his nihilistic descriptions, a boyishness keeps peeking out, cracking one-liners and admiring the amazing if benighted scenery." —*Cleveland Plain Dealer*

"Short-story collections don't come much better than this. *Brief Encounters with Che Guevara* offers pointed prose, nimble revelation, some stunning description of flora and fauna, and a rueful generosity toward a string of well-intentioned bumblers who get in over their heads." —*Philadelphia Inquirer*

"[An] exhilarating first story collection." —*New York Newsday*

"Once in a blue moon you strike gold: a book by an unknown writer that takes you by the throat and keeps you glued to the chair until you are finished. Ben Fountain's *Brief Encounters with Che Guevara* is one of those books. Fountain cranks out stories about our own world as we have never seen it before. Fountain is one of those rare fiction writers who casts his imagination out into the Third World like a gill net and snags all kinds of strange fish that come swimming by. Fountain is a writer to watch; better, a writer to read." —*Buffalo News*

"Despite their various international settings and plots, the stories are not overweeningly ambitious and are rarely emotional or enlightening. If anything, they fall away from conclusions or epiphanies, which may be their most potent aspect." —*Library Journal*

"Ben Fountain writes the kind of stories that Robert Louis Stevenson, Joseph Conrad, and Graham Greene used to write: empty of self-obsession, not melodramatic, and full of complex adventure and off-balance humor. He tells them with cool detachment, his narrative voice never getting in the way of the horror and chaos. These stories have the texture and heft of novels: heavy, sensual atmosphere; the leisure of unhurried telling; and characters drawn in detail." —*San Diego Union-Tribune*

"Fountain is always able to compel the reader to turn the page and discover what happens next. The work of a talented writer pursuing compelling and complicated themes, *Brief Encounters with Che Guevara* is a considerable step in a career worth following."
—*Austin Chronicle*

"Ben Fountain writes deftly about fear and disorientation abroad in his first story collection." —*Outside* magazine

"Comparisons to Graham Greene, though, seem inapt—unlike Greene's characters, Fountain's protagonists represent no threat to anybody. The best stories in *Brief Encounters with Che Guevara* treat these strivers with both gentle irony and sympathy for their fumbling efforts to do the right thing. . . . The ambition and global outlook of Fountain's fiction marks a welcome addition to the literature produced in our state." —*Houston Chronicle*

"At times the stories become so intense that readers will want to stop for breath between them, even as they long to find out where Fountain will take them next. Fountain, editor of the *Southwest Review* and winner of an O. Henry Prize and a Pushcart Prize, is the perfect author to convert people who don't read short stories."
—*Arkansas Democrat-Gazette*

"[Fountain] is a gifted storyteller and his collection will blow your literary socks off." —*Tucson Citizen*

"Grand . . . darkly funny. . . . These stories feature people who are too brave for their own good. Fountain's subject matter is as important as anything you will see on the nightly news. He understands the political situation in a number of countries—including this one." —*Deseret Morning News*

"It is such an unexpected joy, in this age of introspection, to discover a new, resolute American writer with a global outlook. Ben Fountain's sensitive but unflinching stories take us golfing in Myanmar, birding in Colombia, and smuggling in Haiti to present a rogues' gallery of Quiet Americans in uniforms or business suits and a world turned toxic by their hunger for the deal, the dollar, and the (voodoo) dames."

—Jim Crace, author of *Genesis* and *Being Dead*

"I have never read such a geographically diverse collection of stories. Ben Fountain's confidence in taking on real world problems is matched by his reluctance to pontificate or judge. Faced with some of the most benighted landscapes on earth, Fountain's characters manage to remain morally pure and intensely likable — a combination even rarer in fiction than in life."

—Nell Freudenberger, author of *The Dissident* and *Lucky Girls*

"In Ben Fountain's world, sensitive ornithologists kidnapped by South American revolutionaries worry first and foremost about losing their teaching assistant slots, earnest aid workers fall hard for African diamond barons, and second-rate professional golfers find themselves at the reliably scary mercies of Southeast Asian politics. In a word, these stories are weird. In another word, they are brilliant. In each story, Fountain displays a creepy gift for giving form to the (in Fountainese) "peculiarly specific hell that life has a way of devising for us." There are eight specific hells in this exhilarating book — all filled with heavenly language and insight."

—Tom Bissell, author of *Chasing the Sea* and *God Lives in St. Petersburg*

"A necessary collection of short stories brimming with style and wit. From Haiti to Burma to Sierra Leone, Ben Fountain has the storytelling gifts to bring the entire world home to us and a moral compass set to true north."

—Gary Shteyngart, author of *Absurdistan*
and *The Russian Debutante's Handbook*

"In this brilliant first collection, Ben Fountain rides roughshod over territory originally staked out by Graham Green and Joseph Conrad. Wildly plotted, astutely observed, and beautifully rendered, these stories portray a motley band of foreign aid workers and ex-patriots left stranded by the receding tide of the American Empire. But best of all *Brief Encounters with Che Guevara* is riotously funny in the best way. Fountain's stories produce those truthful laughs that come from witnessing the blunt, hard follies of human nature."

—David Means, author of *Assorted Fire Events*
and *The Secret Goldfish*

Brief Encounters with Che Guevara

AN **ecco** BOOK

HARPER ◐ PERENNIAL

NEW YORK • LONDON • TORONTO • SYDNEY

Brief Encounters *with* Che Guevara

STORIES

BEN FOUNTAIN

HARPER ● PERENNIAL

Acknowledgment is made to the publications in which these stories first appeared: "Near-Extinct Birds of the Central Cordillera" in *Zoetrope: All-Story*; "Rêve Haitien" in *Harper's* magazine; "Asian Tiger" in *Zoetrope: All-Story*; "Bouki and the Cocaine" in *Zoetrope: All-Story*; "The Lion's Mouth" in *The Paris Review*; "Brief Encounters with Che Guevara" in *Shenandoah*; "Fantasy for Eleven Fingers" in *Southwest Review*.

A hardcover edition of this book was published in 2006 by Ecco, an imprint of HarperCollins Publishers.

P.S.™ is a trademark of HarperCollins Publishers.

HarperCollins books may be purchased for educational, business, or sales promotional use. For information please write: Special Markets Department, HarperCollins Publishers, 10 East 53rd Street, New York, NY 10022.

FIRST HARPER PERENNIAL EDITION PUBLISHED 2007.

Designed by Jennifer Ann Daddio
Title page photo by Andrew Gunners / Getty Images

The Library of Congress has catalogued the hardcover edition as follows:
Fountain, Ben.
  Brief encounters with Che Guevara : stories / Ben
Fountain.—1st ed.
    p. cm.
  Contents: Near-extinct birds of the central Cordillera—Rêve Haitien—The good ones are already taken—Asian tiger—Bouki and the cocaine—The lion's mouth—Brief encounters with Che Guevara—Fantasy for eleven fingers.
  ISBN: 978-0-06-088558-8 (acid-free paper)
  ISBN-10: 0-06-088558-0 (acid-free paper)
    I. Title.
PS3606.O844B75 2006
813'.6—dc22   2005049507

ISBN: 978-0-06-143842-4 (B&N edition)
ISBN-10: 0-06-143842-1 (B&N edition)

07 08 09 10 11 ❖/RRD 10 9 8 7 6 5 4 3 2 1

For Sharie

Contents

Brief Encounters with Che Guevara

Near-Extinct
Birds of the
Central Cordillera

I extended to the *comandante* the
opportunity to walk the floor
of the exchange with me, and he
seemed reasonably intrigued.
—RICHARD GRASSO, CHAIRMAN,
NEW YORK STOCK EXCHANGE,
BOGOTÁ, COLOMBIA, JUNE 26, 1999

No way Blair insisted to anyone who asked, no self-respecting
bunch of extortionist rebels would ever want to kidnap him. He was
the poorest of the poor, poorer even than the hardscrabble *campesinos*
pounding the mountains into dead slag heaps—John Blair, graduate assistant slave and aspiring Ph.D., whose idea of big money was
a twenty-dollar bill. In case of trouble he had letters of introduction
from Duke University, the von Humboldt Institute, and the Insti-
tuto Geográfica in Bogotá, whose director was known to have con-
tacts in the Movimiento Unido de Revolucionarios de Colombia,
the MURC, which controlled unconscionable swaths of the south-

west cordilleras. For three weeks Blair would hike through the remnant cloud forest, then go back to Duke and scratch together enough grants to spend the following year in the Huila district, where he would study the effects of habitat fragmentation on rare local species of parrotlets.

It could be done; it would be done; it had to be done. Even before he'd first published in a peer-reviewed journal—at age seventeen, in *Auk*, "Field Notes on the Breeding and Diet of the Tovi Parakeet"—Blair had known his was likely the last generation that would witness scores of these species in the wild, which fueled a core urgency in his boyhood passion—obsession, his bewildered parents would have said—for anything avian. Full speed ahead, and damn the politics; as it happened they grabbed him near Popayán, a brutally efficient bunch in jungle fatigues who rousted all the livestock and people off the bus. Blair hunched over, trying to blend in with the compact Indians, but a tall skinny gringo with a big backpack might as well have had a turban on his head.

"You," said the comandante in a cool voice, "you're coming with us."

Blair started to explain that he was a scholar, thus worthless in any monetary sense—he'd been counting on his formidable language skills to walk him through this very sort of situation—but one of the rebels was into his backpack now, spilling the notebooks and Zeiss-Jena binoculars into the road, then the Leica with the cannon-barrel 200x zoom. Blair's most valuable possessions, worth more than his car.

"He's a spy," announced the rebel.

"No, no," Blair politely corrected. *"Soy ornitólogo. Estudiante."*

"You're a spy," declared the comandante, poking Blair's notebooks with the tip of his gun. "In the name of the Secretariat I'm arresting you."

When Blair protested they hit him fairly hard in the stomach, and that was the moment he knew that his life had changed. They called him *la merca*, the merchandise, and for the next four days he slogged through the mountains eating cold *arepas* and sardines and taking endless taunts about firing squads, although he did, thanks to an eighty-mile-a-week running habit, hold up better than the oil executives and mining engineers the rebels were used to bringing in. The first day he simply put down his head and marched, enduring the hardship only because he had to, but as the column moved deeper into the mountains a sense of possibility began to assert itself, a signal too faint to call an idea. To the east the cordillera was scorched and spent, rubbled by decades of desperate agriculture. The few mingy scraps of surviving forest were eerily silent, but once they crossed the borders of the MURC-controlled zone the vegetation closed around them with the density of a cave. At night Blair registered a deep suck and gurgle, the engine of the forest's vast plumbing system; mornings they woke to the screams of piha birds, then the mixed-species flocks started in with their contrapuntal yammerings and groks and crees that made the forest sound like a construction site. In three days on the trail Blair reliably saw fourteen species on the CITES endangered list, as well as an exceedingly rare *Hapalopsittaca* perched in a fern the size of a minivan. He was amazed, and said as much to the young comandante, who eyed him for a moment in a thoughtful way.

"Yes," the rebel answered, "ecology is important to the Revolution. As a scholar"—he gave a faint, possibly ironic smile—"you can appreciate this," and he made a little speech about the environment, how the *firmeza revolucionario* had banned the multinational logging and mining "mafias" from all liberated zones.

The column reached base camp on the fourth day, trudging into the fortified MURC compound through a soiling rain. They hauled

Blair straight to the Office of Complaints and Claims, where he sat for two hours in a damp hallway staring at posters of Lenin and Che, wondering if the rebels planned to shoot him today. When at last they led him into the main office, Comandante Alberto's first words were:

"You don't look like a spy."

A number of Blair's possessions lay on the desk: binoculars, camera, maps and compass, the notebooks with their microscopic Blairian scribble. Seven or eight subcomandantes were seated along the wall, while Alberto, the *comandante máximo*, studied Blair with the calm of someone blowing smoke rings. He resembled a late-period Jerry Garcia in fatigues, a heavy man with steel-rim glasses, double bags under his eyes, and a dense brillo bush of graying hair.

"I'm not a spy," Blair answered in his wired, earnest way. "I'm an ornithologist. I study birds."

"However," Alberto continued, "if they wanted to send a spy, they wouldn't send somebody who looked like a spy. So the fact that you don't look like a spy makes me think you're a spy."

Blair considered. "And what if I did look like a spy?"

"Then I'd think you were a spy."

The subcomandantes hawed like drunks rolling around in the mud. So was it all a big joke, Blair wanted to know, or was his life really at stake? Or both, which meant he would probably go mad? "I'm an ornithologist," he said a little breathlessly, "I don't know how many ways I can tell you that, but it's true. I came to study the birds."

Alberto's jaws made a twisted, munching motion, like he was trying to eat his tongue. "That is for the Secretariat to decide, all cases of spying go to the Secretariat. And even if you are what you say you are, you will have to stay with us while your release is arranged."

"My 'release,' " Blair echoed bitterly. "You know kidnapping is a crime in most countries. Not to mention a violation of human rights."

"This isn't a kidnapping, this is a *retención* in the sociopolitical context of the war. We merely hold you until a fee is paid for your release."

"What's the difference?" Blair cried, and when Alberto wouldn't answer he came slightly unglued. "Listen," he said, "I don't have any money, I'm a student, okay? In fact I'm worse than worthless, I owe twenty thousand dollars in student loans. And if I'm not back at Duke in two weeks," he went on, his voice cracking with the wrongness and rage of it all, "they're going to give my teaching assistant slot to somebody else. So would you please just save us all a lot of trouble and let me go?"

They scanned his passport photo instead, then posted it on their Web site with a five-million-dollar ransom demand, which even the hardcore insurgents knew was a stretch. "Sixth Front gets the Exxon guys," Subcomandante Lauro muttered, "and we get the scientist with the holes in his boots." He became known around camp as "John Blair," always the two names together, *Johnblair*; but *John* got mangled in the depths of their throats so that it came out as the even more ridiculous *Joan*. In any case they couldn't seem to speak his name without smiling; thirty years of low-intensity warfare had given the rebels a heightened sense of the absurd, and Blair's presence was just too fertile to ignore, a gringo so thick, so monumentally oblivious that he'd walked into the middle of a war to study a bunch of birds.

"So tell me, Joan Blair," one of the subcomandantes might say, pointing to a manakin spouting trills and rubatos or the tanagers that streaked about like meteor showers, "what is the name of that species, please?"

He knew they were testing him, nominally probing for chinks in his cover, but more than that they were indulging in the fatuous running joke that seemed to follow him everywhere. Which he handled by coming right back at them, rattling off the Latin and English names and often as not the Spanish, along with genus and all the natural history he could muster before the rebel waved his arms and retreated. But an implacable sense of mission was rising in Blair. He eyed the cloud forest lapping the compound's walls and knew that something momentous was waiting for him.

"If you let me do my work," he told Comandante Alberto, "I'll prove to you I'm not a spy."

"Well," Alberto answered, "perhaps." A man of impressive silences and ponderous speech, who wore his gravitas like a pair of heavy boots, he had a habit of studying his hands while he spoke, slowly turning them back and forth while he declaimed Marxist rhetoric in the deep rolling voice of a river flowing past giant boulders. "First the Secretariat must review your case."

Always the Secretariat, MURC's great and powerful Oz. In the evenings the officers gathered on the steps of their quarters to listen to the radio and drink aromática tea. Blair gradually insinuated himself onto the bottom step, and after a couple of weeks of Radio Nacional newscasts he understood that Colombia was busily ripping itself to shreds. Gargantuan car bombs rocked the cities each week; judges and journalists were assassinated in droves; various gangs, militias, and guerrillas fought the Army and the cops, while the drug lords and revanchists sponsored paramilitary *autodefensa* squads that seemed to specialize in massacring unarmed peasants. In their own area Blair could hear shooting at night, and the distant thud of helicopters during the day. Rebel patrols brought in bodies and bloody *autodefensa* prisoners, while U.S. Air Force planes gridded the sky overhead, reconnoitering the local coca crop.

"Where," Blair asked during a commercial break, "is this Zone of Disarmament they're always talking about?"

"You're in it," Subcomandante Tono answered, to which Lauro added with a mocking snarl: *"You mean you couldn't tell?"*

Some evenings Alberto joined them, usually when one of his interviews was being broadcast; he'd settle onto the steps with a mug of tea and listen to himself lecturing the country on historical inevitability or the Bolivarian struggle or the venemous strategies of the World Bank. After one such broadcast he turned to Blair.

"So, Joan Blair, what do you think of our position?"

"Well," Blair said in his most formal Spanish, "of course I support these things as general principles—an end to poverty, an equitable education system, elections where everyone is free to participate." The officers murmured patronizingly and winked at each other; amid the strenuous effort of articulating himself, Blair barely took notice. "But frankly I think you're being far too timid in your approach. If you really want to change society you're going to have to start thinking in more radical terms."

The group endured several moments of intense silence, until Alberto cleared his throat. "For example, Joan Blair?"

"Well, you're always going on about agrarian reform, but face it, you're just evading the real issue. If you really want to solve the land problem you're going to have to get away from the cow. They're too big, they overload the whole ecosystem. What we have to do is forget the cow and switch over to a diet of mushrooms and insects."

"Mushrooms and insects?" Lauro cried. "You think I'm risking my ass out here for mushrooms and insects?"

But Alberto was laughing. "Shut up Lauro, he gave an honest answer. I like this guy, he doesn't bullshit around—with a hundred guys like him I could take Bogotá in about two weeks."

During the day Blair was free to wander around the compound; for all their talk of his being a spy, the rebels didn't seem to mind him watching their drills, though at night they put him in a storage hut and handcuffed him to a bare plank bed. His beard grew in a dull sienna color, and thanks to the high-starch, amoeba-enriched diet he began to drop weight from his already aerodynamic frame, a process helped along by the chronic giardia that felt like screws chewing through his gut. But these afflictions were mild compared to the awesome loneliness, and in the way of prisoners since the beginning of time he spent countless hours savoring the lost, now-clarified sweetness of ordinary days. The people in his life seemed so precious to him—*I love you all!* he wanted to tell them, his parents and siblings, the biology department secretaries, his affable though self-absorbed and deeply flawed professors. He missed books, and long weekend runs with his buddies; he missed women so badly that he wanted to gnaw his arm. To keep his mind from rotting in this gulag-style sump he asked for one of his blank notebooks back. Alberto agreed, more to see what the gringo would do than out of any humane impulse; within days Blair had extensive notes on countersinging among Scaled Fruiteaters and agnostic displays in Wood-Rails, along with a detailed gloss on Haffer's theory of speciation.

Alberto fell into the habit of chatting with Blair whenever they happened to cross paths in the compound. He would inquire about his research, admire the sketches in his notebook, and generally humor Blair along like a benevolent uncle. It came out that Alberto was a former banker, a *burgués* city kid with advanced degrees; he'd chucked it all twenty years ago to join the MURC. "It was false, that bourgeois life," he confided to Blair. "I was your typical social parasite." But no matter how warm or frank these personal exchanges, Blair couldn't shake the sense that Alberto was teasing him, holding back some essential part of himself.

"You know," Alberto said one day, "my grandmother was also very fond of the birds. She was a saint, this woman—when she walked into her garden and held out her arms, the birds would fly down from the trees to perch on her hands."

"Amazing," said Blair.

"Of course I was just a kid, I thought everyone's grandmother could do this trick. But it was because she truly loved them, I know that now. She said the reason we were put here on earth was to admire the beauty which God created."

"Ah."

Alberto's lips pooched out in a sad, nostalgic smile. "Beauty, you know, I think it's nice, but it's just for pleasure. I believe that men should apply their lives to useful things."

"Who says beauty and pleasure aren't useful?" Blair shot back, sensing that Alberto was messing with his mind again. "Isn't that what revolutions are ultimately about, beauty and pleasure for everyone?"

"Well," the comandante laughed, "maybe. I'll have to think about that."

So much depended on the rebels' goodwill—whether they lived by the ideals they so solemnly sloganized. Blair knew from the beginning that their honor was the best guarantee of his life, and with time he began to hope that he'd found a group of people with a passion, a sense of mission, that equaled his own. They seemed to be authentic *concientizados*, fiercely committed to the struggle; they were also, to Blair's initial and recurring confusion, loaded with cash. They had the latest in laptops and satellite phones, fancy uniforms, flashy SUVs, and a potent array of high-tech weapons—not to mention Walkmen and VCRs—all financed, according to the radio news, by ill-gotten gains from the cocaine trade.

"It's a tax!" the rebels screamed whenever a government spokesman started railing on the "narcoguerrillas" of the MURC. "We tax coca just like any other crop!" A tax that brought in six hundred million dollars a year, according to the radio, a sum that gave Blair a wifty, out-of-body feeling. On the other hand there were the literacy classes and crop-rotation seminars which the rebels sponsored for the local *campesinos,* who looked, however, just as scrawny here as in the nonliberated areas. So was it a revolution *a conciencia,* or just a beautifully fronted trafficking operation? Or something of both—Blair conceived that the ratio roughly mirrored his odds of coming out alive.

The notebook became his means of staying clued to reality, of ordering time which seemed to be standing still or maybe even running backward. The only thing the guerrillas would say about his ransom negotiations was that Ross Perot might pay for his release, which Blair guessed—though he could never be sure—was some kind of inside joke. A group of the younger rebels took to hazing him, *los punketos,* ruthless kids from the city *comunas* who jittered the safeties of their guns whenever Blair walked by, the rapid *click-click-click* cascading in his wake like the prelude to a piranha feed. Sometimes he woke at night totally disoriented, unsure of where or even who he was; other nights it seemed that he never really slept, sinking instead into an oozing, submetabolic trance that left him vague and cranky in the morning. One night he was drifting in just such a haze when a *punketo* burst into the shed, announcing through riffs of soft hysterical laughter that he was going to blow Blair's head off.

"I wouldn't recommend it," Blair said flatly. The kid was giggling and twitching around, literally vibrating—hopped up on *ba-suco* was Blair's guess. He'd probably been smoking for hours.

"Go fuck yourself," said the kid, jamming his gun into the notch behind Blair's left ear. "I'll kill you if I want."

"It'll be thrilling for a minute, just after you pull the trigger." Blair was winging it, making it up as he went along; the main thing, he sensed, was to keep talking. "Then it'll be like having a hangover the rest of your life."

"Shut up you cocksucker, just shut the fuck up. Shut up so I can kill you."

"But it's true. I know what I'm talking about."

"You? You never killed anybody in your life."

"Are you kidding? The United States is an extremely violent country. You must have seen the movies, right? *Rambo? Die Hard?* Where I come from makes this place look like a nursery school."

"You're a liar," the kid said, though less certainly.

"Why do you think I'm here? I have so much innocent blood on my hands, I was ready to kill myself I was so miserable. Then it came to me in a dream, the Virgin came to me in a dream," he amended, remembering how the rebels fell to their knees and groveled whenever the Spanish priest came to say mass, and the *punketos* were always the worst, weeping and slobbering on the padre's ring. " 'Follow the birds and you'll have peace,' that's what she told me in the dream. 'Follow the birds and your soul will know peace.' "

"Bullshit," the kid hissed, clanking his gun into the back of Blair's head.

"I'm here, aren't I? You think anyone other than a desperate man would come to this place? I came for the birds," Blair continued in a lulling voice, "the most incredible birds in the world live here, and they do the most amazing things. For instance, did you know that the bellbird's call can be heard several kilometers away?

In contrast to the puffbird's soft, heavenly whistle, which he sings just once a day, right before dawn. Then there's your famous oilbird who flies only at night, navigating with his headful of radar equipment . . ." And Blair talked on in the most hypnotic, droning voice imaginable, cataloging the wonders of Colombian avifauna until the *punketo* finally staggered off into the night, either entranced or stupefied, it was hard to say which. But when dawn broke and Blair was still alive a weird peacefulness came over him, along with the imperatives of an irresistible conviction. As soon as the cuffs were off he strode across the yard to Complaints and Claims, brushed past the guard, and walked into Alberto's office without so much as a knock. Alberto and Tono were spreading maps across the *jefe*'s big desk; when the door flew open they went for their holsters, a reflex that nearly got Blair's head blown off.

"Go on," he dared them, stepping up to the desk. "Either let me do my work, or shoot me."

There was a heat, a grim fury about Blair that most people would associate with madmen and martyrs. The comandantes eyed the gringo at a wary slant, and it occurred to Blair that, for the moment at least, they were actually taking him seriously.

"Well," said Alberto in a cautious voice, "what do you think, Tono?"

Tono blinked. "I think he's a good man, Comandante. And ecology is important to the Revolution."

"Yes," Alberto agreed, "ecology is important to the Revolution." He tried to smile, to inject some irony into the situation, but his mouth looked more like a fluttery open wound.

"Okay, Joan Blair, it will be as you wish. I give you permission to study your birds."

————

Blair was twelve when it first happened, on a trip to the zoo—he came on the aviary's teeming mosh pit of cockatoos and macaws and Purple-naped Lories, and it was as if an electric arc had shot through him. And he'd felt it every time since, this jolt, the precision stab in the heart whenever he saw *psittacidae*—he kept expecting it to stop but it never did, the impossibly vivid colors like some primal force that stoked the warm liquid center of his soul.

He'd known a miracle was in these mountains, he'd felt it in his bones. For five rainy days he tramped ever-widening circles out from the base, traversing ridges and saddles and moiling through valleys while the armed guard followed him every step of the way. Hernan, Blair guessed, was another of the comandantes' jokes, a slight mestizo youth with catlike looks and a manner as blank and flaky as cooled ashes. By now Blair knew a killer when he saw one; Hernan would as soon shoot a man as pinch off a hangnail, but as they trudged through the gelatinous drizzle together Blair began to get the subtext of the comandantes' choice.

"So how long have you been with the MURC?" he asked.

"Always," Hernan replied in a dreamy voice.

"Always?"

"That other boy," Hernan said in a gaseous hum, "that other little boy they called Hernan, he died. I have been a *revolucionario* my whole life."

Blair studied the youth, then went back to scanning the canopy. Alberto had returned the binoculars but not the camera.

"So I guess you've been in a lot of battles?"

"Yes," Hernan said in his humming voice, and he seemed to reflect. "Yes, many," he added.

"What's it like?" Blair asked rudely, but the kid's catatonia was driving him nuts.

"Oh, it's not so bad. Once the shooting starts everything's okay."

Which Blair took for a genuine answer; five days through some of the most beautiful, rugged country in the world, and the youth showed all the emotion of a turtle. It might not matter what you hit him with—a firefight, a bowl of stew, a trip to Disneyland, Hernan would confront each one with the same erased stare, but when Blair passed him the binoculars on the fifth day, pointing down a valley at a grove of wax palms and the birds wheeling around like loose sprockets, Hernan focused and gazed in silence for a time, then burst out laughing.

"They're so silly!" he cried.

And they were, Blair agreed, they were delightful, this remnant colony of Crimson-capped Parrots whose flock notes gave the impression of a successful cocktail party. The Crimson-capped Parrot, *Purpureicephalus feltisi,* aka Felty's Crimson: there'd been no sightings since 1973, when Tetzlaff et al. spotted a single breeding pair in Pichincha, Ecuador. CITES listed the species as critically endangered, though the more pessimistic literature assumed extinction. That first day Blair counted sixty-one birds, a gregarious, vocal group with flaming crowns and chunky emerald green bodies, their coverts flecked with blues and reds like glossy M&Ms. Sixty-one birds meant that God was good: not only was there a decent chance of saving the species, but if he lived and made it home with his data intact Blair was going to knock the ornithological world on its ass. Over the next few days he and Hernan built a blind of bunch grass and palm fronds, and Blair settled into the grind-it-out fieldwork mode. He charted the foraging grounds, the potential nest holes, the roosts and flyways across the valley; he identified the mated pairs within the flock and noted the species' strong affinity for wax palms—*Ceroxylon andiculum,* itself endangered—and surmised a trophic relationship. They talked constantly, with complex repertoires of sounds, chattering in an offhand, sociable way as they clambered about the canopy or sputtered from tree to tree, their short shallow wing beats batting the air with the noisy ruction of windup toys.

Within weeks Blair had a basic ethological profile. In exchange for the privilege of fieldwork he had to do camp chores every afternoon, but three years of graduate school had inured him to slave labor and subsistence living. In some ways this was better than school: he got room and board, worked with minimal interruptions, and was furnished a local guide-bodyguard free of charge. Hernan proved adept at tracking the birds on their feeding rounds, leading Blair through the forest as they listened for debris tumbling through the leaves, then the fuddles and coos that meant Crimsons were overhead. At the blind he usually lay back on the grass and dozed, rousing from time to time to say amazing things about himself.

"I used to have a girlfriend," he once confessed to Blair in a sleepy voice. "She wouldn't let me kiss her, but she'd bite me on the ear."

In the same vacant drone he told all manner of terrible stories: battles he'd fought, prisoners he'd executed, patrols where his column had come across peasants burned to death or babies nailed to planks. The stories were so patently nightmarish that Blair wondered if Hernan was talking in his sleep, channeling dreams that rose like swamp gas out of his wounded subconscious. Hernan's whole family had been killed when he was twelve, their village wiped out by *autodefensas* for electing a former insurgent as mayor.

"Sometimes I see them," Hernan murmured in a half-doze, one arm thrown over his eyes, feet crossed at the ankles. "Sometimes I'm lying on my cot at night, and I look up and all my family's standing there. And it's like I'm lying in a coffin, you know? My family's alive and I'm the one who's dead, and they've come to my funeral to tell me good-bye."

Blair was so horrified that he had to write it all down, the baroque, spiraling cycles of murder and revenge mixed with his notes on allopreening among the mated Crimsons and the courtship dances of the unattached males, the way they minced around like fops doing a French quadrille. *Sickness,* he wrote in the margin of his notes, *there's a sickness in the world,* along with *parrots the most intelligent and beautiful of birds, also the most threatened—a clue to the nature of things (?)* He wrote it all because it all seemed bound together in some screamingly obvious way that he couldn't quite get. Tramping through the woods he and Hernan kept coming across giant cocaine labs, the thuggish workers warning them off with drawn machetes. The coca fields around the camp kept expanding; radio reports of the fledgling peace talks took on a spectral air, with the MURC insisting on prenegotiation of themes that might be substantively negotiated at a later time. Every few weeks Hernan would go off on a mission, and after three or four days he'd drag in with the other survivors, skinnier, with corpselike shadows under his eyes but otherwise the same, and the next dawn he and Blair would be at the blind, watching the birds greet the day with gurgling chatter. In March the males began to hold territory, and when the females developed brood patches Hernan offered to climb the trees for a look at the nests, a job they both knew was beyond Blair. After a year in the mountains he was a rashy stick-figure of his former self, prone to fevers and random dizzy spells that made his head feel like a vigorously shaken snow globe. Sometimes he coughed so hard that his nose bled; his bowels were papier-mâché, his gums ached, and the sturdiest thing about him seemed to be his beard, which looked positively rabbinical.

"Go for it," Blair answered, and in a flash Hernan was seventy feet up the tree, relaying information while Blair wrote. Clutch, two; eggs, white; nest, about the size of a Guambiano water jar. Hernan had left his rifle propped against a nearby tree; Blair eyed it while allowing an escape fantasy to float through his head, a mini-vacation from the knowledge that if he ran they'd catch him before the day was out. Still, the rifle raised a nagging question: how could he leave, now, in the middle of his research, even if he got the chance? But not to leave might be a slow form of suicide. Sooner or later something would get him, either sickness, a swacked-out *punketo*, or an *autodefensa* raid, or maybe the Secretariat would decide to make a point at his expense. The hard line had lately crept back into the MURC's rhetoric, which Blair guessed was part posturing for the peace talks, part exasperation at the trend of the times. The Soviet Union had imploded, the Berlin Wall was gravel, and the Cuban adventure was on life support, and yet the MURC insisted it would soldier on.

"Some say the end of history has come," Alberto intoned to the journalists. "We can all have different interpretations about what's happened in the world during these very complex years, but the fact of the matter is that most things haven't changed. Hunger, injustice, poverty, all of the issues which led the guerrilla of the MURC to take up arms, they are all still with us."

True, thought Blair. He wanted to believe in the Revolution, in its alleged devotion to reason and justice, but the Revolution wouldn't return his camera for even one day. All of his research would be deemed hypothetical unless supported by a photo or specimen. No photo, no dissertation, and he'd sooner burn every page of his notes than take a specimen.

"I could steal the camera back for you," Hernan offered. "I think I know where they're keeping your stuff."

"What would happen if they caught us?"

Hernan reflected. "To me, nothing—I can just disappear. To you?" He shrugged. "They'd probably cut off your fingers and send them to your family."

Blair considered for a second, then shook his head. Not yet. He wasn't that desperate yet.

When the chicks hatched Hernan went up again, checking out the nests while the parents and auxiliaries seethed around his head like belligerent box kites. One egg would hatch, then the second a few days later; Blair knew the second hatchlings were insurance, doomed to die unless their older siblings died first, and he sketched out a program for taking the second chicks and raising them in captivity.

The Crimsons had saved him, in a way; maybe he'd save them in turn, but he had to know everything about them first. "There's something wrong with us," he told Hernan one day. He was watching the nest holes for the soon-to-fledge chicks and thinking about the news, the latest massacres and estimates of coca acreage. The U.S. had pledged Colombia $1.6 billion in aid—advisers, weapons, helicopters, the whole bit—which made Blair wonder if his countrymen had lost their minds. There was a fire raging in Colombia, and the U.S. planned to hose it down with gasoline.

"Who?" Hernan answered, cracking open one eye. "Something wrong with who?"

"With us. People. The human race."

Hernan lunked up on one elbow and looked around, then subsided to the grass and closed his eyes. "People are devils," he said sleepily. "The only *persona decente* who ever lived was Jesus Christ. And the Virgin. And my mother," he added.

"Tell me this, Hernan—would you shoot me if they told you to?"

"Anh." Hernan didn't bother to open his eyes. "They'd never ask me."

"They wouldn't?" Blair felt an unfamiliar surge of hope.

"Of course not. They always put the new guys on the firing squads, to toughen them up. Guys like me they never bug for stuff like that."

Over the next few days seven chicks came wobbling out of the nests, and Blair set himself the task of tracking the flock as it educated the youngsters. Back in the shed he had notebooks and loose papers crammed with data, along with feathers, eggshell fragments, and stool samples, also a large collection of seeds with beak-shaped chunks scooped out of them. Occasionally Alberto would trek up the mountain to the blind, checking on Blair and the latest developments with "the children," as he'd taken to calling the parrots. He seemed relaxed and jolly during these visits, though his essential caginess remained; he would smile and murmur noncommittally when Blair lobbied to start his captive-breeding program.

"Get with it, Alberto," Blair pressed one day. "It would be a huge public relations coup for you guys if the MURC rescued an endangered species. I could help you across the board with that, like as an environmental consultant. You know we're really on the same side."

Alberto started to speak, then broke off laughing as he studied the wild gringo in front of him. Blair was dressed in scruffy jungle fatigues—his civilian clothes had worn out long ago—and with his gaunt, weathered face and feral beard he looked as hardened as any of the guerrillas. New recruits to the camp generally assumed that he was a zealot from the mythical suicide squad.

"Joan Blair, you remind me of a man I once knew. A man of convictions, a real hero for the cause. Of course he died in Bolivia many years ago."

"Doing what?"

"Fighting for the Revolution, of course!"

Blair winced, then shook off a spasm of dread. "So what about my captive-breeding program?"

Alberto chuckled and patted Blair's shoulder. "Patience, Joan Blair, you must learn patience. The Revolution is a lot more complicated than you think."

"They're negotiating you," Hernan said a few weeks later. "Some big shot's supposed to be coming soon."

"Bullshit," Blair said. The camp was a simmering cesspool of rumors, but nothing ever happened.

"It's true, Joan Blair, I think you're going home."

"Maybe I'll stay," Blair said, testing the idea on himself. "There isn't an ornithologist in the world who's doing the work I'm doing here."

"No, Joan, I think you should go. You can come back after we've won the war."

"What, when I'm eighty?" Blair chewed a blade of grass and reflected for a moment. "I still don't have my photo. I'm not going anywhere until I get that."

The rumors persisted, gradually branched into elaborate subrumors. Just to be safe Blair got all his data in order, but it was still a shock to see the helicopters come squalling out of the sky one day, cutting across the slopes at a sassy angle and heading for camp. Blair and Hernan were walking back for afternoon chores, and if there was ever any doubt about Blair's intentions his legs resolved it for him, carrying him down the trail at a dead sprint. At camp the helicopters were parked on the soccer field, two U.S.-surplus Hueys with the sky blue Peace Commission seal on their hulls. *Campesinos* and guerrillas were streaming into the compound; Blair had to scrum his way through the crowd to get a view of Complaints and Claims, where some kind of official moment was taking place on the steps. Several distinct factions were grouped around a microphone: Alberto and the subcomandantes were on one side, along with some senior comandantes whom Blair didn't recognize, while to their right stood a sleek delegation of civilians, Colombians with careful haircuts and tasteful gold chains. Blair spotted the American delegation at once—their smooth, milky skin was the giveaway, along with their khaki soft-adventure wear and identical expressions of informed concern. Everyone was raked toward the microphone, where a Colombian was saying something about the stalled peace talks.

Why didn't you tell me? Blair almost screamed. A Tele-Nacional crew was filming the ceremony; photographers scuttled around like dogs chasing table scraps. *What about me?* he wanted to shriek, *say something about me!* He tried in vain to make eye contact with the Americans, who'd arranged themselves into distinct pairs. The two middle-aged men stood farthest from the action, robust, toned, country-club types; the other two Americans stood close to the center, a tall, older gentleman with a shrinking hairline and sharp Adam's apple, then the sturdy young woman who was glued to his side, short of stature, hyperalert, firecracker cute. *The international community's show of support,* said the speaker. *A message of hope from U.S. financial circles.* Blair felt one of his dizzy spells coming on, his eyes clouding over in a spangly haze. He slumped and let the crowd hold him up; Hernan had vanished somewhere along the trail. When the delegation began to move inside, Blair watched them disappearing as if in a dream, then roused himself at the last moment.

"Hey!" he yelped in English, "I'm American! Hey you guys, I'm an American!"

Only the woman seemed to hear, flashing a quick, startled look over her shoulder, then continuing inside. Blair started to follow but a guard blocked his way.

"*Alto*, Joan Blair. Only the big shots go in there."

"Who are those people?" Blair asked, craning for a look through the door. Which abruptly shut.

"Well," the guard said, assuming the manner of someone schooling a particularly dense child, "there is Señor Rocamora, the Peace Commissioner, and there is Señor Gonzalo, the Finance Minister—"

"But the Americans, who are they?"

"How the hell should I know? *Peces gordos*, I guess."

Blair didn't dare leave, not for a second, though he could feel the sun baking all the juices out of him. The crowd in the compound absently shuffled about, disappointed without really knowing why. *Fritanguera* ladies set up their grills and started frying dough; a King Vulture scraped lazy circles in the sky. After a while the American woman stepped outside and walked down the gallery to speak to the reporters. Blair brushed past the guard and was up in a second, intercepting the woman as she walked back to the door. Out of instinct she started to dodge him; he looked like a wild man with his castaway's beard and grimy jungle fatigues, but his blue eyes beaming through the wreckage brought her up short.

"Oh! You must be John Blair!"

He could have wept with gratitude. "Yes, I'm John Blair! You know who I am!"

"Of course, State briefed us on your situation. I'm Kara Coleman, with the—" A scissoring blast of syllables shot off her lips. "Wow," she continued, eyeing him up and down, "you look like"—*hell*, she barely avoided saying—"you've been here awhile."

"Fifteen months and six days," Blair instantly replied. "You're with the State Department?"

"No, I'm with the—" She made that scissoring sound again. "I'm Thomas Spasso's assistant, he's leading our group. Thomas *Spasso*," she repeated in a firm voice, and Blair realized that he was supposed to know the name. "Chairman of the Nisex," she continued, almost irritated, but still Blair didn't have a clue. "The *Nisex*," she said as if speaking to a dunce, "the New York *Stock* Exchange."

Blair was confused, but quite as capable as anyone of rational-izing his confusion—he knew that fifteen months in the Andes might have turned his American frame of reference to mush. So maybe it wasn't so strange that the king of Wall Street would turn up here, in the jungly heart of MURC territory. Blair's impression of the stock market, admittedly vague, was of a quasi-governmental insti-tution anyway.

"Right," he said, straining to put it all together. The unfamiliar English felt like paste on his tongue. "Sure, I understand. But who, I mean, what, uh—why exactly are you here?"

"We're here to deliver a message from the financial community of its support for the current peace initiative. Foreign investment could do so much for this country, we felt the MURC might be more flexible if they knew the opportunities we could offer them. And Mr. Spasso has a special interest in Colombia. You know he's close personal friends with Ambassador Moreno."

Blair shut his eyes and wondered if he'd lost his mind. "You mean," he said in a shattered whisper, "this doesn't have anything to do with me?"

"Well, no, we came chiefly with the peace process in mind. I'm sorry"—she realized the effect she was having—"I'm truly sorry, I can see how insensitive that must seem to you right now."

Blair was sagging; all of a sudden he felt very, very tired. "Isn't there something you can do for me?" he softly wailed. "Anything?"

Kara touched his arm and gave him a mournful look; she wasn't heartless, Blair could see, but rather the kind of person who might cry at movies, or toss bites of her bagel to stray dogs.

"Mr. Spasso might have some ideas," she said. "Come inside, I'll try to get you a few minutes with him."

She led Blair through the door, down a short hallway, and into the big concrete room where the comandantes mediated peasant disputes every Tuesday and Thursday. The delegates were sitting in the center of the room, their chairs drawn in a circle as if for a group therapy session. Thomas Spasso was speaking through an interpreter, and in seconds Blair formed an impression of the chairman as a ticky, nervous guy, the kind of intractable motormouth who said the exact same thing no matter where he was. "Peace will bring you huge benefits from global investors," the chairman told the comandantes. "The capital markets are lining up for you, they want to be your partner in making Colombia an integral part of the Americas' economic bloc." He rattled on about markets and foreign investment, the importance of strong ratings from Moody's bond-risk service. The rebels sat there in their combat fatigues and Castro-style hats smiling and nodding at the chairman's words, but Blair saw they could barely hold their laughter in. They didn't dare look at each other—one glance, and they'd lose it—but the supreme challenge came when the chairman invited them to visit Wall Street. "I personally extend to each and every one of you an invitation to walk the floor of the exchange with me," Spasso said, his voice thrumming with heartfelt vibrato. He clearly thought he was offering them the thrill of their lives, but Blair could picture the rebels howling on the steps tonight—*Oooo, that we should have this big honor, to walk the floor of the bourgeois exchange with him!* Even now the comandantes' eyes were bugging out, quivering with the strain of holding it in, and it was only by virtue of supreme discipline that they didn't fall out of their chairs laughing.

Spasso, ingratiating yet oblivious, talked on. "He's very passionate," Kara whispered to Blair, who was thinking how certain systems functioned best when they denied the existence of adverse realities. After a while the Peace Commissioner got to say some words, then the Finance Minister, and then Alberto, who limited his comments to an acknowledgment of the usefulness of market mechanisms, "so long as social justice for the masses is achieved." Then some aides circulated a proposed joint statement, and the meeting dissolved into eddies and swirls as each group reviewed the language.

Kara waited until Spasso stood to stretch his legs. "Mr. Spasso," she called, hustling Blair over, "this is John Blair."

Spasso turned, saw Blair, and seemed to lose his power of speech.

"The hostage," Kara said helpfully, "he's in your briefing kit. The guy from Duke."

"Oh yes, yes of course, the gentleman from Duke. How are you, so very nice to see you."

Nice to see you? Fifteen months in hell and *nice to see you?* For Blair it was like a curtain coming down.

"Sir, John and I were discussing his situation, and while he understands the limited scope of our visit, he was wondering if we could do anything with regard to, ah, facilitating his return home. At some possible future point."

"Well," Spasso said, "as you know we're here in the spirit of a private sector exchange. Though your name did come up at the embassy this morning." He paused as one of the other Americans approached, a fellow with silver blond hair and a keen, confident look.

"Working the final numbers," he told Spasso, waving a legal pad at the chairman, "then we're good to go. Thanks so much for setting this up, Tom."

Spasso nodded and glanced at his watch as the American moved off. People were milling about the big room, talking and bumping shoulders.

"Uhhh—"

"John Blair," Kara prompted.

"Mr. Blair, absolutely. I'm afraid your situation is rather problematic. There are laws"—he looked to Kara for confirmation—"apparently there are laws here in Colombia which prohibit private citizens from engaging in kidnap negotiations. Am I correct on that, Kara?"

"Unfortunately yes, sir."

" 'Aiding and abetting a kidnap negotiation,' I believe those are the words. We're to avoid any action that could be construed as aiding and abetting a kidnap negotiation, those are our strict instructions from the State Department. Which I know must seem rather harsh to you—"

Blair had groaned.

"—but I'm sure you can appreciate the bind this puts us in. Much as we'd like to help you, our hands are tied."

Blair wanted to hit this fool, or at least shake him hard enough that some air got to his brain. "Look," he said in his most determined voice, "they keep threatening to kill me, they say I'm a spy. They could take me out and shoot me as soon as you leave."

"I'm certainly aware of the seriousness of your situation." *Señor Spasso,* someone called from across the room. "Believe me, I am most sympathetic. But any goodwill we foster here today will redound to your future benefit, I'm sure."

Señor Spasso, we're ready.

"Be right there! People are working for your release, I can assure you. Top people, extremely capable people. So hang in there, and God bless."

Spasso joined the general push of people toward the door. "I am so, so sorry," Kara said. She reached into her satchel and pulled out a handful of Power Bars. "Here, take these," she said, thrusting them at Blair. "I'll talk to you before we leave."

Kara melted into the crowd. Blair allowed the flow to carry him out to the gallery, where he leaned against a column and closed his eyes. He could not comprehend what was happening to him, but it had something to do with the casual cruelty of people who'd never missed a meal or had a gun stuck to their heads. Out in the yard the press was forming ranks for another photo op. Spasso and company gathered around the microphone; while they made the same speeches as two hours ago Blair ate his Power Bars and discreetly wept, though after a few minutes he pulled himself together and resolved to make one last plea for help. He scanned the yard and gallery for Kara, then entered the building, where he found her in the big concrete room. She and the other two Americans were sitting with Alberto and one of the senior comandantes. They were speaking in quiet, reasoned tones, their chairs so close that their knees almost touched. Blair was struck by their visible ease with each other, the intimate air which enclosed the little group.

"Oh, John!" Kara cried. "Maybe John can help," she said to the others, waving Blair over. "John, we're having some trouble with the language here, maybe you can help us out."

The blond American stood with his legal pad. "All those years of high school Spanish," he chuckled, "and I don't remember a thing."

"John's American," said Kara. "He's in graduate school at Duke."

"Super!" The man pulled Blair close. "Listen, we're trying to finalize the numbers here and we can't seem to get on the same page. I'm offering thirty-five hundred per fifty unit, fifty thousand board feet in other words. Think you could put that into Spanish for me?"

Blair eyed the scribble of numbers on the pad. "Thirty-five hundred . . ."

"Dollars, U.S."

Blair kept scanning the pad, the numbers teasing him; it seemed important to make sense of the mess. "Board feet . . ."

"It's the standard unit in the industry. One square foot by one inch thick."

"Of board," Blair said. "You're talking about lumber."

"You bet."

"Who are you?"

The man stuck out his hand. "Rick Hunley, Weyerhauser precious woods division."

"You're going to log this area?"

"That's the plan, if we can close this thing."

Blair turned to Alberto, who gave him a squirrelly, sullen look. The honks and woofs of the press conference drifted through the door, and that, Blair realized, was simply a show, a soufflé of airy smiles and empty words. Whereas the deal was happening right here in this room.

"Alberto," he cried in bitter, lancing Spanish, "how could you? How could you even think of doing such a thing?"

Alberto shrugged, then turned away as if he smelled something bad. "Running an army is expensive, Joan Blair. The Revolution doesn't survive on air, you know."

"Christ, look at all the coca out there, how much more money could you possibly need? You're going to wipe out the parrots if you log up here."

"We have to save the country, Joan Blair."

"What, so you can turn it over to these guys?"

"Enough."

"You think there'll be anything left to save when they're done with it?"

"Enough, Joan Blair, I mean it." Alberto flicked his hand as if shooing a fly. "Get out of here, I'm tired of listening to you. Beat it. Where are those son of a whore guards—"

But Blair had rounded on Hunley. "There's a parrot up here," he said in very fast English, "an extremely rare species, these are probably the last birds of their kind in the world. If you guys log up here it's a pretty sure thing you're going to wipe them out."

"Whoa, that's news to me." Hunley and his partner exchanged dire looks; Hunley turned to Alberto. "Comandante, I can tell you right now if we get bogged down in any environmental issues then we're outta here. We don't have time to mess around with that stuff."

"Is not a problem," Alberto said, emitting the gruff sort of English that a bear might speak.

"Well according to your interpreter it is."

"Not a problem, no, for sure, no bird problems here. Forget the birds."

"I won't stand for this," Blair stated flatly. "I don't accept it. You people can't do this."

Alberto's lips cramped inward, holding back a smile, though Blair could see it surface in his eyes well enough, the near-lethal mix of pity and contempt. "Okay, Joan Blair, why don't you stop us," he mocked, but something skittish and shamed began to leak into his eyes, a gray, mizzly vapor that snuffed out all the light. Alberto tried to stare him down but couldn't, and at the moment the comandante turned away, Blair knew: the Revolution had reached that classic mature stage where it existed only for its own sake.

"Okay," Alberto said, reaching for Hunley's legal pad, "I think we can make the deal." He circled a number on the pad and handed it back to Hunley. "For that, okay? For this price we make the deal, but one more thing. You have to take this guy with you."

"No way," Blair said, "forget it. You're not getting rid of me."

"Yes, yes, you are going. We're tired of feeding you, Joan, you have to go home now."

"Go to hell Alberto, I'm staying right here."

Alberto paused, then turned to the Americans. "This man," he said stiffly, pointing to Blair, "is a spy. As a gesture of goodwill, for the peace process, I am giving him to you, you may please take him home. And if you don't take him home, today, now, he will be shot. Because that is what we do to spies."

Kara gasped, but the worldly lumber executives just laughed. "Well, son," Hunley said, turning to Blair, "I guess that means you're coming with us."

Blair wouldn't look at them, Spasso, Kara, the others, he wouldn't acknowledge the smiling people in the seats around him. He kept his face turned toward the helicopter's open door, watching the dust explode as the engines powered up, the crowd waving through the storm of rotor wash. The chopper throbbed, shuddered, shyly wicked off the ground, and as it rose Blair glimpsed Hernan in the crowd, the kid dancing like a boxer as he waved good-bye. In the chaos of loading, he'd slipped through the muddled security cordon and shoved a plastic capsule into Blair's hand—film, Blair had known without looking at it, a 35mm cartridge. The film was tucked into Blair's pants pocket now, while he clutched to his lap the backpack with its bundles of data and artifacts: the first, and very likely the last, comprehensive study of the Crimson-capped Parrot. He hung on as the Huey accelerated, trapdooring his stomach into empty space as it slammed into a sheer vertical climb. The world fell away like a ball dropped overboard, the torque and coil of the jungle slopes diminishing to finely pebbled sweeps of green. The craft pivoted as it climbed, nose swinging to the east, the Crimsons' valley with its fragile matchstick palms sliding past the door like a sealed tableau—from this height Blair could see how easy it would be, nothing at all to rub out the faint cilia of trees. Easy, the sheltering birds just so much incidental dust.

How does it feel? Spasso was shouting in his ear. *How does it feel to be free?* They were rising, rising, they might never stop—Blair closed his eyes and let his head roll back, surrendering to the awful weightlessness. Like dying, he wanted to tell them, like death, and how grieved and utterly lost you'd feel as everything precious faded out. That ultimate grief which everyone saves for the end, Blair was spending it, burning through all his reserves as the helicopter bore him away.

Rêve Haitien

In the evenings, after he finished his rounds, Mason would often carry his chessboard down to the Champ de Mars and wait for a match on one of the concrete benches. As a gesture of solidarity he lived in Pacot, the scruffy middle-class neighborhood in the heart of Port-au-Prince, while most of his fellow O.A.S. observers had taken houses in the fashionable suburb of Pétionville. Out of sympathy for the people Mason insisted on Pacot, but as it turned out he grew to like the place, the jungly yards and wild creep of urban undergrowth, the crumbling gingerbread houses and cobbled streets. And it had strategic position as well, which was important to Mason, who took his job as an observer seriously. From his house he could track the nightly gunfire, its volume and heft, the level of intent—whether it was a drizzle meant mainly for suggestive effect or something heavier, a message of a more direct nature. In the mornings he always knew where to look for bodies. And when war had erupted between two army gangs he'd been the first observer to know, lying in bed while what sounded like the long-rumored invasion raged nearby. Most of his colleagues had been clueless until the morning after, when they met the roadblocks on their way to work.

On Thursdays he went to the Oloffson to hear the band, and on weekends he toured the hotel bars and casinos in Pétionville. Otherwise, unless it had been such a grim day that he could only stare at his kitchen wall and drink beer, he would get his chess set and walk down to the park, past the weary peddler women chanting house-to-house, past the packs of rachitic, turd-colored dogs, past the crazy man who squatted by the Church of the Sacred Heart sweeping handfuls of dirt across his chest. There in the park, which resembled a bombed-out inner city lot, he would pick out a bench with a view of the palace and arrange his pieces, and within minutes a crowd of mouthy street kids would be watching him play that day's challengers. Mason rarely won; that was the whole point. With the overthrow and exile of their cherished president, the methodical hell of the army regime, and now the embargo that threatened to crush them all, he believed that the popular ego needed a boost. It did them good to see a Haitian whip a *blan* at chess; it was a reason to laugh, to be proud at his expense, and there were evenings when he looked on these thrown games as the most constructive thing he'd done all day.

As his Creole improved he came to understand that the street kids' jibes weren't all that friendly. Yet he persisted; Haitians needed something to keep them going, and these games allowed him to keep a covert eye on the palace, the evening routine of the military thugs who were running the country—the de facto government, as the diplomats and news reports insisted on saying, the de factos basically meaning anybody with a gun. Word got around about his evening games and the *zazous* started bringing chess sets for him to buy, the handcrafted pieces often worked in Haitian themes: the voodoo gods, say, or LeClerc versus Toussaint, or Baby Doc as the king and Michèle the queen and notorious Macoutes in supporting roles. Sometimes during these games the crowd grew so raucous that Mason feared drawing fire from the palace guards. And, regardless of the game, he always left in time to get home by dark. Not even a *blan* was safe on the streets after dark.

Late one afternoon he'd barely set up his board when a scrap of skin and bones came running toward him. *Blan!* the boy shouted, grinning wickedly, *veni gon match pou ou!* Mason packed up his set and followed the boy to a secluded corner of the park, a patch of trees and scrub screening it from the palace. There on the bench sat a mulatto, a young Haitian with bronze skin, an impressive hawk nose, and a black mass of hair that grazed his shoulders. His T-shirt and jeans were basic street, but the cracked white loafers seemed to hint at old affluence, also an attitude, a sexually purposed life that had been abandoned some time ago. He simply pointed to the spot where Mason should sit, and they started playing.

The mulatto took the first game in seven moves. Mason realized that with this one he was allowed to try; the next game lasted eleven moves. "You're very good," Mason said in French, but the mulatto merely gave a paranoiac twitch and reset his pieces. In the next game Mason focused all his mental powers, but the mulatto had a way of pinning you down with pawns and bishops, then wheeling his knights through the mush of your defense. This game went to thirteen moves before Mason admitted he was beaten. The mulatto sat back, eyed him a withering moment, then said in English:

"All of these nights you have been trying to lose."

Mason shrugged, then began resetting the pieces.

"I didn't think it was possible for anyone to be so stupid, even a *blan*," said the mulatto. "You are mocking us."

"No, that's not it at all. I just felt . . ." Mason struggled for a polite way to say it.

"You feel pity for us."

"Something like that."

"You want to help the Haitian people."

"That's true. I do."

"Are you a good man? A brave man? A man of conviction?"

Mason, who had never been spoken to in such solemn terms, needed a second to process the question. "Well, sure," he replied, and really meant it.

"Then come with me," said the mulatto.

He led Mason around the palace and into the hard neighborhood known as Salomon, a dense, scumbled antheap of cinderblock houses and packing-crate sheds, wobbly storefronts, markets, mewling beggars underfoot. Through the woodsmoke and dust and swirl of car exhaust the late sun took on an ocherous radiance, the red light washing over the grunged and pitted streets. Dunes of garbage filled out the open spaces, eruptions so rich in colorful filth that they achieved a kind of abstraction. With Mason half-trotting to keep up the mulatto cut along sidestreets and tight alleyways where Haitians tumbled at them from every side. A simmering roar came off the closepacked houses, a vibration like a drumroll in his ears that blended with the slur of cars and bleating horns, the scraps of Latin music shredding the air. There was something powerful here, even exalted; Mason felt it whenever he was on the streets, a kind of spasm, a queasy, slightly strung-out thrill feeding off the sheer muscle of the place.

It was down an alley near the cemetery, a small sea green house flaking chunks of itself, half-hidden by shrubs and a draggled row of saplings. The mulatto passed through the gate and into the house without speaking to the group gathered on the steps, a middle-aged couple and five or six staring kids. Mason followed the mulatto through the murk of the front room, vaguely aware of beds and mismatched plastic furniture, a cheesy New York–skyline souvenir clock. The next room was cramped and musty, the single window shuttered and locked. The mulatto switched on the bare light overhead and walked to an armoire that filled half the room. That too was locked, and he jabbed a key at it with the wrath of a man who finds such details an insult.

"Is this your house?" asked Mason, eyeing the bed in the corner, the soiled clothes and books scattered around.

"Sometimes."

"Who are those people out there?"

"Haitians," snapped the frustrated mulatto. Mason finally had to turn the key himself, which went with an easy click. The mulatto sighed, then pulled two plastic garbage bags out of the armoire.

"This," he announced, stepping past Mason to the bed, "is the treasure of the Haitian people."

Mason stood back as the mulatto began pulling rolls of canvas from the bags, stripping off the rag strings, and laying the canvases on the bed. "Hyppolite," he said crisply as a serpentine creature with the head of a man unfurled across the mattress. "Castera Bazile," he said next, "the crucifixion," and a blunt-angled painting of the nailed and bleeding Christ was laid over Hyppolite's mutant snake. "Philomé Obin. Bigaud. André Pierre. All of the Haitian masters are represented." At first glance the paintings had a wooden quality, and yet Mason, whose life trajectory had mostly skimmed him past art, felt confronted by something vital and real.

"Préfète Duffaut." The mulatto kept unrolling canvases. "Lafortune Felix. Saint-Fleurant. Hyppolite, his famous painting of Erzulie. There is a million dollars' worth of art in this room."

This was a lot, even allowing for the Haitian gift for puff. "How did you get it?" Mason felt obliged to ask.

"We stole it." The mulatto gave him an imperious look.

"You stole it?"

"Shortly after the coup. Most of the paintings we took in a single night. It wasn't difficult, I know the houses where they have the art. A few pictures came later, but most of the items we took in the time of the coup."

"Okay." Mason felt the soft approach was best. "You're an artist?"

"I am a doctor," said the mulatto, and his arrogance seemed to bear this out.

"But you like art."

The mulatto paused, then went on as if Mason hadn't spoken.

"Art is the only thing of value in my country—the national treasure, what Haiti has to offer to the world. We are going to use her treasure to free her."

Mason had met his share of delusional Haitians, but here were the pictures, and here was a man with the bearing of a king. A man who'd gutted his best chess game in thirteen moves.

"How are you going to do that?"

"There is a receiver in Paris who makes a market in Haitian art. He is offering cash, eighty thousand American dollars if I can get the paintings to Miami. A shameful price when you consider this is our treasure . . ." The mulatto looked toward the bed and seemed lost for a moment. "But that is the choice. The only choices we have in Haiti are bad choices."

"I guess you want the money for guns," said Mason, who'd been in-country long enough to guess. There were fantasts and rebels on every street corner.

"Certainly guns will have a role in this plan."

"You really think that's the solution?"

The mulatto laughed in his face. "Please, have you been drinking today?"

"Well." Like all the observers, Mason was touchy about appearing naive. "It took the army a couple of million to get Aristide out, and they already had the guns. You think you can beat the army with eighty thousand dollars?"

"You are American, so of course everything for you is a question of money. Honor and courage count for nothing, justice, *fear*—those people in the palace are cowards, okay? When the real fighting starts I assure you they will run. They will pack their blood money in their valises and run."

"Well, first you have to get the guns."

"First the paintings must be carried to Miami. You are an observer, this is the same as diplomatic immunity. If you take them no one will search your bags."

Mason laughed when he realized what was being asked, though the mulatto was right: the couple of times he'd flown out, customs had waved him through as soon as he flashed his credentials.

"What makes you think you can trust me?"

"Because you lost at chess."

"Maybe I'm just bad."

"Yes, it's true, you are very bad. But no one is that bad."

Mason began to see the backward logic of it, how in a weird way the chess games were the best guarantee. This was Haitian logic, logic from the mirror's other side, also proof of how desperate the mulatto had to be.

"You must," the mulatto said in a peremptory voice, and yet his eyes were as pleading as the sorriest beggar's. "For decency's sake, you must."

Mason turned as if to study the canvases, but he was thinking about the worst thing that had happened to him today. He'd been driving his truck through La Saline, the festering salt-marsh slum that stretched along the bay like a mile-wide lesion splitting the earth. At his approach, a thin woman with blank eyes had risen from her squat and held her baby toward him—begging, he thought at first, playing on his pity to shake loose some change, and then he saw the strange way the baby's head lolled back, the gray underpallor of its ropy skin. The knowledge came on like a slow electric shock: *dead*, that baby was dead, but the woman said nothing as he eased past. She simply held out her baby in silent witness, and Mason couldn't look at her, he'd had to turn away. With the embargo all the babies were dying now.

"Okay," he said, surprised at the steadiness of his voice. "I'll do it."

It turned out that the mulatto wasn't really a doctor. He'd had two years of medical school at the University of Haiti before being expelled for leading an anti–Duvalier protest, "a stupid little thing," as he described it, he'd done much worse and never been caught. As far as Mason could tell, he eked out a living as a *dokté fey*, a kind of roving leaf doctor and cut-rate *houngan* who happened to have a grounding in Western medical science.

He'd cached stolen paintings all over town. Mason never knew when he'd turn up with the next batch, a bundle of wry Zephirins or ethereal Magloires to be added to the contraband in Mason's closet. But it was always after dark, almost always on the nights when the shooting was worst. He'd hear a single knock and crack open the door to find the mulatto standing there with a green trash bag, his hair zapping in all directions, eyes pinwheeling like a junkie's. Mason would give him a beer and they'd look at the paintings, the mulatto tutoring him on Haitian art and history.

"Something incredible is happening here," he might say as they sat in Mason's kitchen drinking beer, studying pictures of demons and zombies and saints. "Something vital, a rebirth of our true nature, which is shown so clearly in the miracle of Haitian art. *Ici la renaissance,*' how strange that this was the name of the bar where Hyppolite was discovered. *Ici la renaissance*—it is true, a rebirth is coming in the world, a realization that the material is not enough, that we must bring equal discipline to the spiritual as well. And Haiti will be the center of this renaissance—this is the reason for my country, the only slave revolt to triumph in the history of the world. God wanted us free because He has a plan."

He could spiel in this elevated way for hours, forging text in his precision English like a professor delivering a formal lecture. If Mason kept popping beers, they'd eventually reach the point where paintings were scattered all over the house; then the mulatto would pace from room to room explaining tricks of perspective and coloration, giving historical reference to certain details. "But the dream is dying," he told Mason. "Those criminals in the palace are killing us. As long as they have the power, there will be no renaissance."

"They're tough," Mason agreed. "They've got all that drug money backing them up. The CIA too, probably."

"But they're cowards. Fate demands that we win."

He wouldn't tell Mason his name; he seemed to operate out of an inflated sense of the threat he posed to the regime. Some nights Mason was sure he'd fallen in with a lunatic, but then he'd think about the chess, or the reams of Baudelaire and Goethe the man could quote, or the cure he'd prescribed for Mason's touchy lower bowel—"You must drink a glass of rum with a whole clove of garlic." Mason did, and the next day found himself healed. If at times the mulatto seemed a little erratic, that might have something to do with being a genius, or the stress of a childhood spent in Duvalier's Haiti. One night Mason suggested a game of chess, but the mulatto refused.

"I don't play chess since I was a boy. The match with you, that was the first time in fifteen years."

"But you're brilliant!"

The mulatto shrugged. "I was third in the national championship the year I was twelve, and when my father found out he threw away my chess set and all my chess books. He said there is no place in the world for a Haitian chess player."

"But if you were good enough—"

"He said I would never be. And he was probably right, my father was a very smart man."

Mason hesitated; the past tense was always loaded in Haiti. "What was he?"

"Doctor. *Opthalmologiste.*"

Again Mason hesitated. "Under Duvalier most of the doctors left."

"My father stayed. He was an eminence. The last Haitian to deliver a paper to the International Congress of Opthalmology." He fell silent for a moment, seemed to gather himself. "If you were noted in your field, that could protect you, but this also meant that Duvalier perceived you as a threat. You could be famous but you could never slip, show that you were vulnerable in any way. One slip, and they'd take you." The mulatto paused again. "My father never slipped, but I think it made him a little crazy. He kept a gun in the house—we lived on the Champ de Mars, and at night we could hear the screams of people being tortured in the palace. One night he took this gun, my father, he held the bullets in his hand and he said to me: This bullet is for you. This one is for your brother. This one for your mama. And this one, for me. Because if they come they are not going to take us alive."

What could Mason say? Any sympathy or comfort he might try to offer would be false, because he'd lived such a stupid life. So he kept his mouth shut and listened, though on nights when the mulatto seemed especially bleak Mason insisted that he sleep on the couch. Sometimes he did; by morning he was always gone. Mason would straighten up the couch, eat his toast and mango jelly, then drive over to the office and get his detail for the day. Some days he drove around in his white 4Runner with the powder blue O.A.S. flag rippling in the breeze: "showing the blue" this was called, letting the de factos know that they were being watched, though after a time Mason realized this was a strategy that assumed some capacity for shame on their part. Other days he was assigned to the storefront office that took complaints of human-rights abuses. Not much happened on those days; it was common knowledge that the building was watched, and walk-in complaints were depressingly rare.

Once a week he'd drive over to Tintanyen and make a count of the bodies dumped out there, and often these were horrible days. Tintanyen was a wide plain of shitlike muck held together by a furze of rank, spraddling weeds. You entered through a pair of crumbling stone portals—the gates to hell, Mason couldn't help thinking—and stepped from your car into a pressure cooker, a blast of moist, dense, unwholesome heat, silent except for the whine of flies and mosquitoes. The mosquitoes at Tintanyen were like no others, an evil-looking, black-and-gray jacketed strain that seemed to relish the smell of insect repellent. Mason and his colleagues would tramp through the muck, sweating, swatting at the murderous bugs, hacking away the weeds until they came on a body, whatever mudcaked, hogtied, maggoty wretch the de factos had seen fit to drag out here. From the shade of the trees bordering the field a pack of feral dogs was always watching them, alert, anticipating a fresh meal. Those dogs, the Haitian driver once confided in a whisper, were de factos.

"The dogs?" Mason asked, wondering if his Creole had failed him again.

Sure, the driver explained. They were *zobop,* men who could change into animal form. Those dogs over there were de facto spies.

Mason nodded, squinting at the distant dogs. *M' tandé,* he said. I hear you.

Each week Mason photographed the bodies, drafted his report, and turned it over to his boss, the increasingly demoralized Argentine lawyer. They were all lawyers, all schooled in the authority of words, though as their words turned to dust a pall of impotence and futility settled over the mission. The weakest on the team gave themselves up to pleasure, taking advantage of their six thousand tax-free dollars a month to buy all the best art, eat at the best restaurants, and screw strings of beautiful, impoverished Haitian girls. The best lapsed into a simmering, low-grade depression: you had to watch, that was your job, to *observe* this disaster, a laughable, tragically self-defeating mission.

"What does it mean?" Mason asked the mulatto one night. They were sitting in Mason's kitchen during a blackout, studying Hyppolite's *Rêve Haitien* by candlelight. The picture was taped to the back of a kitchen chair, facing them like a mute third party to the conversation.

"It is a dream," said the mulatto, who was slumped in his chair with his legs thrown out. The first beer always went in a couple of gulps, and then he'd sag into himself like a heap of wet towels.

"Well, sure," said Mason, "*Haitian Dream,* you told me that." And the colors did have the blear look of a dream, the dull plasma blush of the alternating pinks, the toneless mattes of the blues and grays, a few muddy clots of sluggish brown. In the background a nude woman was sleeping on a wrought-iron bed. Closer in stood an impassive bourgeois couple, the man holding a book for the woman to read. The room was a homely, somewhat stilted jumble of curtains, tables and chairs, framed pictures and potted plants, while in the foreground two rats darted past a crouched cat. As in a dream the dissonance seemed pregnant, significant; the sum effect was vaguely menacing.

"I can't make heads or tails of it," said Mason. "And that thing there, by the bed," he continued, pointing out what looked like a small window casement between the bed and the rest of the room. "What's that?"

"That's part of the dream," said the mulatto, almost smiling.

"It looks like a window."

"Yes, I think you are right. Hyppolite puts this very strange object in the middle of his picture, I think he's trying to tell you something. He's telling you a way of looking at things."

On these nights the gunfire seemed diminished, a faint popping in their ears like a pressure change, though if the rounds were nearby the mulatto's eye would start twitching like a cornered mouse. Here is a man, Mason thought, who's living on air and inspiration, holding himself together by force of will. He was passionate about the art, equally passionate in his loathing for the people who'd ruined Haiti. You don't belong here, Mason wanted to tell him. You deserve a better place. But that was true of almost every Haitian he'd met.

"You know, my father thought Duvalier was retarded," the mulatto said one night. They were looking at a deadpan Obin portrait of the iconic first family, circa 1964; Papa Doc's eyes behind his glasses had the severe, hieratic stare of a Byzantine mosaic. "It's true," he continued, "they worked together treating yaws during the 1950s, every week they would ride out to Cayes to see patients. Duvalier would sit in the car wearing his suit and his hat and he would never say a word for six hours. He never drank, never ate, never relieved himself, he never said a word to anyone. Finally one day my father asked him, 'Doctor, is something the matter? You are always so quiet—have we displeased you? Are you angry?' And Duvalier turned to him very slowly and said, 'I am thinking about the country.' And of course, you know, he really was. Politically the man was a genius."

Mason shook his head. "He was just ruthless, that's all."

"But that's a form of genius too, ruthlessness. Very few of us are capable of anything so pure, but this was his forte, his true métier, all of the forms and applications of cruelty. The force of good always refers to something beyond ourselves—we negate ourselves to serve this higher thing. But evil is pure, evil serves only the self of ego, you are limited only by your own imagination. And this thing Duvalier conceived, this apparatus of evil, it's beautiful in the way of an elegant machine. An elegant machine that may never stop."

"I can see you've thought about it."

"Of course. In Haiti we are forced to think about it."

Which was true, Mason reflected as he made his rounds, Haiti shoved it in your face sure enough. During the day he'd drive through the livid streets and look for ways to make the crisis cohere. At night he'd lock his doors, pull down all the shades, spread twenty or thirty canvases around his house, and wander through the rooms, silently looking. After a while he'd go to the kitchen and fix a bowl of rice or noodles, and then he'd wander around some more, looking as he ate. It was like sliding a movie into the VCR, but this was better, he decided. This was real. With time the colors began to bleed into his head, and he'd find himself thinking about them during the day, projecting the artists' iridescent greens and blues onto the streets outside his car, a way of seeing that seemed to charge the place with meaning. The style that seemed so primitive and childish at first came to take on a subversive quality, like a sly commentary on how the world had gone the last five hundred years. In the flattened, skewed perspectives, the faces' confrontational starkness, he began to get the sense of a way of being that had survived behind the prevailing myths. The direct vision, the thing itself without the softening filter of technical tricks—the vision gradually became so real to him that he felt himself clenching as he looked at the paintings, uneasy in his skin, defensive. An obscure sophistication began to creep into the art; they were painting things he only dimly sensed, but with time he was starting to see a richness, a luxuriance of meaning there that merged with the photos, never far from his mind, in the mission's files of the Haitian dead.

Life here had the cracked logic of a dream, its own internal rules. You looked at a picture and it wasn't like looking at a picture of a dream, it was passage into the current of the dream. And for him the dream had its own peculiar twist, the dream of doing something real, something worthy. A *blan*'s dream, perhaps all the more fragile for that.

He packed sixty-three canvases in a soft duffel bag and nobody laid a hand on him. He had to face the ordeal all by himself, with not a soul to turn to for comfort or advice. There hadn't even been the consolation of seeing the mulatto before he left, the last sack of paintings delivered by a kid with a scrawled one-word message: *Go.*

But Mason was white, and he had a good face; the whole thing was so absurdly easy that he could have wept, though what he did do on getting to his hotel room was switch on the cable to MTV and bounce on the bed for a couple of minutes.

He'd gone from Haiti to the heart of chic South Beach. His hotel rose off the sea in slabs of smooth concrete like a pastel-colored birthday cake, but for a day Mason had to content himself with watching the water from his balcony. When the call finally came, he gathered up the duffel bag and walked three blocks to The Magritte, an even sleeker hotel where the men were older, the women younger, the air of corruption palpable. Well, he thought, here's a nice place to be arrested, but in the room there was only the Frenchman and a silent, vaguely Asian type whose eyes never left Mason's face. There were no personal items about; they might have taken the room for an hour. Mason had to sit and watch while the Frenchman laid the paintings across the bed like so many bolts of industrial cloth. He was brisk, cordial, condescending, a younger man than Mason expected, with a broad, coarse face only slightly refined by a prissy mustache and goatee.

They wore dark, elegant suits. Their hair was smooth. They looked fit in the way of people who obsess over workouts and what they eat. New wave gangsters—Mason sensed a sucking emptiness in them, the void that comes of total self-absorption. It made him sick to hand the paintings over to these people.

"And the Bigaud?" the Frenchman asked in English. *"The Bathers?"*

"He couldn't get it."

A quick grimace, then a fond, forgiving smile; he was gracious in the way of a pro stuck with amateurs. He acted like a gentleman, but he wasn't—it was only since he'd lived in Haiti that Mason found himself thinking this way. Only since he'd met the first true gentleman of his life.

They gave him the money in a blue nylon bag, and he made them wait while he counted it. Later, perversely, he would think of this as the bravest thing he'd ever done, how he endured their stares and bemused sarcasm while he counted out the money. When it was finished and he'd zipped up the nylon bag, the Frenchman asked:

"What will you do now?"

Mason was puzzled, then adamant. "I'm going back, of course. I have to give him the money."

The Frenchman's cool failed him for the briefest moment. He seemed surprised, and in the silence Mason wondered, Is my honor so strange? And then the smile reengaged, with real warmth, it seemed, but Mason saw that he was being mocked.

"Yes, absolutely. They're all waiting on you."

At the house in Pacot he stuffed the cash up a ten-dollar voodoo drum he'd bought months earlier at the Iron Market. Then he settled in and went about his business, staying up late at night to listen for the door, going down to the park in the afternoons to take his daily drubbing at chess. He realized he was good at this kind of life, the lie of carrying on his normal routine while he kept himself primed for the tap on the back, the look from the stranger that said: *Come. Meet me.* Late at night he could hear machine guns chewing up the slums, a faint ghost-sound, the fear a kind of haunting. During the day he would look at the mountains above like huge green waves towering over the city, and he'd think, Let it come. Let it all crash down.

He missed the paintings with the same kind of visceral ache as he'd missed certain women who'd meant something to him. He missed the mulatto in a way that went beyond words, the man whose aura of purpose burned hot enough to fire even a cautious *blan*. My friend, Mason thought a hundred times a day, the phrase so constant that it might have been a prayer. My very good friend whose name I don't even know. The air felt heavy, thick with delay and anticipation, though the slow sway and bob of palm fronds seemed to counsel patience. Finally, one evening, he'd waited long enough. He carried his chess set past the park into the Salomon quarter, an awful risk that the mulatto would surely scold him for, but he couldn't help himself. He had trouble finding the street and had almost given up when it appeared in the ashy half-light of dusk. He turned and walked along it with a casual air. Just a glance at the house was all he needed: the green walls streaked with soot, the charred stumps of the trees, the blackened, empty windows like hollow eye sockets. Just a glance, and he never broke the swing of his stride, never lost the easy rhythm of his breathing.

The next day he went back with his truck and driver, poking around under the guise of official business. He knocked on doors and explained himself; the neighbors shuffled their feet, picked at their hands, glanced up and down the block as they talked. Lots of shooting one night, they said, people shooting in the street. Bombs, and then the fire, though no one actually saw it—they'd rolled under their beds at the first shot. The next morning they'd edged outside to find the house this way, and no one had gone near it since.

When did it happen? Mason asked, but now the elastic Haitian sense of time came into play. Three days ago, one man said. Another said a month. Back at the office Mason went through the daily logs and found an incident dated ten days earlier, the day he'd left for Miami. The text of the report filled a quarter of a page. They had the street name wrong but otherwise it fit, the shooting and explosions and ensuing fire, then the de factos' response to the O.A.S. inquiry. Seven charred bodies had been recovered from the house, none identified, all interred by the government. The incident was characterized as gang activity, "probably drug-related." Mason winced at the words. The line had grown to be a bad joke around the mission, the explanation they almost always got whenever a group of *inconnus* turned up dead.

Still, Mason hoped. He made his rounds each day through the stinking streets, past old barricades and army patrols and starving street kids with their furied stares, and every afternoon he wrote his report and watched storms roll down the mountains like the hand of God. Finally he felt it one day as he was driving home, he just knew: his glorious friend was dead. It caught him after weeks of silence, a moment when the cumulative weight of days reached in and pushed all the air from his chest, and when he breathed in again, there was just no hope. False, small, shabby, that's how it seemed now, the truth washing through him like sickness—he'd been a fool to think they'd had any kind of chance. Inside the house he got as far as the den, where he took the voodoo drum from its place on the shelf and sat on the floor. Wearily, slowly, he rocked the drum over and reached inside. The money was there, all that latent power stuffed inside the shaft—something waiting to be born, something sleeping. He cradled the unformed dream in his hands and wondered who to give it to.

The Good Ones
Are Already
Taken

It was after midight when the plane came smoking down the runway at last, the vast cyclone roar of the C-130 a fair approximation of Melissa's inner state. A cheer went up from the families strung along the fence, the kids in their pajamas and scruffy cartoon slippers, the frazzled moms trying to keep it all together in the heat, hair, makeup, manic kids; they'd parboiled for hours in the parking lot while word kept coming from the off-limits terminal, *Delay, Delay, Delay,* until Melissa thought she'd chew through the chain-link fence. It had been eight months since she'd seen her husband, and every hard-fought minute for this young wife had been the home-front equivalent of trench warfare. They'd even cheated and tacked on an extra ten weeks, *a high honor* the captain said when the rest of the team exfilled in March, *you should be so proud*. Proud, sure, she would have been proud to nail Clinton's draft-dodging ass to the wall, but what could you do? SF WIFE read the T-shirts at the Green Beret Museum, THE TOUGHEST JOB IN THE ARMY, and she supposed she was proud, or would be, once she had him back. Even among the elite Dirk had proved himself special, his surprisingly quick fluency in French and Creole earning him extra duty in the Haitian Vacation, that tar baby of a mission known to the rest of the world as Operation Uphold Democracy.

Chogee boy, she'd written in her last letter, *I'm going to screw you into a coma when you get back.* Melissa was twenty-four, a near-newlywed of fifteen months, and his leaving had been like an amputation—for weeks afterward she'd had missing-limb sensations, her skin fizzing and prickling where her husband should have been. As every man who'd undressed her mentally or otherwise would agree, celibacy was wasted on a body like hers: she had high, pillowy breasts, the compact butt of a boy, and abs you could bounce golf balls off of, a smallish package topped with a pretty heart face and reams of wavy sorrel brown hair. That she was also smart, sensible, and socially well-adjusted didn't save her from serial panic attacks, the fear that sex was an engine that dragged the rest of you along. A month ago she'd been having drinks with friends and found her mettle being probed by an older, handsome man with a shoebox jaw and rapturous muscles straining at his shirt. This was James, ex-paratrooper, ex–special operations, now on private contract with the DOD; his mere proximity, their casual bumping of arms and legs, tripped an all-over sensual buzz in her, a Pavlovian hormone flush that felt like drowning. After that there was lunch, and friendly phone calls at work, then a Happy Hour that ended with her bottom pressed against his cherry red Corvette while his tongue did a soft, sweet crush inside her mouth.

The whoop of his car alarm had wrenched her out of it. She'd driven home in tears, cursing Dirk for being gone and wondering how they'd done it, all those loyal, suffering women down through the ages who'd waited out crusades and world wars, not to mention whaling voyages, jungle and polar expeditions, pointless treks to wherever just because it was there. James kept calling; Melissa resorted to cold showers and masturbation until the captain called from Bragg to say Dirk was headed home, today, now, ETA 2200 hours. She wasn't sure she believed it until he walked off the plane, his sleeves in a jungle roll, beret blocked and raked to the side, head carried with the bearing of a twelve-point buck. Like someone had died, that's how strong the moment was, all that tragic magnitude suddenly floored in reverse—she had to lean into the fence while the earth stabilized, a sob dredging the soft lower tissues of her throat. Then she lifted her head and started cheering.

They lived in a trailer off base, a modest single-wide down a sandy dirt road amid the pine and sweet-gum forest outside Fayetteville, or Fayette-*Nam* as it was known when Melissa was growing up, forty miles down the Interstate. Thanks to the mighty spending power of its military bases, Fayetteville boasted more clip joints and titty bars than any city its size in the U.S., and Melissa's first business as a married woman had been to move beyond the city's trashy outer tentacles. *Aren't you scared out there, all by yourself?* people asked her, other women usually—her mother and sisters down in Lumberton, post-menopausal aunts, friends from high school who'd settled for hometown boys. *Plenty of worse things to be scared of,* she'd answer, leaving unsaid her sense of marriage as a nearer threat than any snakes or feral dogs the woods might throw out. The threat of waking one day to find a very familiar stranger next to you in bed — she felt it sometimes in his lockjawed moods, his slides toward the brute, monosyllabic style that might drive her away in twenty years. Stranger still, and maybe funny, were the shooting sounds he made in his sleep, *pow-pow, pah-pow-pow-pow*, like a kid popping off an imaginary gun. Who was he shooting in that subterranean field of dreams? But he laughed when she razzed him about it in the morning, and that was the Dirk she trusted, the sweet-natured goof who could sing "The Star-Spangled Banner" in note-perfect burps and had a thing for tonguing the backs of her ears. You had to be a little crazy for the Green Berets, hardcore warriors who could kill with their hands thirty-seven different ways.

"Ahhhh." He grinned as he stepped inside the trailer, checking eight months of combat duty at the door. Melissa went up on her toes to smack his cheek.

"How about a shot?"

She'd already set out their supplies on the coffee table, the salt and limes, shot glasses, a bottle of tequila. The jet fuel of passion.

"Well," he laughed, blushing like a prom date, "what I've really been craving is a beer. But let me hit the head first . . ."

They went in opposite directions, he to the bathroom and she to the kitchen. The trailer funneled sound so efficiently that they could talk to each other from opposite ends.

"Everything looks great!" he called from the bathroom.

"It ought to." She opened the beers and quartered a lime while a platter of nachos spat in the microwave. "I've had nothing to do but clean house for eight months."

"Hot water!" he shouted down the hall. "Clean towels! Oh dear sweet Jesus, Dial soap! It's like I've been gone about six years."

"Tell me about it," Melissa said through clenched teeth. She

stuck a lime wedge in the top of each beer. "We've got some catching up to do."

Back in the den, sitting thigh to thigh on the sofa, she let him eat
a few nachos and take a couple of hits of beer before she swung
herself over and straddled his lap, her skirt riding artfully high on
her hips.

"So how does it feel to be home?" she asked, her face six inches
from his.

"It feels pretty good."

She rocked back and had a good look at him. His skin was a
coppery reddish brown, and he was leaner, his few soft edges burned
away. She'd met him three years ago in the law office where she
worked; Dirk had brought in a buddy who'd snagged a DUI, and
while the friend met with counsel behind closed doors Dirk sat in
reception and chatted up Melissa. He talked in the slow, careful
manner of a man chewing cactus—it turned out he was from Valdo-
sta, even farther south—a buff body with soulful, syrup-brown eyes
and little knots of muscle at the hinges of his jaw, but it was his smile
that made her anxious in an intensely pleasurable way, the coyote
guile of it, his cockiness like a knockout drug. Straddling him now,
rubbing his cropped hair and searching his face, she decided he
looked mostly the same—a little dazed, maybe, and definitely older,
his eyes newly creased with crow's feet. Maybe Haiti aged you in
dog years? He was only twenty-eight.

"You've lost weight," she said, kneading his chest and ribs. He
felt as hard as an I beam. "We're gonna have to fatten you up."

"I'm looking forward to that."

She went to work on the buttons of his uniform blouse, flicking
them loose with a picklock's sure touch. Her bottom settled deeper
into his lap; she could feel the loaf rising to meet her there, his
maximum expression straining at his pants—it took only that much

pressure to make her groan. Her mind was going slack, starting to empty out, awareness liquefying to pure sensation.

Dirk gently took her wrists and pulled her away.

"Lissa, stop. We got to talk, babe."

"Talking's for wimps," she murmured, her voice slurred as a drunk's. She came at him again.

"No, listen, I'm serious," he said, and this time he firmly slid her off of him. Her ears were hissing like a lit fuse, and she felt giddy, dizzy with passion and guilt. How did he know? He couldn't know. So how did he know—

"We can't do this tonight," he told her. One of his arms held her shoulders, sympathetic yet sterile, exuding a brotherly tenderness that scared the daylights out of her. "Tomorrow's fine, we can do it all day tomorrow and frankly there's nothing I'd rather do. But to-night I can't." He paused. "I can't make love on Saturdays."

Her lungs collapsed—there was no air, nothing inside to form a response. She found a reserve at the very tip of her mouth. "What are you saying?"

"What I'm saying is—look, it's sort of complicated. But there's one thing I wanna make clear right now, I'm still your husband who loves you more than anything."

Now she was terrified; he'd never talked this way before.

"Something happened down there," he told her, "something wonderful, in a way. And you don't have to be scared, I promise you that. Just be patient, this is going to take a while to explain. Just trust me and everything'll be okay."

"Dirk," she wailed, "what is going *on?*"

She didn't follow any of it at first, the bizarre story he unloaded on her about poison powders and a voodoo priest and his initiation into voodoo society, then some garbled business about a ceremony, and someone named Erzulie. A person, or maybe not quite a person—a spirit? Who Dirk had married somehow? Melissa thought she might throw up.

"You're telling me you got married?"

"Well, yeah. To a god. It's not all that uncommon down there."

Melissa couldn't process the part about the god. "But you're married to *me*."

"And that hasn't changed at all." He squeezed her hand. "I know this is a lot to be laying on you, but trust me, it's okay. We're still married, I still love you, I'm still the same Dirk."

She looked at him: he was, in fact, the same, so much so that it broke her heart.

"If nothing's changed then why can't we have sex?"

"Well, that's only on Tuesdays and Saturdays. Those are the nights I have to devote to her."

"*Devote* to her?"

"Be with her. Sleep with her."

"What do you mean, sleep with her. You mean *sleep* with her?"

"In a way. It's kind of hard to explain."

She felt as if some part of her brain had been carved out, the lobe of reason, logic, reality-based thought. All the normal tools of argument deserted her, and so she sat mostly silent for the next two hours while Dirk described his journey into Haitian voodoo, which began as part of the mission, a standard hearts-and-minds tactic of the Special Forces—contact and co-opt the local power structure. In Haiti this meant befriending the village voodoo priest, who turned out to be one Moïse Dieuseul in the remote coastal town where the team was based. Dirk's near-coherent French made him the team's point man for local liaison, and from their very first meeting Moïse showed a special affinity for the young American.

"He called me his son," Dirk told her, "he said that God had brought us together. At first I thought he was just juicing me, right?

The guy's a survivor, he figured to get on the winning side. But all this weird stuff kept happening between me and him, and after a while I'm like, okay, maybe I need to think about this."

What kind of weird stuff?

Dreams, coincidences, uncanny divinations. Then Moïse proved his ultimate good faith by alerting Dirk to a plot by the local Macoutes to poison the entire Special Forces team, and after that Dirk was staying for all-night sessions, going deeper and deeper into the voodoo. Which led to initiation, revelation, the mystic marriage; the stories were blurring into a hopeless purée when Melissa looked at the clock and saw that it was five a.m.

"Are we talking about a real woman here?"

"This is Erzulie, Lissa, a god, a *lwa*. The voodoo goddess of love."

"But you said there was a woman in a wedding dress."

"Well, yeah, she came down and possessed a woman from the temple, that's how it works in voodoo. She used this woman's body for the ceremony."

Melissa shivered, forged ahead. "So after. After you got, married. Was there, like, sex?"

"Well, no. Yes and no. It's really hard to explain." He paused. "It's more of a spiritual thing."

Melissa sputtered, rolled her eyes — was he giving her the world's lamest line? "Dirk, dammit, for eight months I've been climbing the walls like a good Army wife, and now you're telling me, you, you're telling me, uh . . ." She found herself backing up. "Did you have sex with another woman down there? I mean a live human being, an actual person. Or anything else. Or *whatever.*"

"Why no, baby, it's not like that." He cupped her face in his hands, turned her toward him; she searched his eyes and found them clear amber-colored wells, her own pocket-sized reflection peering back from the bottom.

"No way," he said softly, "you're the only one. You're the only woman on Earth for me."

Dawn broke, filling the windows with pale, milky light. Outside the birds began singing like hundreds of small bells, their notes scattered as indiscriminately as seed. Once the sun rose Dirk was released from his promise, and in the early morning they did make love, though it wasn't the dirty movie that Melissa had been scripting in her head for months. It was, instead, as gentle as a stream washing over them, with Melissa quietly crying as Dirk poured himself out behind a sweet, knowing, mysterious smile.

It had started in dreams. Luscious, full-bodied dreams in which two beautiful women, one white and one black, were making love to him—Dirk put it down to the sexual deprivation of the field, combined with the *Penthouse*-fueled fantasies of any all-American boy. Then the team was tasked to nation-build in Bainet, and Dirk started making the rounds of the surviving power elite, the neurotic mayor, the budding Hitler of a *député*, the effeminate Catholic priest, and finally M'sieur Dieuseul, the locally renowned voodoo man. Moïse received the young sergeant like this was Schwarzkopf himself, inviting him into the shade of his thatched-roof temple where they discussed *la situation* over coffee, the stew of international politics and underground intrigue that seemed more intractable with each passing day. This was grunt-level diplomacy, basic hearts and minds; Dirk was already starting to cut his French with earthy Creole slang, and while they talked he eyed the voodoo gods painted on the walls, the horned, fish-tailed, vaguely humanoid *lwa* like creatures out of Dr. Seuss on drugs, then the snakes twined around the temple's central pole like strands of neon-laced DNA. Voodoo had already become a running joke with the team, *voodoo voodoo voodoo* their simmering code for everything that was weird and wonderful in this brave new world. Then out of the blue Moïse smiled, gave Dirk's knee a friendly pat, and said:

"Maitress Erzulie likes you."

And he proceeded to describe the tag team that was so vividly running amuck through Dirk's dreams—the black beauty was Erzulie Dantor, the white, Erzulie Freda, twin incarnations of the goddess of love. A week later, doing recon in the hills, Dirk and the team stopped in a village where an old woman announced that she could see the Erzulies floating around Dirk. This woman—she was a few spoons short of a full set? A wired smurf of a granny with notched earlobes and crazy African stuff draped around her neck, amulets, stoppered bottles, burlap sachets, and her mouth spraying Creole in an aerosol stream, shouting how *good* this was for Dirk, *two Erzulies!* Meaning his head was well-balanced, his person much favored. The news burned through the market in a flash fire of laughs, *blan sa-a se moun voodoo li ye!* The white guy's a voodoo man!

"So what are they like?" Melissa asked. "These dreams."

"Sometimes they're pretty hot. We're talking wet dreams here."

"*Dirk,* gross."

"Hey, it is what it is, baby, balls-to-the-wall sex. The kind with all that burning truth in it, like you and me got."

"Yeah, right. Nice try."

"Weren't we telling the truth last night?" Cocky as the day she met him, which wasn't to say he hadn't come back a changed man, a more thoughtful, thankful man with a newfound gift for patience, a slackening of the male impulse to domineer. From the first she'd always been the one who tried harder, who sacrificed her pride to his moods and whims and relieved herself with tearful rages in the bathroom, but eight months of living with the wretched of the Earth had returned to her a kinder, gentler Dirk who appreciated the good love he had at home. But those dreams worried her, the sense of forces, vectors of conscience and control that she couldn't see and didn't understand. So can they read your thoughts, she wondered. Can they get inside your head?

"Anyway," Dirk added, "she'll probably start showing up in your dreams too."

Melissa bristled. "I don't *think* so."

"Maybe not, but that's how it usually works. We're all connected now."

And James, was he connected too? He called her at work every few days, "just checking in," he'd say, "just watching out for my girl." "You're a special little lady," he told her. "I want us always to be friends."

"Sure, James, we can be friends."

"Now you tell me if he's not treating you right. I know how tough it can be when a trooper comes home, and if there's anything, well, I just want you to know I'm here for you."

"I appreciate that. But my husband's treating me just fine, thanks."

"If you ever need to talk, we could meet for lunch sometime, or maybe a drink if you want . . ."

Wasn't going off to war supposed to screw them up? And yet she was the one brooding and holding it in, not faking, exactly, but struggling to maintain, putting a happy face on the pressure cooker inside. In their spare bedroom Dirk devised an altar out of an old mahogany cabinet, "so you can shut it when company comes," he explained, "I don't want you to be embarrassed." Inside he stuffed all manner of junk, a miniature yard sale tumbling over the shelves: trinkets, perfumes, a silver comb and brush set, candy, minibottles of champagne and liqueur, a plaster statue of the Virgin Mary. He taped cheap-looking prints of the Virgin inside the cupboard doors, two different Virgins, one black with scars on her cheek, the other white with a jewel-encrusted sword through her heart. At sundown on Tuesdays and Saturdays he lit candles on the altar, sparked up some incense, and played voodoo drum cassettes on the boom box in there, the rambunctious afrobeat burbling through the walls like the world's biggest migraine headache. They'd watch TV curled together on the couch, but when Leno or Letterman started to drag Dirk would kiss her on the cheek, sweetly tell her goodnight, and go padding down the hall to the spare bedroom.

So sign me up for *Oprah*, Melissa thought, the other woman in my life is a voodoo god. The sense of a third presence grew on her like guilt, like it was the haunting of every bad thing she'd ever done. Voodoo, living right here in her house: she was enough of a lapsed Baptist to know what *they* would say. *Cast OFF that demon! Satan get THEE behind! Sur-REN-der is the key that unlocks sal-VA-shun!* Here in the buckle of the Bible Belt religious messages were available in all styles, from sugar-lipped warbling to hillbilly gibbering to the sonic stampede of call-and-response. The susceptible could easily find themselves bombarded by signals, and Melissa was, now, for the first time in her life, though actual religion still seemed strange to her. God was out there somewhere, she believed, and beyond that everything else was up for grabs, but as Dirk told his stories those first few weeks she began to understand a little of it, how a shock to the system might trigger a bizarre religious kick. Though really, was there any other kind? *In your face* was how he summed up Haiti for her, a place where everything happened altogether all at once, food, sweat, shit, grace, god, sex, and death, the raw and the cooked of life coming at you without any of the modern veneers.

"One day we set up a checkpoint out on the highway," he told her, "we were spot-checking all the SUVs for weapons. Then this big flatbed truck comes humping along, and there in the back, piled up in this huge mound are all these cow heads, hundreds and hundreds of bloody cow heads. So after it passes we're all laughing and yelling at each other like, Hey, did you see that? Can you believe that shit? Cause once it was gone you weren't sure you'd really seen it."

She got it, sort of, how fluid and free your mind might become when life took on the quality of hallucination. How that might blow your coping strategies all to hell? Dirk meditated daily in the middle of the den, which Melissa took for a joke at first—Green Berets, *snake-eaters*, did not meditate, nor did anyone else she knew except people from Chapel Hill. "Keeping it real" was how he explained himself; meanwhile Melissa took wary note of her dreams and watched her life fill up with nagging signs and portents. FORBIDDEN FRUIT CREATES JAMS, read the message of the week on Calvary Baptist's streetside sign, which Melissa passed each day going to and from work. A few miles farther on, First Methodist inquired: ETERNITY—SMOKING OR NON-SMOKING? Pondering Satan, carrying on her nominally normal life, she didn't feel so much fear as a kind of fraught spaciness, maybe fear spread thin. Then one Tuesday evening she and Dirk were cuddled on the couch, watching a *M*A*S*H* rerun while voodoo-trance music submarined through the walls. It began as a joke, a tease, Melissa's hand crabwalking up her husband's thigh, sneaking higher and higher until it reached his lap. Dirk smiled without turning from the TV and gently set her hand aside.

Thirty seconds later she was at it again.

"Melissa."

"What?" she cooed, all floozy innocence.

"You know I can't mess around tonight."

"I'm not doing anything," she blandly protested, but she giggled and found him hard when she squeezed again.

"Melissa!" The alarm in his voice hooked something fierce in her. He was helpless, she could fuck him anytime she wanted.

"Melissa, give me a break."

"I'm not doing anything!"

"Yes you are. And I'm asking you to stop it, please."

She jumped him with a vengeance then, scooching up on her knees and grabbing his belt, hanging on as he backpedaled down the couch. They were laughing as she pinned him against the cushions, both of them gasping in strained little bursts.

"Whoa, Lissa."

"Gimme somma that!" She'd freed enough of his belt to wank it around like a lasso.

"Melissa, stop. We can't do this."

"Give it up!" she shouted.

"Come on Melissa, stop." His voice was soupy underneath, losing tensile strength; what man didn't dream of being ravished this way? She had his pants open and was starting her dive when he shuddered and grabbed her hands, pulled her up short.

"Melissa," he said steadily, without cruelty, "enough."

"You aren't sleeping in there tonight." Her voice surprised her, the harpy venom in it—could she take it back?

"But I have to sleep in there."

"Bullshit!" When she pushed she could feel the strength in his hands, how he could snap her wrists like cheesesticks if he chose.

"I made a promise—"

"Uh, hello? I seem to recall you making a few promises to me."

"I did. And I'm not forgetting that."

"Well it sure looks like it to me."

There followed the worst argument of their married lives—the worst, anyway, for Melissa, who couldn't provoke a decent angry word from him. It was like trying to punch out a roomful of shadows, her frustration climaxing with a placid kiss from Dirk and the announcement that he was going to bed.

"You aren't sleeping in there with her!" she rowled at his back. "You aren't!" she cried as he turned the corner. "Dammit, Dirk!"— one final shout before futility overtook her, the realization of how dumb, how utterly clueless you were to think you might control anything about your life. She went to the kitchen and banged pots and pans for a while, then took herself to bed in a wicked funk. After cutting off the lights she masturbated, scraping herself into a shallow, passionless clench which as an act of revenge was a total failure. Then she lay there dry-eyed and completely still, wondering if she could live with this.

Five years ago, at the end of her job interview, Mr. Bryan sat her down in his corner office and gave Melissa what she described forever after as "the talk." "This is a pretty lousy business," said her future boss, a short, cheerfully caustic man with Gucci pouches underneath his eyes and a Little Richard cloud of jet black hair. "We get rapists, murderers, drug dealers, child-molesters, just about every bad deal you can think of walks through that door, and it's our job, it is our *sworn constitutional duty*, to work like hell to get these scumbags off. So. Think you can handle that?"

Melissa was not quite nineteen. She was living away from home for the first time and would have dug ditches not to go back. "Yes sir," she said, "I think I can handle it."

Fayetteville might not be the big city, but it offered all the excitement a small-town girl could reasonably want. In her first several years on the job she was flashed at her desk, had a knife pulled on her, watched a gang fight erupt in the reception area, and called social services on a hooker client who slapped her toddler three times in as many minutes. As an education she couldn't have asked for more, and the strenuous sleeping around she did those first few years, that was part of the education, maybe the main part. At the time she'd felt the truest way to live was by tunneling down to the wildness at your core, though she regularly shocked herself with what she found there. Did other women feel this way? she wondered. She suspected that she had unspeakable things inside her, a black hole of lust that might suck her past the point of no return, and she took her share of hits, pushing the limits of that—plenty of men were more than happy to exploit her sexual nature. Luckily Dirk had come along just as she'd found herself at the cusp of a premature cynicism.

"So whadda we got?" Mr. Bryan asked this morning, puffy-eyed, tie dangling loose around his neck.

"You've got your sanity hearing at ten, the guy who shot his ex's dog," she called through the door to his office. "Then you're due in Judge Hershoff's at eleven-thirty, that's your motion to suppress James Fenner's kilo. Okay, phone calls." She switched to a different pad. "You know Miss Blinn, our stripper? She called and said a hose in her car broke, she'll bring the cash over as soon as she can but it's not going to be today. Artis McClellan's mother called, she said his ankle monitor's giving him infections again. Then Roland Nash, he told me to tell you that D'Shawn Weems is a lying sack of you-know-what, and if he tells the cops what he's been telling you then he's going to beat D'Shawn up and stick his head down a commode."

A sigh like dust drifted through her boss's door.

For the next two hours Melissa answered the phone, typed letters and motions, juggled the walk-ins, and tracked down shifty witnesses. If she didn't singlehandedly run the criminal justice system she kept her end of it from clogging up altogether, this in spite of feeling slightly homicidal this morning. Her emotions were skidding around on a sheet of ice, a big jackknifed trailerful of ire and angst careening through the traffic of a normal day. Dirk had still been asleep when she'd left for work, so their argument was technically still in play; *time out!* she said to herself when James called, feeling something like relief. They made small talk for a while. He called her "angel." His voice was smooth and sweet as hot buttered rum.

"What say you and me grab some lunch today?"

She hesitated.

"It's just lunch, babe, come on. I want to take you someplace special."

Melissa sighed. Mainly it made her sad, what he was offering.

"I don't think I can."

"Don't think you can!" he cried, still cheerful, still glib, but she could feel his anger rising. "You have to *eat*, don't you?"

"Yes, but James . . ." She lowered her voice. "I just don't think I should see you anymore."

"Melissa."

She swallowed.

"We need to talk. That's why I'm asking you out, we need to talk about that night. Outside the bar, when we—"

"I know what we did."

"These aren't casual feelings I have for you. I think we had something special going on."

"Oh James. What we had was a makeout session in a parking lot."

"You know it was more than that. You know where it was heading, if the car alarm hadn't gone off we'd of—"

"But it did. That's life. And my husband's back and I'm in a different place now."

He sucked in a breath. "All right. All right. But I heard about you, I know some people you used to party with. They told me what a little wild-ass you were—"

Her eyes burned. *Dammitdammitdammit . . .*

"—you may be acting the good little wife now but I know what a whore you are, you cocksucking little cunt—"

She slammed down the phone and kicked back from her desk. She would not, repeat, NOT cry, but with this macho bastard stalking her and two sex-crazed goddesses swarming her husband, maybe she was allowed—or maybe she was just getting what she deserved, an evil she'd brought on Dirk and her both. Some dark, avid thing spilling out of herself. *Lay DOWN that sin!* the radio had howled this morning. WARNING, the sign at Calvary Baptist read today, EXPOSURE TO THE SON MAY PREVENT BURNING. Twenty thousand American soldiers had invaded Haiti, and this creature, this succubus, had singled out Dirk as the chosen one. Melissa knew there was someone she could call for help, someone she'd been aware of all along, but this was family, which usually made everything worse. She managed to stall for most of the rest of the morning, then finally plunked the phone book down on her desk. Dialing the number she considered the pause-giving fact that PSYCHICS was right next to PSYCHOLOGISTS in the Yellow Pages.

"Hello?" Her cousin Rhee picked up on the first ring. Melissa launched into an explanation of who she was, Margaret Poole's youngest daughter and thus Rhee's second cousin once removed—

"I know who you are," Rhee interrupted, laughing—she couldn't have been less fazed if they talked twice a day.

Melissa asked if they might meet. To discuss a small, uh, personal matter—

"How about for lunch?" Rhee suggested.

"You mean today?"

"Sure, why not?"

Melissa resisted the thought that Rhee had been expecting her call. They made plans, then Melissa asked how she would know Rhee at the restaurant. She hadn't seen her older cousin in years, and had a fuzzy recollection at best.

"Oh," Rhee laughed, "don't worry about that. I'm pretty sure you'll recognize me."

Her hair was, how to put this? If not orange, then orange-like, sort of a bonfire color. Melissa's cousin turned out to be a short, sturdy woman in her early fifties, with a doughy though pleasant face, smooth, rosy cheeks, and Wedgewood-blue eyes that were happy, direct, and shrewd. They met at the India Palace restaurant near Bragg—Rhee's suggestion, Melissa had never had Indian food but the duskiness of the place seemed suitably exotic. The twangy sitar music on the sound system reminded her of cats in heat.

"Oh *honey*," Rhee exclaimed, clamping Melissa in an eye-popping hug, "I am *so glad* to see you. And just look at you! My God what a gorgeous woman you've grown into!" Hearing her cousin's weirdly familiar mile-a-minute voice Melissa at once felt the undertow of family relations. She dearly loved her family, but after a couple of hours in Lumberton she always felt herself smothering under the ties that bind, all that tightly wound energy compacting on itself like a rubber band ball.

As she followed Rhee through the buffet line Melissa considered her cousin's history, how she'd led a life of exemplary conformity until a falling kitchen light fixture knocked her cold. After that she began acting odd, the oddness consisting, so far as Melissa had gathered, of exercising, backtalking her husband, and learning to play the drums, as well as casually mentioning to family members that she could now channel signals from the other side. Eventually she left her husband and moved to Fayetteville, where to the horror of her kin she set up shop as a psychic. One of the more successful, by all accounts: word drifted back that she was much in demand among private detectives and desperate families, and that her services were not unknown to various law enforcement agencies.

Out of nervousness Melissa loaded her plate, while Rhee took only flat bread and rice. In line they talked about their hometown kin; Melissa felt herself reverting to the mumbly torpor that family always seemed to inspire, but after they'd settled themselves in a booth and unrolled their flatware, Rhee said:

"So you got out. Congratulations."

Melissa sat up; it was like a needle in the spine.

"And you did it while you're young," Rhee went on cheerfully, "see how smart you are? Whereas it took me forty years and a whack on the head to realize Lumberton was going to be the death of me. Genius is wisdom plus youth, you know who said that? Me neither but I'm sure no genius, I blew half my life doing what everybody expected me to. We have to live our own lives and that's what you're doing, I'm just so proud of you! Now tell me about yourself."

Melissa gave the expanded résumé version—home, marriage, work—while Rhee ate her rice and bread in dainty garden-club bites, a style imprint from her previous life. Melissa heard herself describing Dirk as "a wonderful guy"; children were covered by alluding to the thinking-about-it stage. She was conscious of Rhee listening with a level of attention that was gratifying, and at the same time unnerving. She seemed to absorb everything, but behind that sunny, dumpling-textured face you had no idea what the woman was thinking.

"It sounds like you've done just wonderfully for yourself," Rhee observed when Melissa ran out of things to say.

"I've been lucky."

"Yes, lucky." Rhee's smile was wry, and a little distant, as if an old boyfriend's name had come up. "And I trust you're *happy*, Melissa. Because that's what I want for you."

"Well," Melissa gave a weak laugh, "mostly?" Rhee sat there pleasantly, patiently, like a sales clerk waiting for money; after several moments Melissa realized that her cousin wasn't going to break the silence, so there was nothing left to do but spill it.

"You know," the older woman remarked after Melissa had told her about Erzulie and Dirk, "it never ceases to amaze me."

"It doesn't?"

"And yet it happens all the time, this strange and wonderful way of the world which brings a thing and its polar opposite together. Think about it, Melissa—your husband, a white man, a *southern* white man and a warrior from the most powerful nation on Earth, gets connected with a *black* woman spirit from *Haiti*. The goddess of *love*, opposite of *war*. And this isn't just any old fling, they get *married*. Now what could be heavier than that?" Rhee's eyes fired a startling salvo of tears; as if overwhelmed or suddenly drowsy she slumped into the booth's high back, her features flattening into a moonlike mask that Melissa found oddly compelling. After a moment Rhee surfaced with a shake of the head.

"Okay. So how do you feel about this?"

"Well, I think it's starting to make me crazy."

Rhee nodded as if this was the sanest response imaginable. "How's Dirk been treating you since he got back?"

Melissa gazed across the restaurant, suddenly miserable. "It's never been better," she said, clearing a sob from her throat.

"But you're resisting."

"I guess I am."

"Why are you resisting?"

There was a precision to Rhee's voice, a tone of vigorous self-respect, that obliged Melissa to focus her thoughts. To decide what was real in her life, perhaps. "Well, there was a guy. While Dirk was gone." She told her cousin about James.

"So do you care for this man?"

"Not anymore. Not ever, really."

"But you were attracted to him. Sexually."

"Well, yeah. I guess I was."

"Do you think that's strange?"

"I think it's wrong."

"Did you think you were going to go your whole married life without wanting to sleep with someone else?"

"I don't know. I guess I never really thought about it."

Rhee studied her. "Have you told Dirk?"

"No, no, God no, never." Melissa paused. "Do you think I should?"

Rhee shrugged. "Dirk's not having an earthly affair, you know that. Not in the sense he's stepping out with another woman."

"No."

"And it doesn't sound like he's trying to hide anything."

"God no. He wants me to know everything. It's just . . ." She concentrated. "It scares me," she went on, wondering if fear was what it took to make something real. "I don't know what I'm dealing with, what he's brought into the house—whether he's messing around with something evil, satanic. Does that make any sense?"

Rhee's face took on a neutral thoughtfulness, every feature except her smile, which revealed nothing. "Well, based on what you've told me, this Erzulie sounds like a lot of different things. Kind of a slut, a sexpot who's also a saint, sort of a gorgeous Virgin mother—Lord, no wonder he's got a thing for her. But is she evil?" Rhee seemed to double back on herself. "I might need a couple of days to think about this. In the meantime"—she'd caught Melissa's panicked look—"I want you to take it slow. Be nice to Dirk, let him be nice to you. I bet he's dealing with a lot, coming home from a place like that. Try to see it his way as much as you can."

"All right. But what about James?"

"What about him?"

"What if he keeps coming at me?"

"Oh Melissa, that's easy. Just call the cops."

Was there a homegrown voodoo right under her nose, a french-fried North Carolina version she'd been missing all this time? It seemed possible as she made her daily commute, staring out from her car past the orderly fields toward the brooding wall of trees in the distance, that deckle-edged veil of luminous green standing in for the less penetrable jungles of the mind. There was voodoo in Haiti, why not here? With a little prodding Dirk described the ceremonies for her, which sounded chaotic but happy, like swimming in a heavy surf. Melissa tried to picture her very Caucasian spouse dancing in the midst of a couple of hundred Haitians.

"Didn't you feel funny, the only white guy in the middle of all that?"

"It felt good," he said. "I felt like I was home." So where was the evil in all this? Evil was the mini–killing field he and his buddies discovered behind the Haitian army barracks, the twenty corpses they dug up with their trenching tools. Evil was *La Normandie*, the Macoute social club in Port-au-Prince with its snapshots of murder victims taped to the wall. Evil was the hovering presence of death everywhere, the cemeteries with their scores of tiny children's graves. At night, lying in bed after love, Melissa held Dirk's hand and listened to the stories until he drifted off to target practice. *Pow-*

pow-pah-pow. His leave had ended a week ago and he was putting in eight-to-five at Bragg, ramping up for the next big thing. Colombia, Bosnia, the Middle East, or maybe Haiti Part II—the rumors mutated every couple of days. And when he left, what then—she dreaded that. At work she kept getting hangup calls, while on Saturday and again on Tuesday she accepted Dirk's goodnight kiss and sent him off to sleep with his goddess. How did normal people live? She tried to remember. Meanwhile she waited for Rhee's call as if waiting for the results of a medical test, which took more out of her than she realized; when Rhee phoned on Wednesday, Melissa felt the independence she'd nurtured all these years collapse in a sorry heap. *Thank God for family.*

"I'm getting some funny vibes on this," Rhee told her. "And I was thinking it might help if I could spend a little time out at your place? I'd really like to have a look at that altar he's fixed up." They made arrangements for the following day: Rhee would meet Melissa at the office and they'd drive out to the trailer together, grabbing a bite to eat while they were there.

Just your basic lunch date, that was the tone of it. They hung up, and Melissa decided that she didn't feel crazy. It seemed, rather, that reality itself had gone mad, and she was riding her own little scrap of sanity through the cosmic whirlwind.

Thursday was hot and sluggish, the sky hazed over with a scum of cloud the color of congealed bacon grease. The air had a dense, malarial weight—there'd been a rare outbreak near Myrtle Beach, more evidence of global warming—and driving out to the trailer Melissa cranked the air conditioning so high that her spit curls jumped and spun like small tornadoes. They got on the subject of Rhee's boyfriend, a retired Delta Force sergeant who raised competition roses. "He sounds neat," Melissa said, tobacco rows flashing past like shuffled cards. "You guys serious?"

"We're seriously happy," Rhee said, "with the way things are. We've got each other and got our space and that's just fine. Neither one of us is interested in shacking up."

"I hear those Delta Force guys are pretty tough."

"Sure," Rhee answered in an offhand voice. She watched the low sandy hills roll past, the scrubby brakes of saw brier and slash pine. "Men are funny, though. I never met one yet who didn't need to be mothered at least a little bit. And I think people underestimate that side of sex, the maternal side of what goes on in bed. There's a wild thing and there's a needing thing, but nobody ever talks about that needing thing. Makes us all feel too vulnerable, I guess."

"Sex is a swamp," Melissa said by way of agreement. She turned off the paved road onto the mashed-granola track that led to the trailer, the woods closing around them like a green fog. Poplar and pine shafted through the porous undercanopy, the arching sprays of dogwood and pin oak; Melissa believed there was something watchful about deep woods, a biding if not quite sentient presence, like a block of vacant houses. Through the tunnel of trees they could make out the clearing ahead, the light flooding the open space with a jewel-box glow. "How nice," Rhee exclaimed as they pulled into the clearing. The trailer was a long aluminum carton with flimsy black shutters, but Melissa had softened the package as best she could, with azaleas and flower beds planted along its length like piles of oversized throw pillows. Inside she showed her cousin to the spare bedroom, tensing as she opened the door. Today the altar seemed even gaudier than usual, as resistant to reason as a blaring jukebox. Rhee approached it with her hands clasped in front of her. Melissa lingered by the door, wondering what she was supposed to do.

"I guess you want to be alone?"

"Doesn't matter!" Rhee answered briskly.

But Melissa felt an urgent need to be useful. She left, quietly shutting the door behind her, and went to the kitchen to fix lunch, where she reflected on the therapeutic value of staying busy. Which might explain, it occurred to her as she spooned out chicken salad, why the women in her family were such dazzling cooks? A few minutes later she was setting the table and heard a thump down the hall, a muffled fumbling as if a sack of potatoes had hit the floor.

"Rhee?"

In the den the fake-antique clock gave three iron ticks.

"Rhee, are you all right?"

Melissa walked down the hall and tapped at the door. "Rhee, is everything okay?" Melissa cracked open the door to find her cousin spreadeagled on the shag pile, eyes closed, mouth wide to the sky, a blissed-out stoner look on her face. Melissa was to her in a second, kneeling to check her pulse and set a palm to her forehead — her pulse was even, her breathing deep and steady as the tides. Whatever was happening, Melissa decided, was a psychic, as opposed to a medical, episode, and so she sat and eased Rhee's head onto her lap, wiping the slug track of drool from her cousin's chin. There followed a prolonged series of non-moments, an enforced though not unpleasant lull like waiting in traffic for a train to pass — Melissa sat there stroking her cousin's hair and listening to the birds outside the window, the cicadas buzzing like tiny chain saws. A luxurious sense of calm stole over her, a suspension of anxieties both large and small; suddenly the strangeness of things didn't matter so much. After a while she lost all feeling of the floor, as if she were floating, enwombed in her own sphere of weightlessness, and then she realized that she was thinking of Dirk, her rambling and not-very-focused thoughts suffused with an aura of tenderness. She did love her husband, she felt sure of that; a revelation seemed to be building from this basic point, but Rhee's eyes were fluttering open, startled at first, then locking onto Melissa from upside-down.

"Ahhh," she said, smiling through a long sigh. "Melissa."

"Be still."

"No, it's okay, I'm fine. I saw her, Lissa, she's beautiful, she's a beautiful black sister." Rhee was grunting, hoisting herself into a sitting position like a mechanic crawling out from under a car. "I saw the white one too but she was farther back, it was the sister front and center today. Whoa," she ran a hand through her hair, "that was *strong*."

"Are you all right?"

"Sure, just got to get my head back. I'd love some water by the way, and a couple of Motrin if you got it." She was rolling to her knees, determined to stand; Melissa helped her out to the kitchen, where she accepted a chair at the table. "One gorgeous sister," she was saying, "deep, deep black skin, and beautiful braided hair right down to her butt. A killer body, oh my goodness she was something."

"Uh-huh," Melissa said, moving from sink to cabinet.

"Techy," Rhee went on, "sort of a diva, a real queen-bee type. And *old*, she's been around from the beginning. One of the ancients."

"Right." Melissa was glad for this small task to do. "So did she, ah, talk?"

Rhee thought for a moment. "Actually, no! Not that I remember. We just stared at each other for a while. Sometimes it's like that."

"But sometimes they do. Speak, I mean." Melissa placed the Motrin and water on the table and sat.

"Not really *speak*." Rhee's eyes widened as a pill went down. "It's more like sending. Direct thoughts going back and forth."

"Oh." Melissa watched the second pill disappear. She gathered her nerve; there was really no smooth way to say this. "Is she evil, do you think?"

"Oh heavens, Melissa, how should I know? She's a power that's come into your life, a force, a source, a cause, whatever you want to call it. Nature and then some, that's how I look at it." Rhee blew out her lips with a rubbery sound. "Beyond that you've got to work it out on your own. I can help you up to a point, but whether it's good or bad, that's pretty much up to you. You're the only person who can figure that out."

For some reason Melissa was more or less expecting this, a variation on the once-familiar *grow up* theme; apparently adulthood required you to be your own best psychic as well. They ate lunch, though Rhee was logy and barely picked at her food; on the drive back into town she fell asleep. Melissa nudged her awake as they pulled into the law firm's parking lot.

"Are you okay to drive?"

"I'm fine," Rhee said. She seemed a little out of it.

"Are you sure?"

"Yes, yes, no problem!"

"Well." Melissa watched her cousin hunt around for her purse. "Thank you. I don't know how to thank you enough."

"Oh Lissa, what little I did I was happy to do. We're family! And you and I are buddies too, sort of the wild hairs of the clan. But believe me, they all show up at my door sooner or later."

Melissa giggled; she felt relief, along with a burning need to know. "*Who?*"

"Life is so much more interesting than people think!" Rhee found her purse and heaved at the door. "You'd be amazed. Take care, Lissa."

Melissa arrived home that evening to find a message from Dirk on the answering machine—he would be late, a SOC briefing was going to keep him at the base. She changed clothes and went for a run, then started on supper while the sweat wicked off her skin, leaving a gummy residue like tree sap. The dusk was deep enough to see fireflies through the windows when she noticed the silence; usually she put on music and sang while she cooked, but tonight she'd forgotten, a lapse that brought on a fit of self-consciousness. She stopped what she was doing and listened, staring out the window at the trees. After a minute she began to feel afraid, the fear grounded in a near-religious conviction that James was out there in the woods, watching her. Abruptly she turned and stepped across the kitchen to the door; after locking it she stood there with her head bowed, listening, her hand on the deadbolt latch. After a moment she turned the latch again, unlocking it.

So if you really thought he was out there, would you do that? Are you really so brave? she asked herself. She moved down the hall peering into every room, and on her way back, with no real purpose in mind, she stepped into the spare bedroom. There was just enough light for her to make out the altar, the ratty flea-market jumble strewn over the shelves, the cheap comic-book colors of the Virgin prints. She approached the altar and clasped her hands as Rhee had done. The two Madonnas stared back through the muddy light with the vapid self-regard of fashion models.

Melissa stood there for a while, waiting. She became aware of her breathing, the loom of her heart inside her chest. Various aches and itches asserted themselves. Eventually it seemed necessary to speak.

"I," she said, and flinched—the word went off like a gun in the tiny room. I, what—acknowledge you? But that seemed corny, false. She took a breath and tried again. "Maybe I can live with you," she said, wondering if she'd finally lost it, "but I want you to know Dirk is *mine*. I found him first, I married him, he's already taken. And if you think I'm going to give him up . . ."

She felt a tingle, a quilled prickling running up her spine—did that mean anything?

". . . well, you've got another thing coming."

A kind of spasm, a jolt of exasperation almost made her laugh. Was something happening? She felt punchy, loose in the head, and with that came a surge of sisterly affection for this *thing,* this Erzulie who'd turned the world inside-out. Melissa began to see the possible humor in this, and even the Madonnas seemed to take on a merry look, the joke expressed in a crinkling around their eyes, the shadows bundling at the corners of their lips. What, exactly, had she been fighting? She wanted to say some agency inside herself, and she stood there for a time absorbing it, feeling in a sure but as yet inexplicable way that she'd arrived at something. Clarity, perhaps. A sense of scales balancing out. She felt older, and saw how that might be a positive thing. She carried the feeling with her back to the kitchen, wondering as she flipped on the stereo if any of this meant that her life had changed.

Five minutes later Dirk was blowing through the door, leading with his pelvis as he kissed her hello. He got a beer from the refrigerator and popped the top.

"Well, babe," he said, "it's Kuwait."

Melissa screamed.

"Hey, it's not so bad. They got about three million mines laying around from the war, we're gonna show their guys how to dig'em out."

Mines. Melissa resisted the urge to tear at her hair. "When do you go?"

"Not for six weeks." He pulled her close, snaking his hand under the waist of her shorts. "Think you can stand me that long?"

Later that night Melissa had occasion to reflect that sex smelled a lot like tossed salad, one with radishes, fennel, and fresh grated carrot, and maybe a tablespoon of scallions thrown in. The notion came to her as she lay naked in bed, making a tent out of the sheet with her folded knees. Beside her Dirk was nodding in and out while they drowsily reviewed the events of the day. Melissa mentioned that she'd had lunch with her cousin the psychic.

"Psychic," he said in a drifty voice. "I know this lady?"

"You've never met her."

"Hunh. She do voodoo?"

"Well, it's more like she's got her own thing going."

"Wanna meet her," he said, seeming to fade out.

"Sure, we'll have her over before you leave." Melissa shifted, raising peckish sparks from the sheets. "So what's it supposed to be like over there. In Kuwait."

"Hot," he muttered. "Sand. Lotsa camel jocks running around."

"Any voodoo?"

He chuckled, then murmured something she didn't understand. Maybe a minute went by. Melissa listened to a hoot-owl lowing outside. Acres of crickets jangled in perfect time like thousands of synchronized maracas.

"Though in a way I guess it's all voodoo, hunh."

"Wha?"

She hesitated, taking the measure of how she felt; after a moment she decided it felt okay. "In a way it all comes down to voodoo,

I said." She didn't really get it, she told him, but she could handle it. If this was something he thought was important in his life, she would trust him, she would try to understand. Because she wanted them —

"Oh honey I love you *so much*," he blurted, his voice too drastic, almost weepy. For a second she thought he was mocking her, until he went on in that same urgent voice: "Cap'll take it, yeah, Cap's got it under control. No go no show what a bullshitter, intel says it's solid, bro. Roger that, lock and load. Ready to rock."

So he'd slept through her big concession speech. *Pow*, he hupped in her ear, *pah-pow-pow, pow;* target practice had commenced for the night, in semiautomatic mode. Melissa sighed and straightened her legs, the sheet collapsing about them like a giant flower. So in six weeks she would be alone again. The episode with James was a shadow on her mind, like some dark, ominous smudge in an X-ray; she dreaded Dirk's leaving, but something in her was rising to meet it as well, anxious to see if she would manage better this time. For a while she thought about her little drama at the altar, trying to fix in her mind the true experience of it, the tingling immanence that in retrospect had about as much zip as static cling. She didn't know what to think about any of this. Voodoo, desire, oversexed spirits, dreams channeling information like a video stream — if these were real, then the business of who we were transpired mostly in the air around us. You could drive yourself crazy with it, she supposed. Some did; and some found their peace in it? But at least there was this, she thought as she rolled toward Dirk, spooning herself into his concourse of knobs and hollows. This was real, whatever else life might bring — there were, finally, no words for this. Melissa kissed her husband's shoulder, closed her eyes, and waited for sleep.

Asian Tiger

The Myanmar Peace and Enlightened Leadership Cup
was a bush league tournament by any standard, not even regular
Asian Tour but a satellite, the dead-end fringe of professional golf.
Which was where Sonny Grous made his living these days, when he
wasn't missing cuts on the Hooters Tour or hustling hundred-dollar
nassaus in America's suburbs; as a twenty-three-year-old rookie on
the PGA Tour he'd won two tournaments in nine months, which
inspired *Golf Digest* to run a cover story entitled, "GROUS, AS IN
LOOSE." He'd come out of Linwood, Texas, by way of Austin, a big
smiling kid with personality and a long game his peers called how-

itzer-in-a-can. "Like a bouncer in a strip club" was how Fuzzy Zoeller described him, 230 malleable pounds on a six-three frame and an ample, full-bodied face to match, along with blond hair cut in floppy surfer-boy bangs. What impressed him most about being on Tour? "All the free stuff," Sonny replied, "I can't get over all the great free stuff they give us." Balls, clubs, bags, clothes, the whole kit; he didn't mention the free-flowing, practically gratis booze, nor the women who hung around the practice green in every town, auditioning for the players in hair-trigger halters and the kind of shorts that make men sweat. He was dreaming those first few years on Tour, lulled by success and the sexual buzz; by the time he woke up and realized that he was going to have to grind to make it, his slide had already dropped him off the money list.

Everybody had to grind. Nicklaus, Watson, Norman, nobody could coast—once he understood how bloody the competition was, it scared him, the lightning strikes of his rookie wins. Those trophies gradually morphed into weights around his neck, but at this, the quiet-desperation stage of his life, they were his meal ticket, an automatic entrée into every joke tournament and corporate junket in search of anything resembling a marquee name. Myanmar, his agent said, what they used to call Burma, down in the heat-rash crotch of the world. Not the most politically correct place you'll ever see, they were on everybody's shit list for human rights and most of the world's heroin was grown there. It was your classic Third World basket case, complete with drug mafias, warlords, mind-bending poverty, and a regime that made the Chinese look carefree, plus a genuine martyr-saint they kept under house arrest, that sexy lady who won the Nobel Peace Prize—whatshername? On the other hand the generals who ran the country were nuts for golf. After thirty years of incoherent isolation they were building resorts and courses by the dozen, leveraging the sport into hard foreign exchange. Now they were holding a tournament to boost the off-brand national image, but there was a problem: who in their right mind wanted to come? American pros of a certain stature were offered all expenses paid, plus a ten-thousand-dollar guarantee, plus a shot at the sixty-thousand-dollar first prize against what promised to be enticingly tepid competition.

"Do not talk politics," said the agent.

"It's cool," said Sonny, who hadn't voted since the Dukakis tank episode.

"Just get in, play your game, and get out. I've got you a spot in the Ozarks Open in two weeks."

Sonny stepped off the plane in Rangoon—*Yangon* in the official, post-imperialist nomenclature—got a whiff of the dense alluvial air, and thought: home? No, he was about as far as he could get from Linwood and the ditchwater funk of the gulf coast, but Rangoon's scruffy urban mass had a small-town feel, its streets shot through with a rural ethic. The smog harbored startling hits of orchids and manure. Rusting corrugated roofs and moss-streaked stucco seemed to mediate a timeless, more organic state of mind. Roosters could be heard at all hours of the day, and even rush hour lacked world-class conviction, a tinny whirr and chutter that teased his ear like the plinking of thousands of pinball machines.

From the generic swank of his hotel room he could watch Chinese junks gliding by on the river, a wonder surpassed only by the locals themselves, slender, graceful people with cashew-colored skin and hair that flashed midnight blue in the sun. And here was another wonder: they didn't hate him! Poor people who bought their cigarettes by one's and two's, and yet they didn't hold their hardship against him, this loud, lumbering, pink-skinned American whose sheer unsubtlety made the natives cringe and giggle. At Shwedagon Paya he created a stir, cries of *bo gyi,* big guy, pealing in his wake as he followed his guide around the temple complex. At the Wish-Fulfilling Place, a shy, lovely girl dressed in yellow and white approached him and asked:

"Do you love the Lord Buddha?"

"Dollface," Sonny answered, so lonely and touched that he could have scooped her up and carried her home, "I love everybody."

Shwedagon: he'd never seen or even imagined anything like it, a sprawling, technicolor theme park of the soul, ten acres of temples and statues and gem-encrusted shrines surrounding the bell-shaped spire of the towering central *zedi.* Sonny eyed the *zedi*'s dazzling golden mass, its bowl base and tapering vertical flow, and after a while realized that he was looking at the world's largest, albeit upside-down, golf tee. An omen? Meanwhile his guide was intoning the Buddha's main tenets, telling Sonny that life is *∂ukkha,* all pain and illusion; that the cycle of *thanthaya,* death and rebirth, will continue as long as desire remains; and that through *bhavana,* meditation, one might achieve the proper karma for enlightenment and nirvana. *Yes,* Sonny thought, *yes yes all true*—he felt something swelling in him, a weepy and exhausted soulfulness, a surrender that felt like wisdom's first glimmerings, and coming down off the plinth he acknowledged the moment by passing money to every monk he saw.

Thursday morning there were more monks at the first tee, wizened old men in orange robes who stood off to the side quietly chanting. Sonny said a little prayer himself, teed it up, and played lights-out golf for the next four days, dissecting fairways with thunderous three-hundred-yard drives, sticking iron shots like the latest smart bombs, and wielding on the greens not his usual limp putter but a veritable stick of fire. His gallery swelled by the hour, a fun though basically clueless crowd yelling "Tigah numbah one!" for encouragement, and while the reference to Tiger slightly broke his heart he obliged by crushing their fancy new resort course. Sunday afternoon he acknowledged their cheers with a shameless Rocky Balboa salute, but the real prize came after the trophy and the check, when he was ushered into the hotel's penthouse suite to find the council of generals waiting for him. Ah, the generals—after trying to chat them up at the nightly banquets Sonny had come away actually pitying them. What was the point of having power if you were comatose? They were weird little guys, homely men with pot bellies and wispy tinted hair and all the liquid charm of formaldehyde. Sonny took a seat amid the chill of their anti-charisma and listened to General Hla make the pitch: they wanted Sonny to become Myanmar's ambassador of golf, their consultant on matters of tourism and sport and their host to visiting dignitaries and businessmen. As compensation he would be provided a car, a house, reasonable expense money, and a salary of twenty-five thousand dollars a month. "We also request," Hla added as his colleagues came to the edges of their seats, "that you please be available to give us private instruction."

Sure, like he had something better to do? In Dallas his ex-wife was about to impound his car for nonpayment of child support. Back there lay failure and angst, the permanent hangover of a badly blown youth, whereas here he'd gone from zero to hero in a couple of days.

"Gentlemen," Sonny said, laying on his corniest Texas charm, "I would consider it an honor to be your golf ambassador. Just show me where to sign."

By the Tuesday after his victory he had a Mercedes sedan, a fat U.S. Dollar account at the Myawaddy Bank, and a rent-free bungalow at the National Golf Club, an antique gem left over from the days of the British Raj. It was a tight, slyly challenging links-style course with lots of blind approaches and tricky doglegs, while its emerald fairways and parklike woods suggested the moist, hushed intimacies of a tropical greenhouse. Only the military—the "Tatmadaw"— and their relatives and guests were allowed to enjoy the National's sumptuous perks. Fore-caddies chased wayward shots through the trees, while small boys in skivvies waited by the ponds, poised to dive after balls that found the water. In the clubhouse, a tatty but venerable gingerbread legacy, waiters in starched white jackets served up the best in Indian cuisine and premium liquors.

"Dear Girls," Sonny wrote to his daughters Carla and Christie, ages eight and ten. "Your Dad is still a golf bum"—this was their private, semifacetious running joke, his feeble way of defusing his ex-wife's more vicious criticisms—"but he is now making more money than President Bush. I am going to be sending most of it to your mother, so please tell her to stop scaring you about the homeless shelter."

His first day on the job he teed it up with the generals and a delegation of Japanese steel tycoons. *Happy face,* he told himself, *smile, smile, so what if it's golf hell?* He jumpstarted the good karma by thinking about his girls, and nuked a drive on Number One of such rare and aching profundity that everyone present—generals, tycoons, bodyguards, toothless caddies—emitted an awed, transcendent "ahhh" like the dying chords of the world's largest gong. So he was delivering—before they got to discussions about labor capacity and penetrative pricing, the big guys had to bond, and Sonny saw that as his job, supplying the positive vibes. The next day he walked into the pro shop and found a beautiful Oriental vase waiting for him.

"It's for you," said Tommy Ng, the pro-shop pro. He was a slight, melancholy man in his late twenties who'd started life as a Vietnamese boat person and learned his golf caddying at Singapore's Keppel

Club. His English was so rushed and idiomatic that it sounded like change rattling out of a tube.

"Get outta here. For me?" Sonny was afraid to touch it.

"Those guys you played with yesterday, the Japanese. They sent it over."

"Why would they do that?"

Tommy hesitated. "They want to be your friend. They want you to like them."

"Oh. *Oh.*" It wasn't so much a bribe as a, ah, gesture, a little goodwill grease for the wheels. It wasn't long before Sonny realized that a giant corporate ratfuck was happening out on the course. If you wanted to do business in Burma you had to cozy up to the generals, and the best place for that was the National's elegant links. Which put Sonny in a classic trickle-down position: over the next few days he received a case of Bordeaux from Singaporean financiers, a carved elephant from Thai teakwood barons, a kangaroo-skin golf bag from Malaysian gem traders.

"So popular," said Tommy Ng in a voice like dry ice. "Two weeks in Myanmar and look at all the wonderful friends you have."

But Sonny was troubled—these people thought he could pimp for them? He was just the pro, a performing human whose job was to stun them with his mighty swing and tell colorful stories on the verandah after the round. They were all, generals included, relentless jock sniffers, eager for inside information about their favorite pros. *Did you ever play with Palmer?* they'd ask him over drinks. *Was Nicklaus really the best? Tell us about Tiger, is he as good as they say?* If Sonny didn't have an actual personal anecdote he'd make one up, something dramatic or funny to make everybody feel good.

"Don't you find it strange," said a voice behind his back one afternoon, "that a guy from Texas is Myanmar's national champion?"

Sonny was stroking ten-footers on the practice green. He turned to find a tall Caucasian watching him, a slender, well-constructed man with impressive teeth and a helmet of glistening, slicked-back hair. With his chiseled, Waspy features and minimal body fat, he might have just stepped out of a Polo ad.

"I guess," Sonny said, more or less playing along; he didn't much care for people sneaking up on him. "But I'd give it all for a couple of decent cheeseburgers."

The man laughed and introduced himself as Merrill Hayden. He added that they'd be playing together today.

"I saw you at the Masters in '87," said Hayden. His voice had an airy William Buckley trill, the adenoid lilt of gentlemen sailors and champagne sippers. "The day you were paired with Crenshaw. My wife and I followed you through most of the back nine."

"Uh-huh," Sonny said politely.

"You were managing the course just beautifully that day. I think you had a seventy for the round?"

Sonny blinked—who *was* this guy? "That's right," he said. "The next day it got a lot uglier, though."

Hayden laughed. "General Myint tells me you were a tremendous hit at the tournament. The council couldn't have been more pleased that you won."

Sonny assumed that he was being schmoozed again. "Well, I was just playing my game." He crouched over his putt. "So you know Myint?"

Hayden returned a smooth laugh. "Well, you might say that. He's the godfather of my youngest son."

Sonny double-clutched his putt, the ball rolling three feet wide of the hole.

"So how about if you and I partner up today?" Hayden proposed. "Civilians versus the military. Let's see how much damage we can do."

"Sure," Sonny answered in a neutral voice. "Why not."

They played six-ball that day, an old-fashioned Thai Crocodile: Sonny and Hayden took on two pairs of generals, Hla and Zaw on one side and Tun and Myint on the other, the Americans giving both twosomes a stroke a hole. It was an elite, top-heavy group, the council's inner club, and yet the afternoon had a relaxed feel, more like going steady than a first date: there was the sense of things happening on an unspoken level, of an ease and mutual deference between Hayden and the generals that made Sonny careful about what he said. In the five hours it took them to go around, Sonny learned these things about Merrill Hayden: that he owned homes in Aspen and New York City; that he was an honors graduate of Princeton; that he had a high, possibly justified, regard for himself and ran his own merchant banking firm, whatever that was. He was also a three-handicapper with a factory-perfect swing, but after several holes Sonny was laying silent bets that he was even better than that. The man's flubs were just too neat, too picturesque, and had a knack for coming when the press was on. More obvious was his habit of giving the generals every putt within four feet.

"Something stinks," Sonny said. He and Hayden were poking around a monsoon drain on Number Thirteen, searching for Hayden's errant drive. The grass was nasty, glutinous, snaky-looking stuff, nature's nightclub for horny cobras. Sonny swagged his 3-wood to and fro like a minesweeper.

"I don't smell anything," remarked Hayden.

"I'm talking about the game," said Sonny. "If you're gonna roll over for these guys, do it on your own dime."

Hayden was calm. "Come on Sonny, you know how this works."

"I know we're down eight hundred bucks and we shouldn't be."

"Power has its privileges. They expect to win."

"Then they should play better. There's your ball." Sonny turned and walked away. "Hit."

Sonny was out twelve hundred dollars by the end of the day—a month of private school tuition for Carla and Christie, or tennis camp, or a new computer with all the trimmings. He numbed the pain with a couple of quick Tsingtaos while Hayden briefed the generals on drilling activity in the Mekong Delta. Unocal and Royal Dutch were going in hard; British Petroleum was sniffing for prospects down the peninsula. By the time Sonny finished his third beer Hayden had moved into a silky pitch for Tesco Energy.

"They'll pay five million for the seismic data on Block 8, plus a ten million drilling fee per well up front. Myanmar Oil and Gas would have a five-year option to buy in, up to twenty-five percent at the market rate. And if MOGE doesn't exercise the option it still gets the standard royalty."

"We have never done business with Tesco," said General Tun, fondling his ivory cigarette holder.

"No, but you know my standards, and I can tell you they're as solid as any company I've ever brought to you. With a field this size you want the strongest player you can possibly get."

"Delivery," said General Zaw, who was chewing ice. This was a long sentence for General Zaw.

"Delivery's going to follow the Yadana pipeline, Unocal's agreed in principle to let us track their infrastructure. And Tesco's fully aware of the security situation down there. They're willing to wait for the rebels to come to terms."

Sonny sipped beer and watched his fellow American give a seminar in low-pressure sales tactics. Hayden was one of those people who seemed to project a glow, a kind of golden, airbrushed aura that sucked all the money and love to themselves. Never an awkward word, never a misplaced pause; the man fairly crackled with discipline and style. "The company thinks there might be four trillion cubic feet of gas in that block," he was saying. Four trillion cubic feet, worth how many billions? Sonny's mind scrambled zeros like eggs. The generals listened but made no commitment, which didn't seem to faze Hayden. When the party broke up he lingered with Sonny on the pretext of finishing his drink.

"This deal is reaching a critical point," he confided. "I need your help."

Sonny laughed. "Looks to me like you're doing just fine."

Hayden favored him with a patient smile. "Let me put it this way, Sonny—I'm covering your losses today. Whenever we're paired together I'll take care of you."

Sonny despaired; was he about to hit a new low? And yet it didn't seem like a great deal to ask.

"I'm a pro, Merrill. Maybe I'm not so much of a pro anymore, but I never . . ." He felt fluttery inside, vaguely airsick. "That's just a bad habit to get into."

"And I'd never ask you to." When Hayden smiled, Sonny thought, he looked like a man flossing his teeth—it had no meaning except as hygiene. "Just humor me. You understand what's at stake here."

"I guess I have an idea."

Hayden pushed back his chair and stood. "We're talking about five billion dollars' worth of natural gas—does that help clarify your thinking, Sonny? A lot of people want to see this deal happen."

"Right," Sonny said, as grudgingly as he could. If he blew this gig he might as well go back to Linwood and cut grass. "I won't get in your way, if that's what you mean," he added, which seemed good enough for Hayden.

One morning a group of monks took up the lotus position outside the National's main gates, blocking traffic and generally messing up everyone's day until the soldiers hauled them off like so many sacks of mulch. Watching it all unfold from the clubhouse steps Sonny gathered that it was a protest of some kind, a peaceful demonstration against—what? Surely not against golf per se? He found himself transfixed by the monks' seditious calm, their silence in the face of all those honking SUVs.

"The monks don't like us," Tommy Ng remarked. He was standing at Sonny's shoulder, one step up.

"But there were monks at the tournament," Sonny pointed out. "They were blessing us."

Tommy considered. "Different monks."

From time to time rogue faxes came over the clubhouse fax machine, broadsides from international activist groups with FREE BURMA! screaming across the front page. As a joke, or maybe simply because he could, Tommy always showed Sonny the faxes before tearing them up, leering as he flashed the illegal document like the rawest sort of porn. Often the faxes featured profiles on Aung San Suu Kyi, the Nobel Peace Prize winner whom the generals had confined to house arrest.

"You know, I tried to see her one day," Tommy said, so deadpan that Sonny suspected this was another of his colleague's vinegar-thin jokes. "I wanted to ask her what it's like not to leave your house for seven years. Not even a walk around the block—must be weird, hunh? But the cops sort of jumped me when I turned down her street, and they were the mean ones too, you can tell because they wear those really cool Ray-Bans. I was thinking I'd made a pretty bad mistake until the captain found out I could get him a tee time."

Tommy blinked, his version of a rim shot. "We're good friends now," he added in an offhand voice.

Sonny could add two and two; he could connect the dots. Driving around town on his rare days off he could see the cops and soldiers on every street corner, the barbed wire, the checkpoints and goofy mind-control billboards, the signs exhorting the gaunt Burmese to even greater sacrifice. "Our country," a cynical trishaw driver told him one day, "is run by a bunch of dopes." Well, if you say so—the only thing Sonny knew for sure was that the generals cheated like bandits at golf. It shocked him at first, not just the cheating but their utter shamelessness, as if they were entitled to tee their ball up in the rough, or nudge it out from behind the trees or kick it back in bounds, puerile, bush-league, penny-ante stuff that should have been beneath their dignity as national leaders, though with time Sonny began to link another set of dots, a series of interconnecting lines between political power and the most banal sort of personality. He thought of the pro-am round he'd played years ago with George Walker Bush, back in the days when the future president was merely the affable front man for the Texas Rangers. "You know how it is with those Latin players," the young Bush told Sonny with his trademark smirk. "The first thing they do when they get that big contract, they go out and buy their wives a new set of titties."

"Dear Girls," Sonny wrote in the next postcard to his daughters, "for the first time in my life I have bosses, and it has been very interesting to say the least. I have to work almost *every day*—I guess this is what I get for all those years of being a bum, ha-ha! But I have decided that being a boss is the best job to have. Study hard and make good grades so you can be the boss."

Sonny could sense a sea change within himself, a difference of depth, perhaps a broadening point of view. He believed that he was starting to understand how successful people made their way in the world, his learning curve pushed along by the rounds he played with Merrill Hayden. Sonny paid close attention to his fellow American, noting his clothes, his physical ease, his slick diplomatic skills. There was, for example, the way he flattered the generals: Hayden never complimented them directly on the job they were doing, which might imply the possibility of a different opinion, but instead he insisted that they worked too hard, sacrificing their leisure for the good of the country. Yes, the generals would gravely agree, yes, it's true, we live only to serve the people's desire. The day after these rounds an envelope would arrive for Sonny from the Strand Hotel; inside he would find enough cash to cover his losses from the day before, rounded up to the nearest hundred.

It felt sleazy, but Sonny pocketed the envelopes, composing mental notes of apology to his girls. Late one afternoon he was crossing the clubhouse verandah when Hayden called out.

"Sonny, come have a drink."

Sonny walked over. Hayden was sitting with another American, a muscular, compact man in his mid-thirties with short dark hair that covered his head like felt. Hayden introduced him as Kel McClure, from the Embassy. McClure added that he was with the political section.

Everyone sat. Sonny signaled the waiter for a beer.

"So you're the Asian tiger," McClure said.

Sonny had a *duh* moment. "Say what?"

"You're the Tiger Woods of Asia."

"Bro, the only Tiger Woods of Asia is Tiger Woods."

"Sonny's a very fine golfer in his own right," said Hayden. "And a first-rate teacher—he's brought General Myint's handicap down four strokes already."

"Excellent," said McClure, grinning at Sonny. He had black co-

coons for eyebrows and a long, spatulate jaw. The bottom half of his face was blue with five o'clock shadow.

Just then Hayden's cell phone rang. "Excuse me," he said, checking the screen, "I really have to take this. Hello?"

McClure sat back and sipped his drink. He kept drilling Sonny with moronic alpha-male stares.

"You like it here?" he barked.

"Sure," Sonny answered. "Last time I checked."

"I hope you know the future of the country is in your hands."

Sonny laughed.

"You think I'm kidding," McClure said with a straight face, "I am absolutely not, the fate of the nation depends on you. If a peaceful civil society ever develops here golf is going to play a major role in that. It's been documented," McClure paused for a quick, compulsive drink, "a white paper came out of State last year, it's a remarkable study. It showed the overwhelming bias of golf-culture countries toward democracy, free markets, your classic open society. Golf-culture countries rarely go to war, and when they do they never fight each other. Whereas non-golf countries have a much more belligerent profile."

"That a fact," said Sonny, who was pretty sure he was being put on.

"It only makes sense," McClure continued, "golf's the ultimate bourgeois sport. And what do the bourgeoisie want? They want peace. They want order. They want security. They want a social structure that's good for business so they can do what they do best, making tons of dough. That's the civilizing effect of your bourgeois middle class, and without it democracy's basically D.O.A. in Myanmar."

Sonny accepted his beer and took a long drink, grateful for the chance to look away from McClure; with his tense, arcane patter and serial-killer stares, he came across as a marginally presentable member of the Manson family. On Sonny's other side Hayden was negotiating a deal, some sort of exotic oil swap out of Kazakhstan.

"Think about it," McClure was saying, "business is all about re-lationships and trust, am I right? That's why anywhere you go, if you're looking to hook into the deals and big money, the first thing you do is head for the course. Take this guy, for instance"—he nod-ded at Hayden—"the deals he's done the last few years, I bet he's added a couple of points to the GNP just by himself. But he wouldn't have gotten anywhere without golf. That's how he met the generals, how he got their trust. Now he's the go-to guy in Myanmar—any-body looking to do an oil deal here, Merrill's the man who can make it happen."

To Sonny's relief Hayden clicked off and stowed his phone. "Sorry," he said, reaching for his drink.

"I was just telling Sonny how vital golf is to Myanmar's future," said McClure. "How he's positioned to make a real contribution here."

Hayden was nodding. "That's true, Sonny has certainly helped to facilitate some things for me. Which reminds me, Sonny, I've been meaning to get you in the loop on this. We've got an investor group that's putting together their plan for a golf resort down on the peninsula, and we'd like the benefit of your expertise. Tour the site, look over the architect's plans, that sort of thing. I think your name recognition in the golfing world would give the project a real cred-ibility boost."

Sonny almost laughed—name recognition, right, with various bill collectors? "I'm not sure how much I can do for you, but I'd be glad to help."

"Super, that's just great. Does seventy-five thousand sound fair? For your fee, I mean."

Sonny tried to stay cool. "Sure, that's fair. More than fair."

McClure sat back, grinning, spreading his arms wide. "This is outstanding," he declared, "I'm just so proud of you guys. This is exactly the kind of investment Myanmar needs."

Hayden gave him a bland look. "You're more than welcome to go in with us, Kel. We're still accepting investors."

McClure laughed; he started backpedaling with his hands. "Unh-unh, you guys are way outta my league. I'm just a poor boy, remember? Just an honest public servant trying to do his job."

Sonny couldn't sleep. At night the bungalow closed around him like a coffin, a recurring personal drama that was greatly enhanced by the power grid's collapse every evening at ten. No lights, no air conditioning, no civilization of any kind; Sonny lay there grazing the coffin lid with every breath and listening to the wildlife beyond his walls, the jet-turbine roar of frogs in heat, the fricative screech of insect group sex. Together with the slurry flow of thoughts in his head it all merged into a riot of nightly delirium, and yet there were times when he could leave his body and float above it, like a dream where he watched himself from outside—from this perspective life seemed more surreal than ever. *Burma,* he'd whisper, trying to make it real, *Burma, Burma,* the word so loaded and fraught that it might have been a prayer. How, exactly, had he ended up here? And how was he going to get back home? Thoughts of his daughters half the world away made him want to weep, and then there was all the blown money he had to think about, all the people hurt and friend-ships wrecked, the chronic sloppiness with booze and food and sex and the obscene squandering of his God-given talent, the past chas-ing him from his bed like a swarm of killer bees so that the earliest violet-silver blush of dawn often found him out on the putting green

in bare feet and boxers, practicing sixty-foot circus putts to clear
his mind. This one for the British Open, he'd tell himself—*clop*. This
one for the Masters. This for the PGA. As a kid he'd played this
game on his mother's good carpet, honing his skills for the glory that
was sure to come, and now the fantasies came flooding back in spite
of himself, filling the good clean space he was trying to make inside.
Dear sweet Jesus, would he ever outgrow desire, that grasping inner child? Maybe you broke free only if you actually won—it was
hard to imagine that Tiger Woods fantasized about winning the
Masters, though maybe after you won you simply obsessed on it in
reverse, replayed the triumph over and over in your head and inflated the moment to such orgasmic perfection that you drove yourself crazy from the other side.

God, it just seemed so hopeless sometimes. Sonny knew his
mental apparatus was out of control, but he was becoming aware of
a different way, in theory at least. Venturing out from the club on
his days off he saw monks everywhere like a visual reproach, monks
begging along the roads, milling around the shrines, chanting softly
as they walked in single file, offering the world an object lesson in
clarity. There was one group in particular, a pod of wispy, older
monks who hung around Mahabandoola Park, across from the
bank where Sonny wired money home. After his banking was done
Sonny would spy on the monks as they went about their business,
which did not, truth to tell, look like much. Some meditation, a little
begging, the occasional catnap—life for them seemed to be a serene
business, and Sonny watched them for clues as to how this was
done. Desire, he knew, had ruined the first half of his life, and re-
gret, its obverse, was going to ruin the second half unless he figured
out their trick of serenity.

Show me! he wanted to scream at the monks. Tell me how!
Where do I sign up? But something always held him back, some

cultural cue bred deep in the bone: he was American, bad karma was his meat and potatoes. The golf course was where Sonny Grous belonged, out where businessmen plied their billion-dollar deals and dictators played their leisurely rounds, relaxing after a busy day of crushing the masses. And McClure—where did he fit in? He turned up at the club several times a week as the guest of one or another of the National's seedier clique, the members said to be deep into drug-running or selling peasant girls to Thailand for the sex trade. The upper-echelon bottom-feeders, that was Kel's crowd; Sonny assumed that McClure was CIA, though why that was he couldn't exactly say. Late one afternoon he was finishing a lesson with General Tha's son when McClure trudged up to the practice tee with a bucket of balls.

"Pro," he wailed, "I'm suffering, man. Tell me what I'm doing wrong."

"Let's have a look," Sonny said. McClure took out his 6-iron and crashed three straight duck-hooks into the trees.

"Your grip's all wonky," said Sonny. "Roll your palm a little bit to the right, there. And move the ball a little more forward in your stance."

McClure's next shot sailed straight and true. "Holy mother," he sighed, "that's better than a blow job. Grous, you're a genius."

"Hit some more. Lock it into your muscle memory."

McClure hit a few shots. "So how you doing these days, Sonny?"

"Sneaking by. Roll that palm, you're already backsliding on me."

McClure smiled, adjusted his grip. "You seen Merrill lately?"

"He's around. We played yesterday, as a matter of fact."

"How's he doing?"

"Fine. Merrill is always fine."

McClure laughed. "That's our boy." He settled in and swung; the ball pulled left, its curve deepening as it fell. He squibbed another out of the pile and raked it toward him. "You know . . ." He settled in and swung; both men eyed the ball's warped trajectory. "If he nails down that Tesco deal, it'll be the biggest thing this place has ever seen. Bigger than Unocal, bigger than the Yetagun field. And our good buddy Merrill will score the mother of all success fees." McClure selected another ball. "But I'm just wondering, how's he going to handle the generals' end?"

"They seem to have a good rapport," said Sonny, which got a braying laugh from McClure. "Rapport, right, that's good Sonny. I'm sure they have outstanding rapport." He paused and swung. "But how's he planning to get them their five percent, that's what I want to know."

Sonny said nothing. That the generals were getting bribes had always been the assumption, a possibility he'd felt no need to explore. He was just the pro; that other stuff had nothing to do with him. McClure smiled and took a lazy practice swing.

"Five percent of this deal, that's the bomb, man, that's just a shitload of dough. How's he going to move that kind of money without the feds jumping his ass? You know, Sonny, there's all kinds of U.S. laws forbidding that sort of thing. They could probably drag a drug angle into it too." McClure paused for another shot. "By the way, how's the golf course development coming?"

"I haven't heard anything. I guess it's on hold."

"Yeah." McClure was futzing with his grip. "I can't help thinking that's a weird place for a golf course, way down there on the peninsula. With the Karens raising all kinds of hell down there . . ." He swung; suddenly everything was going straight. "Tesco investing in that deal?" he asked lightly.

"I have no idea," said Sonny.

McClure sighed and gave him a pained smile. Sonny sensed that he'd let his fellow American down, and that it was, sadly, no great surprise.

"Well, it's just a notion," McClure said in an easy voice. He hit a few more shots, then reached for his bag. "Thanks for the lesson, pro, I think we got it licked. Man, some days I just love this game."

The following Monday Hayden walked into the pro shop and handed Sonny a check for seventy-five thousand dollars, drawn on the account of First Asia Golf Development Corporation.

"We're good to go," he said. "Dr. Maung's going to do the design for us, we're flying down this Thursday to walk the site. General Myint and General Tun are coming too. You free to join us?"

Sonny glanced at the check. Seventy-five thousand dollars — college for Carla and Christie, at least a year or two. "Sure," he said, "I'm available."

Sonny was trying to recall the last time he'd been on a helicopter. Was it '93? '94? The Buick Open in '94, he decided, though that chopper had been a bucket compared to this one, a sleek teal-and-purple corporate job stocked with Cokes and Evian water and fresh *bei moq* cakes. Each seat came equipped with a headset and intercom jack, along with instructions in seven different languages; no explanation, however, was given for the pilots, who wore the combat fatigues of the Tatmadaw — they'd simply climbed aboard with everyone else and powered out. Within minutes Rangoon's scrap-heap jumble had given way to the mudflats of the Sittoung River, and then to the gulf, the sludgy discharge from the river gradually shading into paisley swirls of electric green and blue. If Sonny leaned forward he could spot their military escort, three olive-drab helicopters raked across the sky in a taut diagonal. Helmeted gunners hunkered down in the open side doors, bucking the wind like bugs on a windshield.

Hayden's voice crackled over his headset. "We'll cross the Gulf of Mottama here," he said, holding a map over his shoulder for Sonny to see. "Then we'll follow the coastline almost to Dawei. The property's just north of there."

Sonny nodded and tried to look as useful as possible. He was sitting in back with Dr. Maung, a tiny, intense Thai of advanced age whom Hayden had introduced as the dean of Asian golf course architects. At the moment Dr. Maung was drawing furiously on a pad, sketching a par-three hole with a wraparound pond.

"Sucker pin," Sonny said, pointing to a bulge on the green. "You're luring them in."

Maung grinned maniacally. "Bogey theah, unless you veddy veddy lucky."

"For this course?"

Maung nodded.

"Lots of water out there?"

Maung shrugged and tapped the end of his pencil. "Good erasah."

The headset muffled the engine to a hurricane roar. The sky was cloudless, suffused with a dull, milky film like an eye obscured by cataracts. They made landfall over Kyaikkami and tracked the peninsula due south, following the coastline with its ragged trailing edge of islands. To their right the sea unspooled in fine-grained sheets of blue; to their left the highlands rose in an abrupt green wall, the ridgelines overlapping in sinuous folds.

"What do you think?" Hayden asked, twisting to catch Sonny's eye.

"Real nice!"

"It's paradise," Hayden corrected. "And we're going to be the first."

Sonny drank a Coke. Maung kept sketching fantasy holes. Staring out the window put Sonny in a mild trance, a low-level fugue in which blocks of minutes passed without solid content. Presently the Unocal pipeline scrolled into view, a jigsaw puzzle of tanks and pumping stations and industrial outbuildings. A ruler-straight gash marked its route into the highlands.

"Almost there," Hayden said, checking his watch. "We're making good time."

They turned inland and crossed a series of brilliant green hills, the foliage breathing out light in a phosphorous haze. A small flash caught Sonny's eye, then another, yellow pinpricks winking amid the green. He watched fondly, brain simmering with sleepy fascination.

Hayden's voice fizzed through the intercom, laconic, mildly amused: "Don't look now, gentlemen, but I think we're under fire."

Without warning the helicopter pitched hard left, then seemed to freefall a couple of hundred feet. Dr. Maung started babbling in frenzied blips and chortles as if his internal circuits were shorting out. Puffs of smoke rose off the hills like dandelion heads; one of the pilots was shouting at Hayden, who'd swiveled his headset off one ear. After a minute he nodded and swung the headset into place.

"Looks like we've flown into a little jungle rumble up here," he told Sonny and Maung. "The army's flushed out some rebels from their rabbit hole. Anyway," Hayden tapped his window, "there's our golf course. We ought to be good to land in a couple of minutes."

Sonny heard himself laughing. "We're going to land down there?"

Hayden was brisk. "That's what we came for."

Minutes later they were clambering from the helicopter onto a broad, grassy hilltop with a view of the sea. The area was pocked with craters and chuckholes from a recent bombardment, the grass scorched in jagged starburst patterns. One of the military helicopters had already set down; General Myint, General Tun, and their entourage were gathered at the crest of the hill, surveying the jungle to the east with binoculars. The other two helicopters were skimming a distant ridge, engines keening with a high-pitched weedeater whine.

BOOM.

"Jesus Christ!" Sonny cried, ducking.

"Mortars," said Hayden, unfolding a topographic map and orienting himself. Dr. Maung was at his side with sketchpad in hand, busily scanning the terrain with binoculars. Machine-gun fire began rattling in the middle distance.

BOOM BOOM, two explosions in quick succession. "What the fuck!" Sonny cried, ducking again. The impact was just amazing, like trash-can lids banging down on his ears.

"It's farther away than it sounds," Hayden said, giving Sonny a casual glance. Small-arms fire clattered in catchy snare-drum rolls, and after the next mortar rounds the only thing that Sonny really wanted to do was lie down in the grass and twitch for a while. The battle seemed to be happening on the next hill over.

"All right, Sonny," Hayden said, "here's the deal. We're acquiring everything from the top of this hill down to the high-tide line. Our northern boundary"—he glanced at the map, then pointed to a distant saddle ridge—"is there, and our southern line runs somewhere along that valley. That's around nine hundred hectares in all, which gives us more than enough area for a first-class destination resort. Dr. Maung, what's your assessment?"

"Excellent," announced the architect. With the binoculars at his eyes, sunglasses atop his head, he had a buggy, mutant look. "Is mined?"

"No mines that I'm aware of," Hayden answered.

BOOM BOOM, the next bundle of mortar rounds left a tingly, empty feeling in Sonny's balls. The helicopters were strafing the ridgeline now, guns nattering in the distance like band saws. Smoke drifted across the hilltop in rags and tatters, leaving a bitter aspirin taste in Sonny's mouth.

"Merrill," he observed with all the calm he could muster, "there's a war going on out here."

Hayden laughed. "You mean this never happened when you were on the Tour?"

"Well," Sonny began, but he lacked the heart to finish.

"Relax, Sonny, everything's under control. The good guys have the situation well in hand."

BOOM BOOM BOOM.

Sonny would have given all his hair for a beer just then. Instead he trailed after Hayden and Dr. Maung as they tramped around the hilltop surveying the country, Hayden expounding on the big-picture themes while Dr. Maung supplied the details. There would be dhoob grass on the fairways and serangoon on the greens, Harrison bunkers, Old Course hummocks and swales—they seemed to be working off a design anthology of golf's greatest hits. "Tanks," Maung kept saying, driving Sonny to despair until he realized that the doctor was talking about *ponds.* Or was he? Reality was doing a taffy-pull with Sonny's brain, twisting his mind into gooey tag ends and strings, but something was happening here that went beyond mere madness. He could accept that either he was nuts or they were, fine, but this wasn't how you went about designing a golf course. You brought in engineers, you brought in surveyors, you slogged through the muck of the forest primeval and mapped it out yard by tedious yard, but to stand up here and conjure holes out of thin air—no, this wasn't real, this was a joke of some kind.

BOOM BOOM.

But maybe that's what being crazy is, Sonny thought, it's when everybody gets the joke but you. And if you slipped and let them know you didn't get the joke, what then? A phalanx of helicopters thundered low overhead, stuffed to the skids with government troops. Flare smoke fumed around the crest of the hill, a candy-purple cloud with a toxic glow. Somewhere a two-way radio was ranting to itself.

"So what do you think?" Hayden had turned and was smiling at him.

"By God," Sonny gushed, "it's just gorgeous up here. I don't think I've ever seen a better place for golf."

"Sonny, I'm so glad you agree. What do you think about Maung's idea for saucering the greens?"

"Hey, it works for me."

BOOM BOOM BOOM. Sonny grinned, even made a suggestion or two. He might be nauseous and faint with nervous shock, but he could maintain, absolutely he could maintain, he could fake like his life depended on it. Presently they made their way up to the crest of the hill, where the generals and their aides were surveying the battle. General Myint lowered his binoculars.

"Are you happy, Mr. Hayden?"

"Yes, thank you, General, very happy. We've accomplished what we came to do."

Billows of smoke were rising off the hills to the east, blotting the jungle like clumps of dirty soap suds. The helicopters kept making runs through the valleys, their heavy guns chattering in dense counterpoint. The rebels, whoever they were, were getting slaughtered — Sonny pulled himself together for a careful face-check, noting the bland, almost bored expressions of everyone around him. So maybe that was the joke, not being horrified. Pretending that all this was not simply good, but normal. Maybe you felt the urge to scream and rage around, maybe you even felt like that would be the normal thing to do, but you sucked it up and stayed cool. Because out here the critical thing was to play it straight. To go along, to get the joke. To concentrate, he realized with something like revulsion, on golf.

Two weeks later the *Myanmar New Light* announced the deal in a front-page story, Tesco's acquisition of the drilling rights to Block Number 8. "A glorious transaction in which all patriots rejoice," reported the *New Light* in its usual court-eunuch prose style. "In their wisdom the cherished leaders of our guardian Council have ensured the fulfillment of the People's Desire."

The monsoon season had begun, bringing deluges the likes of which Sonny had seen only in Biblical-epic movies. Banded kraits and pit vipers sought out the high ground of the greens; frogs choired outside Sonny's window at night, serenading him like Mormons on a rapturous drunk. He passed the days hanging around the clubhouse, doing card tricks for the caddies, staring at the rain, and helping Tommy Ng with the pro-shop inventory, tallying up their stock of overpriced golf clubs and polo shirts. The opposition continued to ambush the clubhouse fax machine, their broadsides appearing at all hours of the day. SLAVE LABOR ON UNOCAL PIPELINE read the headline on one; someone had scrawled *MURDERERS* across the top.

"Is it true?" Sonny asked.

"Is what true."

"Murderers. Slave labor."

Tommy considered this as he shredded the fax into pencil-thin strips. "You know, Sonny, this is what I think. I think most days the truth is just another possibility."

"Dear Girls," Sonny wrote in his third postcard to Carla and Christie, "it is the monsoon season and it rains *all the time*, my dandruff is starting to turn green and yesterday I saw a guy with a bunch of animals, two of every kind ha-ha. I miss you miss you miss you and I love you *this* much, how far it is from here to Texas, that's how much. Send towels, love Dad."

Sonny supposed that he was depressed, or terrorized, or posttraumatically stressed, some condition of a dire psychological nature that was supposed to happen only to other people. He'd felt like this ever since his day at the war; that adventure was never totally out of his mind, and he found himself replaying it at various speeds and angles, trying to get at the slippery essence of it. Which was, he began to guess, a transaction of sorts, a meeting of the minds. The joke he'd failed to get. Once the shooting stopped they'd choppered over to the next hill and joined the generals for a tour of the battlefield. The rebel bodies had been placed at the edge of a clearing, eleven or twelve in all as best Sonny could tell, although "bodies" seemed much too civil a word to describe the things he'd seen up there.

Ground beef was more like it. Human roadkill. Blood sausage. What he dreaded more than anything was being dragged out there again, which was why, the few times he'd seen Hayden since, he hadn't mentioned the resort. Several days after the Tesco announcement Hayden showed up again, late on a Tuesday afternoon when the rain had slowed to a stupefying drizzle. The course was too wet to play, but the range was open, and as Sonny filled a bucket of balls, he offered his congratulations on the Tesco deal. Hayden smiled and nodded, graciously modest, then took his bucket and headed for the practice tee. Twenty minutes later McClure walked into the pro shop.

"Yo Sonny."

"Hey, Kel." McClure was wearing a coat and tie. He had the keening, bright-eyed quality of a dog about to be unleashed.

"Is Merrill still around?"

Within a moment, more or less, Sonny had organized his thoughts, figuring people like Kel just knew these things.

"Ought to be. He went up to the range a few minutes ago."

McClure nodded. "Come on, Sonny. I want you to see this."

They followed the stone path out to the practice tee. A couple of maintenance men were squeegeeing water off the putting green, the mist swirling around them like shower steam. Farther along they could see Hayden alone on the tee, methodically hitting balls. He stepped out of his hitting stance when he saw them coming.

"Kel. Sonny." He took in McClure's office clothes. "Something wrong?"

"Not at all," said McClure, crossing the tee with a definite spring in his step. "I was just passing by, thought I'd congratulate you on your brilliant deal."

"Oh, well, I appreciate that. Thank you very much for saying that, Kel." Hayden smiled, the corners of his lips folding down as if to signify irony, indulgence. Surely he knows McClure is crazy, Sonny thought.

"Pretty soon you'll be richer than Bill Gates," said McClure.

Hayden chuckled, a feathery social sound. "I can't say I'm unhappy with our compensation, but what really pleases me is seeing the deal come together, getting all the pieces to fall into place. For me that's where the real satisfaction lies."

McClure laughed. "I bet it is. But I was just wondering, what happened with the golf course?"

"The golf course."

"Your development, the big course down in Dawei."

"Oh, that." Hayden frowned and looked away, gave his club a poky Bob Hope swing. Whenever any of them moved, the turf squelched underfoot like sloppy sex.

"Well, that's on hold for now. We hit a few snags."

"Oh my. Tell me about it, maybe I can help."

"I really don't think—"

"No, please. I insist."

They were still cordial, Sonny noted hopefully. You could still pretend it was a normal conversation, though there was an edge to it, a nervy undertone like a key sliding back and forth along a wire. "Well, you know," Hayden began, "we all run certain risks doing business here, it's just the nature of the beast. Certain elements of society—how should I put this? What you'd call the gangster element, for lack of a better word. The people who make their living outside the rules. Still, you know, I thought we could deal with that. We took precautions, we thought we had the right people in place. But when we funded the purchase money into escrow . . ." His voice trailed off; he swiped the grass with a one-handed swing. "What can I say? The deal changed, but nobody told us. The bottom line is the wrong people got that money."

"The wrong people," McClure said in a bright voice. "Sonny, do you know who the wrong people are?"

Sonny shook his head. It was like an invasive medical exam, you just wanted it to be over.

"The wrong people, Sonny, those are the guys you and Merrill play golf with. The fucking wrong people were supposed to get that money."

"That's not what happened at all," Hayden objected, trembling, his face turning pale and fierce—it was, Sonny thought, a fairly dead-on display of righteous indignation. "Absolutely not, this was a clean deal. We went over those funding instructions with a fine-tooth comb—"

McClure was laughing. He stood there with his hands on his hips and laughed at Hayden.

"—every step we took we had our lawyers sign off and I've got the documentation to prove it. Nobody can claim we weren't dealing in good faith."

"I'm sure that's true, Merrill, I'm sure you jumped through all the hoops. I just wanted Sonny to know he was your window dressing. I think people should know when they're being used."

"Nobody used Sonny."

"Right. You just hauled him out to a combat zone for his own good."

"We contracted for Sonny's services in good faith. And he was well-paid for his time, I might add."

"Well, yeah, that's true, Sonny did get a check out of it. Good for Sonny, but what about your investors, Merrill? What do you say in a situation like this, how do you make it up to them? Or, hey, maybe you already did. Maybe there's a bigger picture I'm missing here."

Hayden was curt. "Everyone understood the risks."

"I bet they did." For a moment it seemed as if McClure might grab Hayden's throat, but then he laughed, a kind of bark like a chain saw starting up. "All right, I'm done. I think I made my point. Come on Sonny, I'm sorry I dragged you out here."

But he wasn't sorry, not really; he seemed quite pleased with himself as they started toward the clubhouse. Halfway down the path a thought occurred to Sonny.

"Should I give the money back?"

McClure laughed. "No, Sonny, you keep that money. I'd rather you have it than those assholes."

Sonny was confused. "But aren't I in trouble?"

McClure had almost stopped laughing, but this set him off again. "Nah, you aren't in trouble, nobody's in trouble. Look, I don't give a damn how Merrill got that deal, I just don't want him thinking he can pull that shit without me knowing. Unh-unh, not on my watch. That's the one thing I won't give him. Plus, you know, I sort of hate the son of a bitch." With an amiable, stinging slap to Sonny's back, McClure veered off toward the parking lot. "Later, pro, I'll give you a call. We'll get together sometime and hack it around."

Sonny walked into the pro shop with the dazed air of a man trying to remember where he'd left his pants. Tommy Ng was spinning a ball on the face of a sand wedge, a zen thing he could do for hours.

"Sonny, are you okay?"

Sonny sat on the stool behind the counter. He still had his money, he still had his job—so why did he feel so bad?

"I think I'm going crazy," he said.

Tommy popped the ball into his hand. "Oh, gee, for a second I thought it was something serious. Crazy, sure, that's nothing, sooner or later everybody goes crazy around here." Tommy waited a couple of seconds for Sonny's comeback; when nothing happened he spoke again, more gently now.

"Hey Sonny, you want a beer? It's almost Happy Hour, why don't we go get a beer."

"Yeah," Sonny said. He was trying to reconcile the two pictures in his head, his daughters side by side with crazy McClure. Why he'd think of his kids just now he couldn't say, but the pain of their absence seemed to have a different feel—like a tumor in his gut?

Like he wasn't allowed to hope. Outside it had started raining again. Back in the locker room the generals were playing cards. Sonny stared at the rain and decided he would never understand anything.

"Sure," he said to Tommy. "Let's drink a beer."

Bouki
and the
Cocaine

Syto Charles saw the go-fasts before anyone. They started coming in the spring after the peacekeepers left, always at night, always running very fast, spearing out of the south with a shrill, concussive roar that he didn't take for anything but trouble. Soon every Haitian on the southern coast knew about the boats from Colombia, how they crossed the sea in ten bone-crunching hours with the payloads of cocaine and gangster supplies that their partners on the Haitian side needed to set up shop. Michelet, the police chief of Marigot, could be heard on the air six times a day denouncing this new and barbarous threat. "Anyone with informa-

tion should please inform us," he woofed on Radio Lumière, his
voice deep but warbly, lacking tonal weight. "We need every citizen's vigilance to help us fight this terrible scourge." Planes came
and went from Jacmel at all hours of the night, the planes, people
said, that were hauling the drugs to America. Rival gangs were
shooting it out in Port-au-Prince, while in the mountains above the
capital, Miami-style mansions were crowding out the farms.

"Ah-ha," said Lulu, watching a go-fast pass a quarter mile off
their bow, streaking south through the soupy predawn light. Syto's
younger brother Louis was a strapping man in the prime of life, by
nature both happier and more caustic than Syto. The same graceful-
ness that made him attractive to women also made him a first-class
hand on the boat, though lately he'd been calling himself an artist
and had grown increasingly slack about catching fish. "So those are
the bums who are ruining the country."

Syto was kneading a piece of coral out of one of their nets. "In
case you haven't noticed, the country's already ruined."

"They just come and go like that and nobody stops them?"

Syto frowned at the net. "You're welcome to try."

For a moment they watched the go-fast, an open-hulled flange
with a low profile and three podlike heads tucked behind the windshield. Great rooster tails of foam vaulted off the stern; the boat was
beautiful in the purplish gray light, beautiful in a cold, cruel, luminous way.

"Fout," Lulu muttered, then with a bit more malice, "just look at
that boat." He glanced sourly over his shoulder at their own rig, a
shallow-draft sloop with a bamboo mast and all manner of junk
strewn about—nets, homemade oars, crumbling Styrofoam buoys,
a sack of rocks for throwing at the occasional thief. "So how do they
do it?" he asked. "They meet their guys on shore and pass it off?"

Syto shrugged. "Sometimes, I guess. Sometimes they just leave it there."

"They *leave* it there? They just dump it on the beach and hope their guys show up?"

"Well, on the rocks over at Bois Rouge. Up inside the cove."

"You've *seen* it?"

"Yeah, sometimes in the mornings. I'll go over there for *chèvrèt* and see the sacks up on the rocks."

"Hell, man, why didn't you pick them up?" Lulu was padding along the gunnel like a big cat; in a moment he had the tiller and was sheeting in the sail, the mast creaking as it cupped the wind.

"Lulu, wait a second."

Lulu swung the boat around and aimed for Bois Rouge.

"Lulu, wait." Syto's fear had more to do with breaking safe, numbing habits than rousing the ire of some ruthless gang. "Lulu, come on. What are we supposed to do if we get the stuff?"

"You have to ask? We're going to give it to the cops, of course."

Bois Rouge was a narrow teardrop bay with a rind of beach packed into the heel, rock clusters flaring across the sand like the rusted-out hulks of old wrecks. They found three duffel bags draped across the rocks, a hundred kilos in each, each kilo triple-wrapped in thick, clear plastic. The brothers loaded up the bags and sailed for Marigot; by mid-morning they'd landed on the mushy beach, hired a couple of kids with a wobble-wheeled *bouret* and carted the bags to the police station, the former pus yellow barracks of the Haitian Army redone in searing white with snappy royal blue trim. These were the new civilian, postinvasion police, recruited and trained by the Americans to be the guardians of the dawning democratic era, and as the brothers waited in an outer office Syto reflected that, yes, there was definitely a different feel about the place.

It wasn't just the paint job, the matching desks and chairs, the glossy validation of fax machines and computers. The old police used to shuffle and slouch around like a bunch of punks—until they wanted you, and then they moved pretty quick—but this crew carried themselves with the same crisp air as the people over at the tax office.

And yet here was Michelet running the place, Michelet with his oblong, strangely blunted head, like a coffee bean squeezed between your thumb and forefinger. A man of medium height, with brisk, officious eyes and the cinematic mustache he'd worn in the army, the pencil-thin wisp like an advertisement for how well the world should think of him. As a soldier he hadn't been known as one of the high-profile rapists or torturers, though he'd slap the odd chicken thief around now and then. He'd been clean enough for the Americans to recycle into the police, a professional who could brace up the situation long enough for the *blans* to pound their chests and leave.

"Well?" he said, stepping into the room, raising his chin at the scruffy fishermen. "Well? What is it?"

Lulu laughed, wasting a little more of Michelet's time. "We heard you on the radio," he said to Michelet. Several policemen had gathered around. "About the go-fasts, you know? We heard you telling everybody you wanted vigilance. Well," he kicked his bare foot against the sacks, "here's your vigilance."

Michelet frowned, then nodded at the duffel bags. The youngest cop fell to his knees and cinched open one of the bags. He looked inside, pulled back for a brief, hysterical giggle, and looked again.

"It's cocaine."

"Bullshit," said Michelet, but he dropped to his knees and peered into the bag, lifted out a kilo with both hands. "Where did you find this?" he barked at the brothers.

"At Bois Rouge," Lulu answered. Syto just watched. He remembered Michelet; the *chef*, of course, would not remember Syto. "On the rocks over at Bois Rouge. We saw the go-fast leaving and we went in and took it."

Michelet attacked the other two bags, wrestling each one open, raking out the top layer, then thrusting his arm all the way to the bottom. He was sweating when he sat back and looked at the brothers, as moist and trembly as a virgin on the cusp. "So tell me," he said, simpering, practically gagging on his smile, "did you happen to see any more of these?"

Syto sailed out alone to do his fishing that night, as regular in his work as the seasons and tides. He fished during the full moon like everyone else, and he fished during the waning moon when no one else bothered, and under the new moon, which was even worse, and before hurricanes, which was sheer futility, but since his daughter died several years ago, catching fish wasn't so much the point. Most nights the only other boats he saw were go-fasts. If he was working close to shore they'd aim for his boat, perhaps attracted by the light from his *lampe-batterie;* Syto would go on setting his hooks and lines and ignore the banshee shriek bearing down on him, and when they saw it was a fisherman they'd cut to the side, the hull flashing sleek and pale in the night.

Tonight he baited his string of hooks with *pisket* and chicken guts, spotlit the water with his *lampe-batterie,* and then drifted, not so much thinking about things as biding with a certain awareness of his life. *Réfléchi,* that was better than direct thinking for the world of problems you could never really solve. The problem of contraband, for example, or the confusions of politics, or the trouble that came of needing to eat every day. Or the death of children, a cruelly regular thing in Trois Pins. He and his wife had lost four, the first three as infants and the last, Marie-Lucie, when she was almost seven.

That one was never far from his mind, a petite, clean-limbed, willful little girl who'd insisted on starting school at age five, nagging her father until he enrolled her at Marigot's ramshackle École Supérieure. One day she'd been skipping rope and singing out her lessons, and the next she was trembling with fever on her mat, her ankle blanched and puffy as a rotten fish. By morning both legs were swollen, her eyes glassy and distant. Syto borrowed a neighbor's chestnut mare, wrapped Marie-Lucie in a towel, and cradled her across the saddle, and they didn't climb down until the shambling little horse carried them all the way to Jacmel. On the road Marie-Lucie went out of her head with fever, talking and singing with such familiar exuberance that Syto thought he would go insane with grief. At the clinic the doctor shook his head—no antibiotics, the embargo had seen to that, there wasn't so much as an aspirin to be had. They gave Marie-Lucie a bed and Syto a mat; that night the life poured out of her like water from a pail, and the next day, cradling her body again across the saddle, Syto didn't so much want to die himself as to lie down in a ditch and wait for time to end. People walking along the road understood at once; they stopped, took off their hats, and bowed their heads, and many called him "brother" and offered a prayer. But just as he passed the *Avant-Poste* in Marigot, the soldiers on the gallery had burst out laughing. A whole row of them lazing there in the shade, chairs tipped against the wall, rifles propped nearby; Syto remembered Michelet among them, Michelet with his sergeant's stripes and prissy mustache, his trousers tucked smartly into gleaming boots. At that moment Syto had felt murder in his heart—*how dare they*—and then he realized they weren't laughing at him, they hadn't even noticed him passing by. One of the soldiers had simply told a joke—it had nothing to do with him, and yet their laughter cut deep, rankling over the years, his mind playing the sound of it over and over as he rode the ocean swells at night.

Within a week all the Marigot cops were driving Land Cruisers. Michelet himself had paid cash for one of the big fine farms near Cyvadier, or so the rumors went; eventually he went on the radio to defend himself. "All contraband has been sent to headquarters in Port-au-Prince," the chief declared, and he, personally, "God's creature and servant," was directing the local drug interdiction effort, "in concert with the American antidruggists."

People shrugged; the truth was right before your eyes, but what could you do? "Our problem," Lulu said on the boat one day, "is that we're chumps. We let those guys run all over us."

"Don't talk like that," Syto objected, reaching over the side for a handful of water to splash on his head. It was a hot, cloudless day; the water around them was the same dazzling blue as the sky, so that at times Syto had the unsettling sensation that they were floating free in space. "We're fishermen, we earn ourselves an honest living. Have a little respect for yourself."

"Respect? Come on Syto, it's like Bouki and Ti-Malice and we're poor dumb Bouki, those cops are driving around laughing at us." Every Haitian grew up listening to the old tales about dimwitted Bouki and sly Ti-Malice, an operator who was always taking Bouki to the cleaners. Though it seemed you were supposed to feel sorry for Bouki, Syto had noticed how people took smirking pleasure in Ti-Malice's cons and scams.

"Well, I don't have any regrets," he said. Though he was just as disgusted as Lulu, he wouldn't admit it. "We tried to do the right thing."

"You try to do the right thing, that's a good way to starve." Lulu paused to light a cigarette. "Bouki starves while Ti-Malice gets nice and fat."

Syto didn't need it, Lulu's reminders of just how degrading life could be, but Syto also knew this: after Marie-Lucie died he would have gone crazy if it hadn't been for Lulu mouthing off on the boat, cracking jokes about their luck, the fish, the world, or Lulu falling down possessed because of the rhythm of the waves, or Lulu sitting in the stern and saying things like "I think that Man is the shadow of God" or just smoking and being a bum, so that Syto had to jump up and scold him instead of quietly fishing until he broke in two from grief. But one morning Lulu announced that he was an artist, and now he spent most of his days painting the dreams he had at night, making dark, blobby pictures that seemed to rise out of an underwater realm in his head. When he got three or four together, he'd go hang around the square in Jacmel and try to sell them to the *blans* who wandered through, aid workers, mostly, sometimes a dazed tourist or two.

"Tell me this," Lulu went on, mumbling now. He was using both hands to coil the *pisket* net, which required him to hold the pull line in his mouth; between the rope and the dangling cigarette there wasn't much room for talk. "Does Esther know about the drugs?"

Syto considered. "I think so."

"You *think* so? You mean you told her?"

"Well, no."

"Did she start talking?"

"You know she hasn't."

Lulu spun the net outward with a twist of his arms, the net flaring, smacking the water like a fond kiss. "Well if you didn't tell her and she isn't talking, how do you know she knows?"

"She may not talk, Lulu, but that doesn't mean she's deaf. She goes to the market, she listens to the radio. She knows what's going on."

"Too much *chagrin*," Lulu said. The net was sinking through the water as if drifting off to sleep. "Too much sadness, I really feel for her. I guess if you guys could have another kid . . ."

Syto shook his head. The midwife said there would be no more children; Marie-Lucie's birth had torn Esther too badly. Lulu fell silent for a time, watching the water, then he gave the net an exploratory tug.

"How much do you think those drugs were worth?"

"I don't know," Syto answered. "A lot, I guess. If you believe the radio."

For a moment the only sounds were the water's slap and gurgle, the creaking of the mast like a bone out of joint. Both brothers were thinking the same thing, and each knew the other was thinking it, but neither was willing to say the words.

"She needs a change in her life, Esther," said Lulu, and he began drawing in the net. "And you too, Syto, you're in a major rut." The net surfaced, a fist of sardines clumped at the end. "But change is always hard, that's a true fact. And speaking for myself, I'm a peaceful man."

For two weeks Lulu didn't miss a day on the boat, and he talked about money so incessantly that Syto wondered if his brother had gone *boujwa*, money-crazy. "You know," Lulu would say, "in a way it would be terrible to have a lot of money. All these people hanging around, all these women in your bed, you'd never know if it was you they liked or just your money." *Moneymoneymoney* like an itch on his tongue, this from a man who claimed he could hear dogs chuckling to themselves and who the voodoo gods favored with frequent possessions and dreams. One day as they were hauling in the lobster traps, Lulu said, "You know, Syto, I don't think it was the devil who tempted Jesus. I don't think the devil was out there with him at all, those forty days in the wilderness. That was just Jesus all by himself, *oui*. Nobody out there tempting Jesus but Jesus himself."

Syto was worried for his brother. He was worried for them both, but when they found another load of contraband—four duffel bags this time, in the shade of the trees that rimmed Pointe Boucan—Lulu studied the situation a moment, then said:

"I don't even want the shit."

"Well I sure don't want it," said Syto. "So what do we do?"

A black and green dragonfly skittered past their heads. The sea rustled against the rocks like a cow scratching its back. "No way we're giving it to the cops," said Lulu.

"No."

"So is there any *politicaille* we can halfway trust? Even this much." Lulu flashed the tip-end of a finger.

"How about Méreste?" Syto suggested.

Lulu made a gagging noise.

"He used to be a priest."

Lulu's head tipped forward, conceding this.

"He's Lavalas," Syto said, invoking the once-revered name of President Aristide's party.

"I thought he was MPP."

"Whatever, I can't keep them all straight anymore."

"Okay, we might as well. He's probably our best shot."

Senator Jean-Mario Méreste received Syto and Lulu in his walled compound on the outskirts of Jacmel. Dressed in a white guayabera and drapey linen slacks, he accepted the contraband with a furrowed brow, praising the Charles brothers' steadfast civic spirit and respect for the law. Within days, as if by coincidence, the senator's entourage was flaunting Uzi machine guns as they tooled around town in new Toyota pickups. Senator Méreste had acquired a Mercedes SUV, and was being mentioned on the radio as a possible presidential contender.

Well, what could you do. The evenings he wasn't fishing Syto sat in his meditation place under the almond tree, and while the leaves dropped around him like exhausted birds he tried to put the whole business out of his mind. Neighbors came by to gossip and sympathize, and often Esther sat with him under the tree, silently stitching up the shredded nets he brought in. She never spoke—she'd had the *pa-palé* disease ever since their daughter's death—but it wasn't a surly or raging silence, Syto knew that now. At first he'd thought she was angry with him, which he understood—wasn't he furious with himself? Though why that was he couldn't exactly say. But with time he began to suspect that her silence had nothing to do with him, that she was performing an act of intense devotion like the nuns who pledged themselves to mindfulness of God, adhering to a passion so pure and strict that their lives amounted to a form of prayer.

It demanded respect, this kind of silence; he no longer tried to trick her into talking, though it was lonely, having a wife who never spoke. They were in their quiet mode under the almond tree one evening when their neighbors hustled up carrying Lulu in a sling. His eyes were swollen shut, his face resembled pulped fruit, and from the whistling in his chest Syto knew that several of his ribs were broken. The neighbors had found him slumped in the Jacmel town square, blubbering with pain and delirious rage. They got him into a tap-tap headed for Marigot, and on the way, revived by water and a couple of hits of rum, he told them how he'd stood outside Méreste's gate, denouncing the senator in such livid terms that his thugs had no choice but to rush out and beat Lulu down in the middle of the street. Lulu's strength seemed to return as he told the story; by the time the tap-tap pulled into Marigot he'd miraculously rallied enough to break away from his friends and dash to the police station, where a confrontation with Michelet led to his second beating of the day.

"I think the cops would've killed him," said Alcide, one of the men who found him in Jacmel. "But we told them he was crazy, he didn't know what he was doing."

Lulu grabbed his brother's arm and pulled him close. "I'm not crazy," he told Syto in a clenched hiss. "I'm just looking for a little justice in this life."

"See what I mean?" said Alcide, rolling his eyes. "Totally nuts."

In the days that followed Lulu's girlfriends worked in shifts, nursing him through the hell of his healing pains. They arrived according to some unspoken schedule, always carrying a pot of griot or fried plantain, and there was hardly any unpleasantness among them, at least until they were sure he was going to live. After several weeks he was strong enough to move back to his house; meanwhile Syto sailed out on the hot summer nights and grimly did the fishing for both of them. At this time of year the fish were always sluggish, the *baret* and snapper yet to make their runs; Syto had to sail out five or six kilometers to make a decent catch, out where wicked squalls whipped through several times a night and salvos of flying fish exploded from the dark, stinging like clusters of tiny whips. Late one afternoon he piled his gear into the boat and headed out to sea, rowing first into the cut at Cayes Caiman to pluck sea urchins off the rocks for bait. It was a hot, bright day, the light a harsh actinic blue. He fetched his boat up on the scrap of beach, then hunted among the sluices and tidal pools for *chadwon*, the waves swatting the boulders with sharp, crackling sounds. He was picking his way along and not thinking of much when the duffel bags caught his eye, three of them laid in a row at the edge of the woods like cooling loaves. He scrambled up the beach and stood over them, blinking, swaying, strangely short of breath. Sunlight pulsed off the water in glittering barbs. Cicadas rowled in the woods that skirted the beach, the big, solemn trees looming at Syto's back like a congress of village elders. For several moments he thought about Michelet and Méreste, and Lulu's savage beating, and the soldiers' cruel laughter and the shame of being a Bouki, but there was really no need to convince himself. The second he saw the stuff he knew he was going to take it.

"You're asking *me?*"

Lulu was sitting under the lean-to in his yard, a rough shelter of palm fronds he'd woven together to keep the rain and sun off his head while he worked. Crinkled tubes of paint, old cans stuffed with brushes, half-finished pictures propped on wobbly easels— Lulu sat on a stool in the middle of it all and painted.

"Lulu, come on. I'm just asking for a little help here."

"Forget it man, I've had it with drugs. I did the right thing and it almost got me killed."

Syto sagged, pulled up a chair, and eyed his brother's latest painting. A tall, skinny black man in a top hat and tails was grinning while a cane field burned in the background. With his fancy clothes, his sunglasses and smart walking stick, this had to be Gédé, the voodoo god of death who doubled as the oversexed lord of misrule. He seemed to be dancing a little jig while the fire raged at his back, delighting as always in chaos and havoc. Papa Gédé was one of the *lwa* who'd come with the ancestors from Africa and had sustained them through the bitter times of slavery and beyond. Even now, in the globally networked age of computers and cell phones and transnational crime, the *lwa* refused to fade away, refused to abandon their *serviteurs*. Syto could no more imagine negotiating life without them than he could without his eyes or the guidance of his reason.

"Lulu, I'm dying here. I've got no idea what to do with the stuff."

"You should've thought about that before you took it."

"Listen, the only thing I was thinking was I didn't want those guys to get it."

Lulu seemed to soften at this. He was dabbing jots of red into the lurid night sky; since his beating he was using a lot of black and red.

"Where is it now?"

"I dug a pit in the Erzulie house, under the altar."

"How much?"

"Three bags, like the first time."

Lulu blew out his cheeks and reached for a different brush. Tiny human silhouettes took form inside the fire, either dancing or dying, it was hard to say which.

"Does Esther know?"

"She helped me hide it."

Lulu painted for a minute, then sighed. "Okay, brother. I'm listening."

"Well," said Syto, "I was thinking we should get in touch with Nixon. He might know some people who could help us out."

"Nixon? He's just a kid!"

"He's a grown man, Lulu, you're forgetting. And he's family. We need a guy we can trust."

Lulu considered as he touched up Papa Gédé's mouth, limning the teeth so that his smile took on the raucous leer of a skull. "Nixon. Okay."

"But I can't go myself, Michelet's watching me. And I bet he's watching you too."

The brush froze in mid-stroke. "You mean he knows?"

"I think he'd take me if he knew for sure, but he's suspicious. His guys keep driving by."

"Shit, Syto. This is serious."

"No kidding. So we better get somebody to Port-au-Prince quick."

They sent word to Nixon through one of Lulu's girlfriends, a *marchand* who traveled to Port-au-Prince every week with loads of oranges and limes to sell. In the meantime Syto put on his slackest Bouki face and went about his business, which at the moment involved dragging his boat up on the beach for caulking and repainting, a yearly chore that kept him near his house and also out in circulation among his neighbors. If Michelet wanted him, Syto reasoned, he'd do the snatching when Syto was alone. As it was Land Cruisers full of flunky cops eased through the village several times a day, a heightened presence that naturally made people talk. Working there on the village commons of the beach, Syto heard the rumors like everyone else, that a local had gotten hold of a load of contraband. And he noticed how pleased his neighbors seemed about this, how they laughed and jittered around in a hyper way whenever they talked about putting one over the cops.

When Michelet came it was in the full light of day, alone, pulling up to Syto's house in his government-issue Nissan pickup. Syto and Esther were just finishing their midday meal under the almond tree; Esther looked at Syto with utter calm, her eyes more eloquent than years of talk. *He can't touch us,* her face implied, and it was true, Syto realized — since their daughter died they had nothing to lose. He felt the fear snap off him like a hat snatched by the wind.

"M'sieu chef des gendarmes," he said with goofy formality, walking over to the truck. "This is certainly an honor."

"Hello, Charles," Michelet said, politely enough. "I want to talk to you." From his truck he surveyed Syto's small *lakou:* the cleanswept yard, the one-room house with its neat kitchen garden, the crooked hut set back among the scrub trees. Syto had built the hut years ago as a devotion to the goddess Erzulie.

"Of course, m'sieu le chef."

"I want you to tell me about the cocaine," said Michelet.

"Of course, m'sieu le chef. Which cocaine, please?"

Michelet's teeth did a slow, decalcifying grind. For all his power he looked whipped sitting there in his truck, like a man in serious trouble with his wife. "We heard that a load of contraband was dropped at Cayes Caiman last week. On Thursday. And you were seen there on Thursday."

"Yeah? Hmmm, I don't know, m'sieu le chef. Cayes Caiman, yeah, sure, I go over there sometimes, it's a good place for *sirik* and *chadwon*. But you know I'm not so good with days. Thursday, you said?"

Michelet gave him a hooded, menacing look. "You were seen, okay? We know you were there. So if you know anything about that contraband, you better tell me."

"M'sieu le chef, of course I will tell you about any drugs I see. Whenever I see anything I go straight to the police, just like the time me and my brother brought the sacks to you. Let the past be your guide, please, m'sieu le chef. You know we're men of honor here."

Michelet's face turned positively saurian. "Yeah," he grunted, "let's talk about your brother. How is his health these days?"

Syto eagerly bobbed his head. "Fine, good, sure, he's going to be okay. No problem there, m'sieu le chef."

"He deserved it, you know, that punishment he got. Those were some pretty bad things he was saying about me."

"Oh my brother," Syto wailed, tilting his face toward the clean aqueous light of the trees, "listen, my brother goes a little crazy sometimes. You know he's an artist? Yeah, he's one of those crazy guys. But we're watching him, don't worry about a thing, chef. He won't be bugging you anymore."

Michelet scowled. He pondered a moment, then snuffed his nose. "Charles, it's not a good idea to mess with me."

"No, m'sieu le chef."

"We've got the Americans breathing down our necks on this, they're screaming at us to shut down the go-fasts. So if you know anything, you better tell me." He knocked the gear into reverse. "And if you don't, stay the hell out of my way."

Syto was already nostalgic for his previous life, when all he'd had to worry about was coaxing a living from the fished-out waters off Trois Pins. "You take even the little fish like this?" a *blan* once asked him, one of the aid guys who occasionally came around to pester the fishermen with stupid questions. Syto had shrugged and stared at his feet, somewhat cowed by the *blan*. "Well, sure," he'd answered. "If I don't take it, somebody else will." And that's what it was coming to, Syto reflected, either you took what you could or you starved to death, but fishing was a relatively obscure arena. The whole world, on the other hand, was mad for drugs. He worried so much he thought his head might explode, and by the time Nixon finally showed up, Syto was more than ready to get rid of the stuff.

He came in the middle of the night with three of his friends, all of them burly, glowering, coal black youths with stylish silky clothes and gold chains around their necks. Lulu was with them; it had been years since Nixon visited Trois Pins and he couldn't remember his way in the dark, finally stumbling onto Lulu's hut by chance. Nixon had been born in Port-au-Prince under Duvalier *père,* when a rumor was going around that the American president was planning to visit; the boy's mother, Syto and Lulu's older sister, had named her son after the great man in hopes of winning an audience and maybe a break for her son. No visit had ever materialized, and only such breaks as Nixon could conjure for himself out of Haiti's thin air of opportunity. In recent years word had drifted back through family channels of the fortune Nixon made during the embargo, buying gas over the Dominican border and running it into Port-au-Prince on armed trucks.

Now he was said to own gas stations and a fleet of tap-taps. Little Nixon, Syto thought as he stared at the bull-necked tough across the table, Nixon the skinny, sickly kid whose mother used to ship him off to Trois Pins whenever he needed fattening up. First he asked for a tumbler of water, which Esther placed before him on the table. Nixon took a pinch of the powder, dropped it into the glass, and pushed it into the light of the single candle. The crystals sank, then vanished before they reached the bottom. Next he placed some powder on a piece of cigarette foil and held it over the candle, the stuff melting and bubbling like cane syrup, liquefying into brown goo. Now he pinched out a thicker wad of crystals and scraped them into a line on the wooden table. He took a slim golden reed out of his pocket, hunched over the table, and proceeded to introduce the drugs to his nose.

Lulu shot Syto a horrified look—*You suck it up your nose?* Nixon sat back and smiled in a distant way; fireflies seemed to be floating inside his eyes. "Uncle," he said, "where did you get this?"

Syto told him. Nixon seemed to know all about the go-fasts.

"How long have you had it?"

"About a week."

"Who else knows?"

"Only us. But the cops are hanging around, they're suspicious."

"Anybody else? What I mean is, any *étrangers?*"

"No, only Haitians. Just us and the cops."

"How much is it worth?" Lulu asked. His eyes shone like lacquer in the candlelight.

"The going rate's four thousand," Nixon told him. "Four thousand dollars U.S."

"For one sack?" Lulu cried, delighted, but Nixon frowned and glanced at his friends. Then he turned back to his uncles and spoke very slowly.

"That's four thousand," he touched the kilo bag on the table, "for one of these."

When Syto heard that, he assumed he was going to die. There was too much money involved, too many desperate people, but the next moment he was thinking: is this what a black man has to do to get a little respect? Risk your life, as Lulu had done when he denounced the government thieves? As Nixon had done running his contraband gasoline? And he sensed the same motive in Méreste and Michelet, that they'd taken the drugs as a matter of self-respect—you were either a chump or a thief, those were your choices in this world. Syto despaired, knowing he'd never be able to explain his sense that they were all, however improbably, on the same side.

"We need help," Syto said, staring at Nixon over the candle. "We can't do this alone."

"Well," Nixon said, "there's a problem. I think I know the people who brought this in. For me to take it back to Port-au-Prince when these people still have a claim on it—I can't do that. It's too direct, I wouldn't be able to walk the street. There's a way we can do it, but you have to get it to Port-au-Prince yourself. Once it gets to Port-au-Prince we can wash it, but until then I can't touch the stuff."

Syto wanted to weep. "There's three hundred kilos here," he said, waving at the sacks that seemed as big as tanker trucks. "The cops are watching every move I make."

Nixon frowned; he was sympathetic, to a point. "Uncle, I hope you think of something soon. And if you don't, I suggest you put these sacks in your boat and go dish them in the sea."

It was tempting. There were moments during the next few days when Syto felt like dishing the drugs or himself into the sea, whichever would bring the fastest relief. People began to talk of strangers cruising the highway, slick-looking characters from Port-au-Prince who were nosing around the local beaches and coves. The cops continued to harass Trois Pins with their presence, and Michelet brought the pressure in other ways: the next several nights a U.S. Army helicopter thundered over the village, its spotlight scything through the palms and huts as a canned Creole message blared from the loudspeaker. The Americans had done this before, during the invasion, when they'd rained words of goodwill down on the people; now they were giving lectures, reminding the people of Trois Pins of their patriotic duty to surrender drugs and criminals to the law. At times it seemed to Syto that the helicopter was parked on top of his house, shattering his mind with its demonic *whacka whacka whacka* while the voice droned on like madness itself.

"Yeah," Lulu said one afternoon, "they're trying to get inside your head. They're trying to drive you nuts."

Syto's jaw was still tingling from the percussive effects of last night's visit. "Well, they're succeeding. I'm not sure how much more of this I can take."

Lulu studied his brother with solemn eyes, then went back to his painting. He was working on four different pictures at once, various incarnations of Gédé propped on chairs and easels with Lulu pivoting on his stool in the middle. All month he'd been painting Gédés, anticipating a big demand from the nonexistent tourists as Papa Gédé's fête and All Souls' Day approached.

"So what are you going to do, brother?"

"I don't know." Syto pulled a chair into the shade of the lean-to. It was early afternoon, the air thick as paste; a couple of houses away someone was noodling on a drum. "I'm empty, man. I can't even think."

"Michelet still hanging around?"

"Esther took a bunch of eggplant into Marigot yesterday. He stopped her and searched through all the baskets."

"That bastard."

"It's only a matter of time, Lulu."

Lulu was painting a funeral procession of dancing Gédés, the coffin borne aloft at a rocking, joyous angle. Syto looked closer: inside the coffin a handsome couple was screwing for all they were worth.

"I tell you what I think," said Lulu. "I think you ought to dish it."

Syto groaned.

"Yeah, slip out on the boat while everybody's doing Gédé and dump it, just get rid of the shit."

"I can't do that."

"What, are you kidding me Syto?" *Bop buh bop bop brrrrp*—the drummer burned into the sexy, driving beat of the *banda*, Gédé's song. Lulu's hands trembled for a second, then stopped. "You want to die for a bunch of junk you suck up your nose?"

"No, but I don't want to live as a fool either."

"Syto, man, nobody's calling you a fool." *Brrrr-rup bop bop.* Lulu's eyes flickered and rolled back; the drum was edging him toward possession, but he gasped and shook his head, pulled out of it. "We aren't cut out for this stuff," he continued, clearing his throat. "Listen, even Nixon won't mess with this and he's tougher than any Macoute. And us, we're just *paysan*, okay? That's just who we are and there's no shame in it, we were born to serve God and live unimportant lives. So forget the drugs, Syto. Let those thieves fight it out."

"I just don't want them to have it, that's all."

"Neither do I," Lulu snapped in a thrumming, nasal voice, the voice Gédé took when he possessed someone. Lulu slumped as if unconscious, then shook himself awake. "So dump the shit," he said, more or less himself again. "Just dump it and be done with it."

"That's not good enough. They almost killed you."

Lulu frowned and turned to a different painting, a Gédé leaning forward with his hands on his cane, butt thrust between the tails of his frock coat. He was diddling his pink, rather dainty tongue at a group of high-toned bourgeois women.

"That was my affair," Lulu said, techy, annoyed. *Brrrrp-bup.* "I went kind of crazy that day."

"Maybe I'm a little crazy too," Syto said, scaring himself. "Just once in my life I'd like to stick it to those guys."

Lulu abruptly pushed to his feet, the stool flying backward as he swagged and reeled around like a spooked horse. He was trying to fight the god coming into his head, but Lulu succumbed so easily to possession—a little drumming could do it, a little dancing and rum, or at times the mere sight of someone else who was possessed. "Look," he said, his voice a high-tension drone, "this is your affair, you're the one who took the stuff. You tell me the plan and I'll help you, but it's not my deal. You have to decide, Syto." He tried to walk, but one of his legs stayed rooted to the ground. He heaved at it like a stubborn tree stump, then lurched off, dragging the leg behind him.

"But I'll tell you this," he said over his shoulder, "you better figure out something fast. Because when I look at you lately, I'm seeing crosses in your eyes."

Lulu shuffled into his hut; Syto heard him collapse on his mat, and soon a slurred, restive muttering drifted back through the door, the hiccupy *ke ke ke* of the gravedigger's chant. Syto felt the skin along his spine prickle, a hundred tiny needles jabbing to the bone. He stared at the paintings. Think of something, he told himself. Think.

Syto Charles bought a seat on the last tap-tap out of Jacmel on All Hallows' Eve, just as the Gédés were starting to appear on the streets. Waiting in the bus with his hat pulled low he watched them emerge in their absurd clothes, their faces crudely smeared with white greasepaint. They went around harassing people with their jokes and stupid songs, air-humping the women with their fluid hips. The victims shrieked and played along, but even as they laughed they stiffened and shrank away, uneasy in the living presence of death.

At sunset the tap-tap finally trundled forward, Syto bowing his head and saying a silent prayer of thanks. His big cardboard box was secured on the roof, sealed with tape, additionally bound in sisal twine, and labeled "Café" on every side. He was stunned to have made it out of Marigot, much less Jacmel, but he'd counted on the confusion of the holiday to give him a small bit of cover. As the tap-tap left the city and climbed into the mountains it passed streams of people dressed all in white, groups of voodoo *dévoués* walking to their temples with a Gédé sometimes prancing along, teasing the crowd. Looking out across the mist-bleared valleys and hills Syto could see bonfires fluttering on the peaks, the dusk rising to them from the folds and hollows like a gray green swamp seeping out of the earth.

Jacmel's huddled lights were far below now, disappearing and reappearing as the road switchbacked, finally vanishing for good when the mountains shouldered in. Syto tried not to hope, which as the miles ticked by became an act of will like holding his breath: every once in a while he had to let go. Through it all he continued praying to Jesus and Mary and the voodoo *lwa*, praying not for success, not even for the safety of his skin, but for a truer deliverance, whatever that might be.

Which was, he supposed when the warning shots came, just as well. The Land Cruiser swung wide and overtook the bus on a desolate mountain curve, the cops hanging out the windows and waving their pistols, screaming at the bus driver to stop. That higher deliverance, then, that's what he should strive for—Syto felt strangely unburdened as he stepped off the bus, almost wise, as if he'd finally grasped the point of life, and the only thing he really wanted now was to see Esther one more time. Michelet ordered the passengers to line up with their baggage, and as the people went about organizing themselves the cops were seized by a kind of authoritarian fit, charging around the road and kicking and screaming, cuffing women and children no less than the men. Michelet himself stood off to the side silently quivering, simmering in his own little world of rage. The passengers gradually fell into line with the guardrail at their backs, the rail skirting the lip of a dark ravine with a woodcut silhouette of mountains beyond. Syto was conscious of the faint thump of drums in the ravine as Michelet made his way down the line and stopped.

"Syto Charles."

"Oui, m'sieu le chef."

Michelet cast a brief, seemingly thoughtful glance to the side, then wheeled and struck Syto a lashing blow. The other passengers turned away with a resigned moan.

"What is this?" Michelet screamed, kicking the cardboard box.

Syto tried to shake the blue sparks out of his eyes. "Coffee, m'sieu le chef. To sell in Port-au-Prince." He thought Michelet was going to hit him again, but after a gruesome pause the *chef* snapped at his men to open the box. One of them sheared through the top with a nasty-looking knife, then the others pulled out two heavy burlap sacks. At a nod from Michelet, his deputy slashed them open with a single stroke, the sacks stuffed so tightly that the fabric burst with a lightning rip, releasing a dense arcing spew of—

Coffee. For several moments Michelet could only stare. He stepped into the road and scuffed at the beans, then shook the sacks until every last particle had rattled free. He turned and gaped at the crowd as if this were a dream, then his eyes fixed and hardened, coalesced with a plan. He advanced on Syto, drawing his pistol as he came. The other passengers inched back, and even the cops seemed to cower and avert their eyes. Syto had turned his face to the stars and consigned his soul when two buses suddenly blew around the corner, horns wailing, boom-box drums blaring, a profound, gurgling hum underlying it all like steam boilers about to explode. The buses pulled up with their lights on high-beam, wallowing in a backwash of diesel exhaust. The doors flapped open; cops and prisoners squinted into the void, and the next moment a swarm of Gédés was tumbling out the doors, coming at them like a horde of demented undertakers.

No, Syto thought, *keep going*, but in a moment he saw that it was out of his hands. The Gédés danced into the road singing and clacking their teeth, gleefully farting as they went for the officers. Many of Syto's fellow passengers were possessed at once, lurching about until they were caught by their neighbors, then coming to with saucered eyes and sucking cheeks to exchange ritual greetings with their fellow Gédés, vigorously shaking both hands and twirling around, blowing mists of pepper-rum in one another's face. Soon the road was filled with leering, chanting Gédés, most of them strutting about in fashions from the nineteenth century. They wore tattered frock coats with thickly padded shoulders, top hats, wing collars, a stray spat or two; several men sported veils and full-length evening dresses. They stole the officers' hats first thing, then demanded food and money and tried to pick the cops' pockets. A group of six or seven Gédés was roughly hustling Michelet—so changed was Lulu by the crisis of possession that Syto barely recognized his brother, an especially eloquent Gédé who was praising the formidable pungency of Madame Michelet's *coco*, the savory little stinger that was her *langèt*.

"Get out of here!" Michelet screamed. "This is a police matter!" The Gédés immediately tossed off pompous salutes, then marched around with their canes thrown over their shoulders, spouting idiotic orders as they circled Michelet. Several others ran off and pre-

tended to bully the crowd, which inspired shrieks of laughter up
and down the line. Michelet weakly raised his gun, but how could
he kill the god of death? His deputies were gagging and clutching
their throats, having inhaled the mists of pimento-steeped rum—
more noxious than the mace they carried on their belts—which the
Gédés were swilling and blowing at each other. The *chef*'s hat was
gone, his shirt blotched with rum and spittle; he took a faltering step
toward Syto, then clenched and spun about with a retching sound,
eyes goggling as he fought the god in his head. The last Syto saw of
Michelet, the *chef* was bellowing at his harried deputies for rum as
they bundled him toward the refuge of their truck.

"Come with us!" Lulu shouted to the crowd. "We're going to the
palace to see the president!" The passengers cheered and gathered up
their parcels, and soon the convoy was barreling through the countryside, the Gédés hanging out the windows and singing dirty songs,
roiling villages from the mountains to the capital. Syto had the ad-
dress in Port-au-Prince where they were supposed to go, but neither
Lulu nor the delighted driver would hear of it until they'd driven up
the Champ de Mars and stopped in front of the palace. The park was
full of late-night revelers, the nucleus of a riot of collective joy that
erupted when the Gédés poured off the buses. The startled guards
refused to open the gates, but the crowd chanted so robustly that the
president was flushed at last from the palace. Flanked by bodyguards,
laughing and mugging like it was all a big joke, he made a short, dull
speech about the manifest uniqueness of the Haitian people, then
passed five-gourde notes through the fence to each Gédé.

So even presidents must acknowledge the primacy of death.
Once they had their homage the Gédés left willingly enough, Syto
coaxing them onto the buses and directing the lead driver to the
house in Bellevue, where Nixon and his gang herded everyone inside. As the god departed each man's head a somewhat dazed Trois

Pins fisherman took his place; once he'd recovered, his jacket and pants were removed and turned inside-out, revealing a system of compartments sewn into the lining. After a lifetime of mending battered nets and sails, the women of Trois Pins were expert seamstresses. Each niche was rolled and tufted so that the lining was smooth, not the slightest bulge visible from the outside. Every man had smuggled eight to ten kilos in his clothes; Gédé's extravagant costume had carried the weight, and while possession had not been part of the plan, the men were elated to learn that the god had been in their heads. In short order a celebration commenced, a fiery *bamboche* with singing and dancing and gallons of rum. Nixon kept standing on chairs and making sentimental speeches; Lulu wept and laughed and hugged his brother a hundred times, and every couple of minutes they drank a toast to Syto, who was sitting with his chair tipped against the wall so that they couldn't slap him on the back anymore.

Syto, he was happy, sure. But mainly he just wanted to go home.

Lulu laughs at him sometimes. He'll be sitting there watching Syto, then for no apparent reason he'll break up laughing and say, "I still can't believe it."

"Believe what?" Syto asks.

"Nothing, brother. You're just funny, that's all."

In some ways life is easier, though filled as always with worry and risk. Everyone in Trois Pins has a new house now, concrete-block structures with running water and stout zinc roofs that purr in the rain. After several weeks in her new house, Esther started to hum, and lately she's been singing in a close, cautious voice; the change, as Lulu predicted, has done her good, though Syto knows he has to be patient. Most of their neighbors have new boats as well, with big outboard motors that boom them along, but Syto kept his old gaff-sail rig. He doesn't do so much fishing these days, anyway. Every month Nixon sends him money from the Texaco station they own together, more money than Syto could earn in a year of fishing. He turns over half to Esther, and most of the rest he gives away or spends on ceremonies for his *lwa*.

So life is easier, but Syto knows he can't relax. From time to time Land Cruisers ease by his house, and at night the American helicopters buzz Trois Pins as they head out to sea—they shoot at the go-fasts now, the marksmen dangling from the hatch with their high-powered rifles, though lately the go-fasts are shooting back. Syto knows their nightly flybys are a message, just as he knows Michelet will take him if he gets a chance. And while he has no knowledge of the classified files in Langley, Virginia, concerning the drug-running franchise of one "Cito Charle," Syto nevertheless suffers sometimes from "eyes," the general fretfulness and anxious feelings you get when too many people are talking about you.

He doesn't doubt that sooner or later they'll come for him—the Americans, perhaps, or the gangs or the cops. Meanwhile Syto watches his back, and at night he thanks God for another day of life and prays for the soul of his daughter in heaven. The last time Marie-Lucie appeared in his dreams, she was fourteen or fifteen, a trim, pretty girl wearing loafers and the plaid uniform of the École Supérieure. She had books and a looseleaf binder in her arms, and she smiled at Syto as she entered the yard.

"How is school?" Syto had called to her in the dream.

"I'm studying mathematics!" she answered brightly.

"Mathematics!" Syto cried, impressed. Marie-Lucie joined him under the almond tree, and Syto was happy while they sat together looking through her books, even as he realized it was no more than a dream.

The Lion's Mouth

Jill arrived at the Royal Sierra every evening around six, took a stool in front of the TV at the open-air bar, and passed the time watching the news and quietly drinking herself stupid while Starkey did deals out on the terrace. In the last few weeks this had become her favorite thing to do, watching cable news and drinking while the day faded out, feeling Starkey at her back like a snug bedfellow. She had a theory about this, a half-serious notion that she could sense his presence without turning to look, as if he gave off a subtle heat or smell to which she'd grown peculiarly attuned.

"Kushay-o, Miss." Bazzy was dressing a tray of drinks with

pineapple and cherries, smiling as Jill slid onto the stool. She was a good customer—patient, soft-spoken, pretty, white. A friend of Starkey's. It was like being a member of a club.

"How's the body, padi?"

"Not so bad. Way you-sef, Miss?"

"Not so bad. Can I get a rum-cola?"

"No problem, Miss."

A breeze like moist velvet blew off the ocean, and for several minutes after sunset the sky filled with brilliant silver blue light, as if rinsing itself of the day's corrosive glare. The Royal sat on one of the peninsula's remotest points, a cheap concrete shell with a nice beach and a crumbling veneer of tropical luxury. No one touched the pool for fear of cholera; weeds and debris were overtaking the neglected grounds, and mold billowed over the walls in complex swirls like countries on a sprawling fantasy map. The Royal was, however, possibly the safest place in Freetown, and certainly, to Jill's mind, the most degenerate, the hotel of choice for the louche community of foreigners who viewed Sierra Leone as an opportunity. A clutch of coal black whores sat on a couch near the bar, boldly eyeing every white man who walked through the door, while a few more girls were trolling the terrace. Last year the front line had been a few miles south, and though the rebels had been driven out months ago shooting could still be heard at night, the U.N. skirmishing with the holdouts or freelance gangs. In the mornings bodies occasionally washed up on the Royal's postcard-perfect beach.

"Rum-cola, Miss."

"Thanks, padi."

The news segued from the American presidential campaign into a story on the wealth effect, the triumphant affluence that the U.S. was enjoying thanks to its high-tech genius and the long bull market. Jill felt discouraged, if only briefly; she'd let the greatest money-grab in history pass her by, though even if she'd been living in the States all this time, she would have done her best to ignore it. She had a congenital distrust of money and luxury, her militant asceticism further aggravated by a very low tolerance for boredom. How did you get the money from there to here? First of all you had to care, and caring, as far as Jill could see, was an accident of birth, just as her own predilection was an accident, a random number that came up. Her father cared about money, very much so; she'd grown up more than comfortably on Connecticut's gold coast. She had a brother at Salomon Brothers who apparently cared, and an entrepreneur sister who was getting rich off the software she cooked up in a Tribeca loft. So much on the one hand, so little on the other; often she wondered what kept the world from going up in flames. *Do you think they'd cut my funding if white people were dropping dead?* She'd written that to her mother, who'd written back: *Come home. We have hungry people in America too.*

She turned on her stool and caught Starkey's eye; he was deep in conversation with a glistening black man, but not so deep that he couldn't manage a little irony for Jill, a smug shadowing around the corners of his lips. They were talking diamonds, probably, though it could be anything, palm oil, bauxite, shrimp, titanium, rubber—for a country with a ruined economy, there were an awful lot of deals around, and Starkey, who'd lived here on and off for years, seemed to have a paying role in most of them. And he made it look so easy, a revelation for Jill, who'd always viewed the getting of money in terms of hassle and guilt. "Don't work hard, work smart," he told her in his plummy English voice, and that was part of it, the mellow, cheerful voice that made the things he said sound so reasonable. He gave people hope, he made them feel close to something real, this in a place that kept threatening to slide past zero.

Presently he excused himself and came over to the bar. Physically he wasn't much, a short, thick-legged man with a blunt, fleshy face and thinning hair dyed an improbable midnight black. He had an embarrassing taste for gold accessories, and most days dressed for business in shorts, espadrilles, Hugo Boss golf shirts—resort-wear, here in one of the world's genuine hellholes. Shed of his clothes he was worse than she'd expected, his body pale and soft as a mitt of dough, shot through with a vestigial stringiness. What had surprised Jill as much as anything was how little all this mattered to her.

"How's the time, Bazzy?"

"Eh boss, I manage small-small. You want Sassman's?"

"As long as you're pouring." Starkey brushed Jill's hand, a ges-ture that managed to be both casual and intimate. "So what's the news at home, love?"

This was a running tease, his insistence on seeing her devotion to the news as a bright girl's interest in current events. They both knew she watched mainly for the sedative effect.

"Oh, they're still getting rich," she said. "And wondering which Third World country they need to bomb next. Being an American these days, that's sort of like being a walking joke, right?"

"Come now, no one holds you responsible. Have you had any-thing to eat?"

She shook her head.

"Then join us. Come have dinner and forget the news."

"I would," she said in mock distress, "but I never know what to say to your friends."

"Nonsense, you're perfectly charming. All of my friends adore you."

Adored, sure; white women of any description were in short supply. "Who's that black man you were talking to?"

Starkey accepted the drink from Bazzy; his hands around the

glass were like plump beef filets. "That's Kamora. The diamond officer at the heliport."

"I knew I'd seen him somewhere. So he's a friend too?"

"After a fashion. He dropped by with a bit of news."

"Good or bad?"

"Well, you'll probably be pleased. Though it's not so nice for me." Starkey cut her a look; in the dim light of the bar his eyes were wine-dark. "They arrested a man in Antwerp today, someone from Ferrin's outfit. Trying to pass a batch of Salone diamonds, apparently."

"You're kidding."

"I am not." Starkey's face was grave. "Rather a shock, isn't it? Everyone knew the ban was good PR, but nobody thought they'd actually try to enforce the damn thing."

For months pressure had been building for an industry embargo on unregistered diamonds out of Sierra Leone, the "blood diamonds" that kept the rebels in operation. Years ago the RUF had charged out of Liberia pushing some vague Marxist rhetoric about liberating the country, their rationale for an agenda that mainly involved robbing, raping, and murdering every peasant they could get their hands on. They kept their columns well-stocked with ganja and coke, and it was the rebel foot soldiers—most of them teenagers, some no older than ten or twelve—who'd filled the DP camps with amputees. "Chopping," they called it, their signature practice of hacking off one or both of their victims' arms. "Short sleeves or long?" they were said to taunt as they raised their machetes.

"Go on, Jill. I give you permission to gloat."

Jill was staring stonefaced at the TV. To feel conflicted at this point was impossible—there was no conflict, not when she thought about the suffering she'd seen.

"I'm not gloating. I just don't see how they can do it."

"They can't," Starkey agreed, "but they could definitely slow it down. And trade's been sketchy enough as it is the last few months."

Jill sipped her rum. "So what are you going to do?"

"Oh," he said easily, "no sense running off in a panic. I'll stick around a bit, see if they're serious."

"And if they are?"

He consulted his drink. "Suppose I'd have to follow the trade in that case. Mono or Guinea, that's where you'll see the stones turning up."

"Gee, Starkey, you'd actually cut out on us? Think of all the great fun you'd miss around here."

His laugh was phlegmy, coarse, as raw as Bazzy's blender pulverizing ice. "Well yes, I really should think about that. All the fun one might miss in dear old Salone." He turned fond as his laughter trailed off, his eyes tender, fixed on hers as if he meant to coax out some sort of therapeutic truth. Jill turned back to the TV—she felt, rather than heard, the faint break of his sigh, his feathery chuckle as he leaned in close.

"Do you know how good you look right now? You're a gift, Jill, that's what you are to me. You're just amazing, love."

She felt warm, slack; her eyes went slightly out of focus. Was this what it felt like to be loved? Before Starkey she'd never let anyone talk to her this way, and lately she had trouble remembering why.

I want the hardest place—she'd actually said that when she signed her contract. She'd spent two years in Guatemala with the Peace Corps, then three years in Haiti with Save the Children, and after that she wouldn't be satisfied with anything but the very worst. *I want the hardest place*—on any given day that was usually Sierra Leone, "the mountain of the lion," a small, obscure West African country known mainly for its top-quality kimberlite diamonds and the breathtaking cruelty of its civil war. She'd signed on as country project director for World Aid Ministries, a Protestant umbrella group that specialized in long-term food relief; a religious vocation wasn't necessary for the job, only a tolerance for what might be charitably called spartan living and a masochistic attitude toward work. So here was the joke: she'd come to Salone determined to lead an authentic life and instead had discovered all the clichés in herself. She wanted to be stupid. She wanted to be rich. She wanted to be lazy, kept, indulged—this was where her fantasies took her lately, mental explorations of the guiltless life. Starkey was rich, and old enough to be her father, a package of clichés that neatly fit her own. She'd tried to pick a fight with him at the Embassy party where they met; anyone in diamonds should have been her natural enemy, but something benign in his eyes, the patient sag of his face, seemed to express a basic decency. She felt calm in his presence, she felt safe; without much fuss she'd gone back to the Royal Sierra with him that night, and it had quickly developed into a standing thing, Jill driving over every evening and staying the night. Her friends in the NGO community thought she'd lost her mind. Maybe I have, she told herself, maybe that's what crazy is. Despising precisely those things you're most attracted to.

"So Jill, you really like this guy?"

She was sitting on the cinderblock porch outside her office, skimming the registration binder that Dennis Hatch had brought over from USAID. Sometime in the next few weeks she would be leading a small convoy through the southeast, delivering resettlement packages in advance of the planned repatriation of refugees. That is if the situation held—if the RUF honored the Lomé Accords, if the U.N. peacekeepers could hang onto their weapons, if the rainy season held off and her drivers stayed sober. If a hundred different things she couldn't control came together at a single moment in time.

"I suppose," she said absently, flipping pages. Each sheet contained the vital statistics for a single family. Age, height, weight, arm circumference—numerical stick figures.

"He sure must like you." Dennis was looking through the door to her office, admiring the electrical inverter that Starkey had donated. "Is it possible the word 'whipped' could apply here?"

"I'm not clear how much seed rice is going into the package."

"Well, we're still elaborating our information on that." After ten years in the development field, Dennis had mastered a sardonic form of bureaucratese that Jill found alternately funny and maddening.

"Can you even give me a definite date?"

"Negative."

Dennis folded himself into the straw-bottomed chair beside Jill's. He had the lean, near-haggard body of a fanatic runner, and was good-looking in a nerdy sort of way, which was more or less Jill's type. His intelligence and contempt for authority made him her natural ally inside the system, and since he'd arrived in-country a year ago their friendship kept threatening to be something more. But their timing was off, their rhythm, the intangible whatever; all those late nights they'd sat up talking and drinking, and he could never bring himself to make a pass. She knew he wasn't gay, so what did that make him? Barely relevant, that's how it struck her lately.

She turned to the budget at the front of the binder. "One-forty per ton for transport."

"Can you live with that?"

"You offering better?"

"Nah."

Jill shut the binder. "Then I guess I'll have to live with it."

Several women from the sewing co-op passed by with snacks they'd bought from the street vendors outside, the women greeting Jill and Dennis with shy hellos. The co-op was housed in a building at the back of the compound, a sideline to the project's core food-relief mission. A year ago, in an absurd expense of time and energy, Jill had followed an inspiration and put the co-op together, converting the warehouse space, cadging basic supplies, plucking forty women from the refugee camps and putting them to work making skirtlike *lapas*. The project's main warehouse faced the office, a large cinderblock structure with a sheet-metal roof and rolling metal doors at either end. Everything in sight reflected Jill's rage for order: the stone paths, the neatly thatched baffas and sheds, the flame trees she'd planted about the grounds for shade. Beyond the walls lay a world of squalor and chaos, but here she'd managed to carve out a small island of control.

"So how's your beau these days?" Dennis asked in a chipper voice.

"He's fine."

"What's he say about the embargo?"

"It's bad for business."

Dennis laughed. "Duh, Jill. But good for the country. Hopefully."

"He doesn't deny it."

"You know the U.N.'s set up checkpoints on all the roads out of Kono. And anybody flying in from the interior is basically subject to a strip search."

"It's still a joke, there's no way they can stop it. You can hide a million dollars' worth of stones in a tube of toothpaste and still have room for most of the toothpaste."

"Well, I guess you'd be the expert now."

"That's just common sense, Dennis, it doesn't take any expertise."

He flashed her a vicious look, out of all proportion to what she'd said. She had to check an impulse to apologize.

"Christ, Jill, what do you see in this guy? I'm saying this as a friend—"

She turned away.

"—somebody who really cares about you. These are not good people you're hanging around with, okay? They're into a lot of nasty stuff, they're basically bleeding the country dry and that's against everything we're working for. It just makes me wonder where your head is at."

Jill was calm; she felt as if she was floating above the argument. "So who do you want me to hang around?"

"Look, all I'm saying is I'm worried about you. It doesn't fit, you and this guy, every time I try to picture it I come up blank. I just think you being with him is a symptom of something."

"Well, yes. Sex is usually a symptom of something."

Dennis winced. "All right, okay, I'll shut up now. I know I'm way out of line." He ran a hand through his hair. "Not that anything I've said matters anyway."

Jill acknowledged this with a half-smile; she realized that Dennis mostly made her sad these days.

"You know," he said, "as long as you've got this guy wrapped around your little finger, you might hit him up for a contribution to the co-op."

"Nope. It just doesn't work that way."

"Has anything come through?"

"Handicap International turned us down last week—I guess they don't believe there's such a thing as one-armed seamstresses. CRS said no, Global Relief, everybody. They're sending all their money to Kosovo now."

"Well, Kosovo's hot these days. And a lot of people have pretty much written off Salone." He stretched a leg, gingerly popped the knee. "How much longer can you keep it going?"

"A couple of weeks. Maybe a month if we really string it out."

"If you give me the numbers I'll try to get something for you. Enough to keep it going till some real money comes through."

"Aisha's got the books," Jill said, rising at once. "Come on."

The co-op was housed in a narrow concrete building with barred windows along one side and rough wooden tables arranged in rows. Wicker baskets full of country cloth and *gara* were placed at each row, and the women worked in teams of two, one woman stitching while the other held the cloth; in a matter of weeks they'd grown so proficient that each team could sew as fast as any able-bodied seamstress. On a good day the co-op turned out over two hundred garments, but the stuff sold too slowly piecemeal, and the Lebanese traders wouldn't buy in bulk until they were satisfied the peace was going to hold.

Jill always felt a kind of compression when she stepped into the co-op, a crowding of awareness that made her hushed and anxious while at the same time lifting her out of herself. How believers might feel when they entered a church—it had something to do with suffering, she suspected, but beyond that she lacked the energy to analyze it. While Dennis and Aisha went through the books Jill tallied and stacked the morning's output of clothes, looking over the room while she worked. Her gaze inevitably lingered on the women's stumps; on some level she never really stopped thinking about that,

though for a long time she'd tried to deny her obsession, this thing
she had—which seemed shameful, vaguely pornographic—for visu-
alizing her own mutilation. "It go red when you chopped," one of
the women had told her. "Everyt'ing go red, red, like your mind on
fire." Jill was sure she would die of horror if it happened to her;
most did, ostensibly from shock or loss of blood, and how these
women had survived was beyond her comprehension. Not just survived—how they seemed capable at times of quite genuine joy.
Lately Jill had seen them laughing and chatting as they worked,
edging back toward something like normal life. They had no idea
that she was a couple of weeks away from shutting them down.

"I can't make any promises," Dennis said as she walked him
across the compound to his jeep. The street noise beyond the walls
roared like a slow avalanche.

"You know I appreciate it," she said, and felt hopeful enough to
try a joke: "Feel free to puff up the numbers all you want."

"Well, you know that's never a good idea." He didn't smile—did
he think she was serious? At the jeep he turned and studied her so
intently that she feared some sort of ridiculous scene.

"Jill."

"What." She avoided his eye.

"Are you sure you're okay?"

"I'm fine, Dennis."

"I don't know, you just seem awfully tired lately. Frankly I think
you're depressed, not that it's any of my business. But a lot of us are
concerned."

This affected her more than she might have expected. She had
to swallow, then consciously smooth out her breathing, but even so
the irony didn't sound quite right. "Well, I may be having a normal
reaction to this place."

"It's still depression, Jill. If I were you I'd be putting some thought into that."

Sometimes at night, when they were alone in his room, Starkey would take out a batch of diamonds and instruct her on the finer points of valuation. He seemed to enjoy the ego-boost of mentoring her, the role-playing and not-so-subtle sexual subtext, and Jill went along with it, amused, not uninterested, though the diamonds themselves were disappointing. In their rough state they were such chalky little nubs, airy nothings that rattled around your palm like baby teeth, and yet they put him at the center of something vital. At night she watched him empty his pockets as he undressed, spilling out scraps of paper, cocktail napkins, matchbook covers, all with names and phone numbers scribbled on them. By eight the next morning his cell phone was going, and by nine he was meeting people downstairs, receiving them on the terrace like a little king. She was starting to see the point of it, how making money might actually be interesting, and how the more you made the more interesting it could be. And lately another revelation had come to her: Starkey was responsible only for himself. This was, she thought, the great luxury of business, of a life devoted solely to making money; it seemed strange to her, exotic in the way of forbidden things, until she remembered that this was how most people lived.

Yet in his way he took care of so many people—or was that simply part of working smart? He was extravagant with gifts and favors, a soft touch for beggars, and he tipped as if bent on keeping the whole staff afloat. He had a trade-school education—mechanical drafting, he'd confessed—and talked enough about his past for Jill to get the sense of a hardscrabble childhood, so different from her own. He wasn't at all touchy or bitter about it; he seemed to take real pleasure in the narrative of what he called her "American" life, the big house, the horse stables, good schools, college. In bed he had definite ideas about what he wanted, though he never pressed, never insisted. He didn't have to, Jill reflected, laughing to herself, feeling the heat rising into her neck and face. She supposed that's what a nice man did for you.

"Look at those bastards."

She was at the bar, sipping her third drink of the evening. Dennis Hatch slid onto the stool next to her, jutting his chin at the TV; CNN was running a story on the latest crop of tech billionaires.

"What are you doing here?"

"Meeting." His eyes stayed fixed on the TV. "Kind of makes you want to puke, doesn't it."

"In a way you've got to hand it to them. They had the energy, they went for it. They pulled it off."

"You got any money in the market?"

"Not a cent."

"Me either." He laughed. "I can't wait for the damn thing to crash."

Jill supposed she sympathized; supposed she even agreed. "So who are you meeting?"

"Some WFP honchos from Conakry, we're tightening up the strategic stocks plan. Just in case."

"Could be a good move."

"Star beer," Dennis said to Bazzy, then he turned on his stool to look over the terrace. The tables were packed with an ecumenical mix of whites and Africans. Thrashing, bass-heavy music played on the sound system, while waiters hustled up and down the steps with drinks. A stunning hooker with blond cornrows passed two feet in front of Dennis, raking him out of the corner of her eye. He turned to Jill with a smirk.

"Always a party at the Royal."

"Somebody's gotta do it."

"How come you're sitting up here?"

She followed the line of his gaze to Starkey's table, where the people and chairs were stacked three deep. "He's having office hours."

"So?"

So—she felt like a whore when she sat at his table? "I'd just rather sit up here."

Dennis turned back to the bar; they talked shop, traded gossip about their fellow expats, speculated on the political situation. Jill didn't mention the co-op; she made herself wait for Dennis to bring it up, and when he didn't she was gradually given to understand that there would be no money from the government. Despairing as she nodded and sipped her drink, maintaining, minimizing the personal side; by now it was second nature. Presently Starkey walked over to the bar, giving Dennis a bland smile as he ordered a Sassman's. Jill introduced the two men.

"Ah, USAID," said Starkey. They shook hands around Jill. "Still a growth industry, what?"

"Unfortunately yes."

"I should think the only one in Salone at the moment."

"I don't know, I understand you diamond guys are doing pretty well."

"On the contrary, they've put a ban on our product. Or haven't you heard."

"I didn't think a little thing like the law slowed you guys down."

Jill kept her eyes on the television, one hand on her drink. She wasn't especially shocked that they'd gotten into it, just surprised that it happened so quickly.

"Please," said Starkey, "let me enlighten you. My man's sitting up in Koidu with six months' worth of stones and I can't get to him even if I wanted to. And everyone here is in the same boat, we're all slowly bleeding to death. Another month or two of this and we'll be closing up shop."

"Cry me a river," Dennis said through his teeth.

"Beg your pardon?"

"Cry me a river, it's an expression. Basically it means all you guys can go fuck yourselves."

"Oh. Well. That's awfully sentimental of you."

Dennis snorted into his beer.

"You think I'm being facetious? I'm quite serious actually, the whole embargo concept is a sentimental crock. It gets the human-rights chaps all warm and fuzzy, but what it's really about is De Beers keeping a lock on the market. Seems so righteous of them, lobbying for the ban and all that—they'll shut down the juniors in the name of good citizenship, then they'll move in and open up the tap again. It's all a farce, son, a sham. I shouldn't think a smart fella like you would need me to explain."

"It's never clean," Dennis said. "I sure as hell don't need the likes of you to tell me that."

"Yes, well said, it's never clean. But you're wrong if you think things are actually going to change. People will buy and sell diamonds as always, my friend. They'll just be different people. Well," he hoisted his drink at Dennis, "cheers."

Starkey turned to leave, but Jill caught his arm.

"Stay," she murmured, tightening her grip. "Don't mind him. Just stay."

Dennis blanched; Jill wondered what it meant that for once

she felt no pity for him. He turned away, then looked back as if he couldn't help himself. "Screw you guys," he finally muttered, and left.

"Oh dear," Starkey fretted, watching Dennis make his way across the terrace. "I do hope I didn't spoil anything for you."

"It doesn't matter." Jill smiled and pulled him onto the stool next to her. She almost laughed; for the first time in months she felt clear about things.

"If you can get your guy down to Bomi," she said, "I'll bring those diamonds in for you."

"Get out. How would you manage that?"

"We've got some trucks going up-line next week, we'll be in Bomi one of those days. If your guy can meet me there I'll get your diamonds."

"Really, Jill, you have no idea—how would you get past the checkpoints?"

"You think they ever mess with me?"

He acknowledged this with a thoughtful nod. "You know the U.N.'s not the only risk."

"So pay me. Pay me for my trouble."

He looked at his drink.

"This is business, just treat it like a business deal. What's the going rate for something like this?"

Starkey hesitated. "Three percent."

"Which comes to?"

"Quite a bit, if Petrik's got what he says he's got." He looked up from his drink. "This is for your project, isn't it, your sewing shop. For Christ's sake, just let me give you the money."

"If you had it to spare, but you don't. And I wouldn't take it anyway."

"Say I agreed to let you go—what would you do for security?"

"I'll have the trucks and crews, just like always. Anything else I'd just draw attention to myself."

Starkey looked bleak, like a man imagining his own funeral. "What about your moral objection to all this?"

"Like the man said, it's never clean."

Starkey chewed the inside of his cheek for a moment. It occurred to her that he must be desperate to consider this; either that, or the challenge appealed to him, the sheer balls of letting her go alone.

"I'll need to hop down to Joburg for the cash, which you'd have to ferry in. So you see, you'd be on the spot both ways. With no security to speak of."

"I'll be under the radar, look at it that way." She laughed and squeezed his hand, wondering how much the rum had stoked her mood. "I can handle it, okay? I've done lots and lots of really hard things in my life, I don't see why I can't do this too."

"Well," he said a bit sadly, lifting the glass to his lips, "no one ever said you lacked potential."

It began, as it always did, with rumors—they started several days before she left Freetown, hints of movement, something stirring upcountry, the stories rippling through the capital in barely perceptible waves. The rumors swelled and took shape as the trucks began their swing through the southeast, and soon she was hearing it on the radio news: the RUF had surrounded peacekeepers in Magburaka and Makeni, effectively holding the towns hostage, and more peacekeepers were turned back on the road to Bendu, faced down by a bunch of kids with automatic weapons. Testing, prodding, seeing how far they could push before the U.N. pushed back—that was Jill's rationalist take on the situation, though at the depot in Kabili the Irish priest's explanation was like a slap in the face: "The devil is hungry again." The devil, or whatever psychopathic gods lived out there—Jill was beginning to hate them all. The news became something else she was responsible for, along with her drivers' morale, the insane logistics, the neverending drama of flats and breakdowns. The strategy she'd developed over dozens of these trips was simply to keep going until something made her stop, and when the Ghanian officer confronted her at the Falla depot she thought that perhaps the time had come. She thought she was busted—he was that formal, that menacing with his small squad in tow, and Jill was spacey from the heat and four nights of short sleep. He got off on a tangent about rogue kammajohs and disarmament centers and reports of "demonstrations" in the area, and it took her a while to realize that he was talking about the rebels. She almost laughed—oh, them? In that same formal shout he asked if she would accept an armed escort to Makela.

By then she already had the diamonds. They were in a cloth pouch stuffed at the bottom of her daypack; she'd gotten them the day before, while the trucks were unloading at the Bomi depot. She'd slipped away on the pretext of delivering some letters, crossed the square by a small cinderblock mosque, and followed the street past rows of mud-brick houses and sludgy garden plots. Except for a few pot-bellied children she was alone on the street—people, dogs, goats, every other living thing had sought shelter from the sun, and peering out from under the bill of her baseball cap Jill watched the street vibrate under the onslaught of light, its outlines shimmering like a half-formed mirage. In two minutes her blouse was soaked through with sweat. No one could handle sun like this for long, and she concentrated on her breathing and the motion of her legs, pulling awareness into herself as a way of saving strength. She was not, she noticed with some satisfaction, very afraid; the dense bricks of cash in the daypack gave her a sense of purpose, their heaviness pleasant on her shoulder, somehow steadying. Presently she saw what she was looking for, a hand-painted sign announcing the CHAZ=3 BAR wired to a tamarind tree by the street. She passed through a gap in the palm-thatch fence and followed the path up to the bar, a small wood-frame structure with a rusting metal roof and bushpoles supporting the porch overhang. The door stood open, the interior a bruise of shadows; she didn't falter until she heard voices inside, and then she was scared in spite of all the guarantees, in spite of Starkey's calm coaching and her own resolve. Afraid, and suddenly weary to the point of despair; this was part of the deal now, the drag-weight of fear. Another thing she'd have to carry for the rest of the trip.

She kept going because she couldn't think of anything else to do. Petrik was there, a wild-haired Russian for whom the payoff seemed to be a mere sideline, a distraction from the main business of the day, which was convincing Jill to go back to Koidu with him. "I'm rich," he declared, slouching against her—they were sitting thigh-to-thigh on a plank bench. Four Leonean soldiers sat at the table with them, dark, strapping men in camouflage fatigues who fell out laughing at everything Petrik said. His security, Jill guessed, the hired help; Petrik scowled but otherwise ignored their hazing.

"I'm rich," he insisted as the soldiers cracked up. "I know it looks not possible but is true, seven years I do nothing but work! Seven years in this shithole, one more year I take my money and I go home."

"Good," said Jill. She'd accepted a warm orange Fanta. The soldiers and Petrik were pouring gin from a filthy plastic jug, everyone sluggish and greasy-looking in the heat. The old lady who ran the place sat at the next table over, a tiny, frizzle-headed woman with immense earlobes. From time to time she reached for the jug and poured herself a drink.

"You tell Starkey, I do one more year for him."

"I'll tell him," Jill said.

"Stay with me," the Russian said, begging her with puppy eyes. "I go crazy for you baby, I take care of you. When you with me you don't worry for nothing, okay?"

"I have to go back. I'm sorry."

"I give you everything baby, you know it's true!"

"I'm sorry. I promised Starkey I'd be back in two days."

"Fuck Starkey, he's not the boss around here!" The Africans howled and slapped the table. "Me! Only Petrik is the boss in Kono! Just stay one night baby, I go nuts for you. Only one night Petrik asks you for."

"I can't," Jill said, wondering how much choice she had in the matter.

"Just one night. Please baby."

"I'm sorry. I have people waiting for me."

To Jill's horror he slumped over and started sobbing, which inspired a fresh surge of laughter from the Africans. The old lady chattered happily in Sherbro; she and the soldiers regarded Petrik and Jill with no more worry than they'd show a couple of dogs by the road. When it became clear that nothing was going to happen soon, Jill turned to the soldier with the most stripes.

"Please," she said, "talk to him. Tell him I need to go."

The soldier eyed her a moment, then leaned over and thrust his hand into the white man's pocket with a brusque, almost sexual familiarity. He pulled out a blue cloth pouch and handed it to Jill over Petrik's head; she pulled out the shrink-wrapped bricks of American currency and passed them back, then stuffed the pouch into the bottom of her daypack. She started to rise but the Russian grabbed her arm.

"Please baby." His face wrecked, pathetic; strings of dry, cottony spittle stuck to his cracked lips. "Give me one kiss and I let you go. Just one kiss baby, it's not so much."

It seemed the fastest, easiest way to go, but when she bent to kiss him it wasn't without some shading of mercy. As her lips met his she reflected that she'd never kissed a crying man before. She shuddered, but didn't rush; the Africans hooted and clapped. They were still laughing when she started down the path.

They left Falla at two in the afternoon, traveling west through a lush, monotonous country of remnant rain forest and abandoned rice paddies. Jill rode in the Mazda doublecab with Pa Conteh, while Pa's son Edmund followed in an ancient Mercedes flatbed. Jill had left Freetown with nine trucks, sending them back to the capital on successive days as their loads were delivered. After Falla the Mercedes and Mazda were empty as well; this was the first leg of the homeward trip, and as the potholes and gullies slung her around Jill considered the crude irony of the situation. Up ahead, the U.N. escort; down by her feet, blood diamonds. To gloat on it, even to think it, seemed like bad luck, though she knew that Starkey, a fearless collector of Third World ironies, would relish the story. In this she supposed she would always fail him as a student.

Pa kept riding the bumper of the U.N. jeep, trying to hurry it along. The Ghanian soldiers stared back with scathing indolence.

"These guys," Pa said in a disgusted voice, "what's the problem with these guys?"

"Take it easy, Pa. We don't want to run over the U.N."

Pa grunted; like most Leoneans he was scared of the dark and loathed the prospect of traveling at night. He was a small, wiry man with a flat-nosed Mende face, easily the best in Jill's spotty talent pool of drivers. A good mechanic, fluent in Mende and English, and so ferociously loyal that he embarrassed her at times; if Pa had a fault it was his tendency toward pessimism, though Jill reasoned that in most situations he was merely advocating the realist point of view.

"We going to Makela?" he asked for the third time.

"That's the plan."

"Lots of soldiers in Makela."

"According to the officer."

"We stay the night."

"I think that would be the smart thing to do."

He eased off the accelerator, momentarily reassured. Jill kept the daypack on the floor, half-consciously nudging it with her shoe from time to time. They gradually passed into a series of gently rolling hills, the peaks as round and mossy green as turtles' backs. The rich mineral smell of wet earth filled the cab; dense stands of fetid jungle alternated with grassy fields, the country almost oppressive in its luxuriance. Clusters of mud-wattle huts punctuated the route, their roofs freshly thatched, with staked fields beyond, but Jill could count the human beings she saw on one hand. They'd heard about the trouble and taken off, either to the towns or deep bush; the loneliness of the country, its still, desolate air, set off a hum in her head like a blank tape, and she was glad when the Ghanians passed them off to a detachment of Indian peacekeepers. There were two jeeps now, eight soldiers in all, and the Indians were considered the most professional contingent in the U.N. force. The lead jeep swung around and pulled even with the Mazda, the heat rising off their engines in cellophane waves.

"You are going to Makela?" the officer called up to Pa. He was fit, in early middle age, with alert, hawkish features and a trim mustache. His face and khakis were powdered with rose-colored dust.

"That's right."

The officer smiled when he spotted Jill in the cab; his next words seemed directed at her. "We're going to pull over for a bit, there's some business near Makela we need to sort out." His starched, precise English made her think of Starkey. "Nothing to worry about. I shouldn't think we'll be long."

They followed the jeep off the road and parked under a stand of locust trees. So here you are, Jill thought, slowly jamming the daypack under the seat with her feet. Stuck here with your head in the lion's mouth, and nothing to do but sit still and wait. Edmund walked up to bum a cigarette and get the news; they passed the water jug around, then he went back to his truck to nap. Jill settled her head against the seat and tried to relax. A dull, dry ache had taken root behind her eyes, and amid the full-body throb of general soreness there were pockets of quite specific pain, as if she'd been struck here and there with a baseball bat. She wanted to sleep but her eyes kept flipping open, gazing past the umbrella of trees to the field beyond, then the low forested hills in the distance. The arc of the horizon, the glaring, empty sky, gave her the sense of being trapped in a vast bowl of light.

"Eh, Miss Jill, how long we going to sit?" Pa was fingering the juju bundle around his neck and staring at the soldiers, who didn't seem to be in any rush. The officer and sergeant were looking through a stack of maps, the officer speaking occasionally into the jeep radio. The other soldiers stood around with their helmets off, smoking and slapping at flies.

"No idea, Pa. It's their call."

"What they doing?"

"Scoping out the situation, I guess."

"Time to go," Pa muttered gloomily, squinting at the sun. "Too many killing man out here. You just sit, after a while they gonna find you for sure."

Jill reflected that riding with her number-one driver could be downright depressing sometimes. She rested her head against the seat and watched a flock of herons turning loops above the field, their bodies startling white against the background of green. Their elegance, the serene, fluent curves of their flight, seemed to merge into the ongoing stream of her longing, the desire—only lately admitted—that she very much wanted to go home. She'd chosen this life because she couldn't imagine any other way, but over time, without her strictly being aware of it, the dead stares of the thousands of amputees had served to drain all the purpose out of her work. Those stares, the aura of hopelessness that always settled over the camps, implied that they knew something Jill didn't, a basic fact that had taken her years to understand. They were finished, their lives were over—if not now, then soon, and this applied to virtually every other Leonean as well. Her work was a delaying action at best, a brief comfort and hope to a very small few—she was handing them a glass of water through the window while the house burned down around their heads. She couldn't save them, she couldn't save anyone but herself, which made her presence here the worst sort of self-indulgence, her mission a long-running fantasy. In this light Starkey began to seem pure to her, his career an ideal she might aspire to. There was truth in that kind of life, a black-edged clarity; more than anyone else she'd ever met, he seemed to operate with a firm understanding of what was and was not possible. Such knowledge seemed to her the key to happiness, or failing that, a way of being that might be plausible, and for a time, sitting there in the sweltering truck, Jill felt as if this version was within her reach.

She could have it, but she would have to quit this kind of life, and the co-op was the deal that would let her walk away. That was the sequence she worked out sitting there in the truck, as if one couldn't happen without the other—as if the whole moral concept could be bought off with a bribe. She'd take her payoff from Starkey and turn it over to the co-op, and only then would she be allowed to leave.

She had no memory of dozing off; there was only a blank, then the thing that shouldered her out of sleep, wakefulness a half-beat behind the fear. She opened her eyes to see the herons flapping toward the treeline.

"Shhh!" hissed Pa Conteh. "You hear that?"

A faint clattering in the distance, bursts of automatic fire like nails raining down on a sheet-metal roof. With a word from their sergeant, the soldiers pulled their rifles from the jeeps and formed a loose perimeter around the stand of trees. The officer was talking steadily into the radio now, taking notes, shuffling through his stack of maps. No one seemed rattled or panicked, Jill noticed; they'd simply gotten extremely efficient in their movements.

"Rocket," Pa murmured when the explosions started. RPGs, standard with the rebels—Jill had learned about rockets the year before, while she sat out the fighting in the basement of the Cape Hotel.

"It's getting closer?" Pa asked.

"I think it is."

For the next twenty minutes they sat and listened while the gunfire grew more distinct, an excruciating exercise in self-control. Pa groaned and shook his head; Jill jammed the daypack farther underneath the seat and made herself sit completely still. Finally the officer climbed out of his jeep and walked toward the truck. His name was stenciled over his right breast pocket, *Sawhey;* he was folding a map as he came, bending it back along the creases as he approached Jill's door.

"So sorry for the delay." His voice was calm, matter-of-fact; Jill felt herself release a breath.

"That's all right."

"Apparently the situation is quite serious," he continued in the same conversational tone. "I'm afraid that Makela is out of the question today. We have a sizeable garrison in Guendu, however," he laid the map on her windowsill and pointed to a town, "and we believe the roads are clear. I strongly recommend that we proceed there."

"Could we just go back to Falla?"

"No. Apparently the situation has deteriorated there as well."

"Wow." Jill laughed without exactly meaning to. "That was fast."

"Yes," Sawhey said briskly. "So it's Guendu, then?"

"Guendu's fine. Whatever you say."

"We would like to make a detour, here," he went back to the map, "we've been asked to evacuate a small NGO group in this location. Would you be willing to carry them in your lorries?"

"Of course."

"That would be most helpful. Let's proceed then."

They followed Sawhey's jeep as it turned and headed east, back the way they'd come; as the Mazda made its lumbering U-turn, Jill could see columns of smoke rising to the west. They drove for several miles, then turned south and took a trail through the deserted countryside, their route little more than a confluence of dry streambeds and overlapping ruts. After an hour of crawling along in low gear they came to a highway, the road littered with chunks of macadam and broken rock. They turned west, the low sun blinding them now, an orange ball raging just above the horizon; after several miles they followed Sawhey's jeep onto a dirt road marked by crumbling stone gates. The road wound through a narrow belt of grassland, the jungle framing the margins like sheer canyon walls.

Ahead Jill could see a set of smaller stone portals with a cyclone fence stretching to either side, then a surreal cluster of ranch-style homes. Tennis courts, a basketball hoop, the angled stanchion of a high-dive—she'd seen such places before, self-contained bits of sub-urbia plopped down in the bush to house foreign logging or mining engineers. She started to ask Pa if he knew this place when a flash of movement caught her eye. A man, shirtless, in torn camouflage pants, had stepped from the trees, then fifteen, twenty, thirty wild-looking men were strung along the edge of the bush, waving rifles and machetes and screaming at the trucks.

"Shit," said Jill. Pa Conteh was grimly muttering to himself. Not just her mind but her whole being seemed to spool down—as if watching from some far remove, Jill saw one of the rebels lift his gun and fire into the air. Pa, Jill, the soldiers in the jeeps, everyone flinched, raising a howl of laughter from the rebels. In the jeeps the soldiers swung their rifles toward the rebels, barrels held at forty-five degrees. Jill braced for more shots but no one fired.

"Jesus, Pa."

He was muttering something over and over, shaking his head as if resigned to the dreadful worst. They passed through the stone portals and followed Sawhey's jeep toward the houses. Jill could see people huddled in the interior courtyard, a crowd of Africans sitting or crouching low. Something was off, she could feel it as the truck approached—the place was shabby, barely holding together, and that glimpse of the crowd had left her strangely unnerved. Pa parked in such a way that her view was blocked.

"Do you know this place?"

He shook his head, unable to speak just then. They glanced back and saw the rebels sauntering toward the fence, laughing and jeer-ing as they crossed the field.

"I don't think I'm gonna see my wife again," Pa said.

Jill felt so wretched that she wanted to hug the old man. Sawhey and two of his men disappeared between the houses; the other soldiers formed a line among the jeeps and trucks. Soon Sawhey reappeared leading an older, heavy white woman by the arm, the woman sobbing, pleading with him in a guttural smear. She was a nun: bareheaded, dressed in men's work clothes, but a nun nevertheless—after years in the relief business, Jill could spot them at a glance. The other soldiers came behind with two more nuns, both of them weeping as messily as the first. A handful of black women followed with quick, controlled steps, looking neither left nor right as they hurried toward the truck.

The first nun stumbled and fell to her knees. Sawhey launched into a complicated slapstick routine, pulling here, gathering there, straining to manage it all; after several seconds of this Jill jumped out of the truck and jogged toward them. As she cleared the corner of the nearest house the courtyard was gradually revealed to her, the crowd seething, roiling in place like a termite mound. Some were weeping, some babbling or laughing to themselves, others rocking back and forth or wringing their hands—the process of understanding was like a slow electric shock, a gathering jolt that finally brought her up short. She had the nun under the arm by then, but she wavered, undone by all those lunatic faces.

"Come on," Sawhey gasped, "help me."

Jill heaved, the nun lurched to her feet. The three of them staggered toward the truck.

"Do you speak Dutch?" Sawhey panted. Jill shook her head.

"They're Dutch," he managed between breaths, "there were supposed to be more." The other women were climbing into the back of the Mazda. "I think everyone bolted but these." With Pa pulling from inside, they managed to hoist the nun into the Mazda's cab. Jill turned and started back toward the courtyard.

"Get in the lorry," Sawhey told her.

"What?"

"Get in the lorry," Sawhey repeated.

"What about them?" Jill motioned toward the courtyard.

"Our orders are to evacuate staff."

Jill took a step toward Sawhey. "You're going to *leave* them?"

"Our orders are to evacuate staff."

"Good God." Jill looked past the trucks—the rebels were strung along the fence like outraged crows, cawing, bending over to show their asses, rattling the steel mesh with their machetes. They knew the soldiers wouldn't shoot unless attacked.

"Don't you know what they'll do to these people?"

"It's out of my hands. Get in the lorry, please."

Jill turned and ran back to the courtyard. She stopped at the edge of the crowd and went through the motions of making a count, though she knew there were far too many for the trucks. Physically they looked fit enough—they were well-fed, and most of them had decent clothes and shoes, but below that line of thought she was struggling, unsure what kind of claim they had on her. How flawed were they, how deficient; how deep their lack of essential human stuff, and could she live with herself if she walked away and left them to this lavish butchery. There would be no limits here, she knew that in her bones. Here it would be a pure Brueghel vision of hell, cretins and lunatics left in the care of compulsive torturers. They didn't even have their reason to protect them, the scant, maybe infinitesimal shield of being able to meet their tormentor with a sane eye. Better to go ahead and shoot them, she thought. Better to have the soldiers machine-gun the lot than leave them for the rebels to carve up.

"Miss." Sawhey had appeared at her side with an enlisted man—

did they mean to drag her off too? "Please, Miss, we need to leave at once."

"How far is it to Guendu?" she asked sharply.

"Fourteen kilometers," he answered with supreme patience. "Please, I insist that you come with us at once."

"We'll walk them out. We'll put as many on the trucks as we can and the rest will have to walk."

Sawhey blinked; it was as if she'd jabbed him with a pin. "My orders are to evacuate staff."

"And you'll evacuate staff, nobody's telling you not to evacuate staff. But you can bring out everybody else too."

He seemed to hold his breath as he glanced over the crowd. "It can't be done."

"Of course it can. We'll make a column, we'll put the jeeps and trucks at the front and the back and everybody else will be in the middle. It'll be slow but we can make it."

For a split second his discipline cracked, his face collapsing as if punched from inside. "Don't you think I would save them if I could?" he cried. "I can't handle these people, I don't have the men. Even if we try that mob will fire before we reach the first gate."

"They won't if they know you'll fire back."

He seemed to plead with her now. "I don't have enough men, can't you see that? Perhaps they'd wait until dark, perhaps we'd get that far. But as soon as night falls we'll be slaughtered."

It surpassed her, simply carried her along—in some clenched part of herself she registered surprise, a faint grace-note of wonder as it happened.

"No," she told Sawhey, "I can fix that. Those people aren't going to touch us."

Later, playing it back in her mind, she found that whole blocks of memory had been lost to her. She couldn't recall getting her day-pack from the Mazda, nor stepping into the open away from the trucks, away from the thin, sheltering line of soldiers. There must have been an exchange, an understanding of sorts, because she started down the road with a vague sense of assurance, a mental imprint of their rifles coming to bear. Then it was all jump cuts and pieces of things, fragments spliced one after another—the awful heat, the scything birdsong in the bush, her nausea and a sharp copper taste in her mouth. How the sun threw orange shafts of light across the road, shadow and light alternating like flattened stairs, and how the rebels fell silent when they saw her coming. Like a switch had been thrown, that sudden, then her despair when they rallied and started in again, howling, obscenely urging her on.

At a certain point she lost the sense of her feet touching the ground. Things went away, spinning off as if gravity had lost its hold—mainly it was about not showing fear at precisely those moments when you were most afraid. Eyes, mouth, voice, strict control of the pressure points, because fear was a tacit form of consent. She was close enough now to see the lumps in their skin, the juju bundles they'd sewn into themselves. They wore rags and tatters of clothes but fairly bristled with weapons; they were boys, teenagers most of them, red-eyed, heads swiveling as they drifted toward the gate. Giggling, clearly messed up on something. Several pointed their guns at her and laughed.

She stopped on a line even with the two stone portals. "Who's the head man," she called in a neutral voice, pitching it between request and command.

There was more laughter. "You a long way from home," a voice answered.

"Sure, padi. But don't you know I'm trying hard to get back there."

The youth who'd spoken waved down the road with his gun. He was tall and gaunt, bare-chested, his thin Fullah face edged with decorative scars. Bandoliers wreathed his body like a fashion state-ment—*gangsta,* that was the style they aspired to. Tupac Shakur was their Haile Selassie.

"Walk on," he said in a jeering voice. "Nobody stopping you."

"Yeah, that would be fine, I appreciate that. But what I'm ask-ing is you let my friends come with me, saby? Let them pass, all these people good people here. Nobody here you need be making trouble with."

The youth laughed; she watched his eyes range past her shoul-der, scanning the soldiers at her back. The rest of the mob stood slack-jawed and goggling, their stares like cigarette burns on her skin.

"You and de soldiers, I leave you go outta de goodness a my heart. Everybody else got to stay, das de order. We in charge of security in all dis place now."

"Come on padi, these people sick. Let these people go to Guendu for the doctor."

"We got doctor," he said, raising a laugh from his friends.

"Let them go, nobody but simple people here. Nobody here go-ing to make any trouble for you." When the youth just stared, Jill added: "I'll pay."

He wasn't impressed. "What you pay," he snapped.

She pulled the cloth pouch out of her daypack, loosened the drawstring, and poured a spoonful of diamonds into her hand. "This now," she said, showing him her hand. "And this later," she lifted the pouch, "when we get to Guendu."

The youth came forward several steps, close enough for Jill to hear the asthma in his chest. When he saw what she had he went blank for a moment.

"Yah." He swallowed, came a few steps closer. "You give me everyt'ing now, you free to go. Give me everyt'ing now and all dese people free to go." When she refused he made a childish swipe at her hand, then played it for a joke when she pulled back. He was laughing, trembling slightly as he glanced from her to the soldiers, trying to solve the hard calculation they presented. The cost of taking them, and his own chances in a fight. Whether he'd be among the lucky when it was all said and done.

"Do the trade," Jill said quietly. "You're a very rich man if you do the trade."

His eyes got busy—diamonds, soldiers, then back to the diamonds. Working the numbers so hard she could hear them squeal. He licked his lips, took one last look at the soldiers, and carefully held out his hand.

Most were manageable. The nuns told them to walk and so they walked, lapsing into a one-track catatonic state in which the next step forward was the only thing. Others, though docile enough, were prone to wandering off or sitting down in the road, and it was a struggle to keep them focused and moving with the group. Those who couldn't be managed at all—the violent, the contrary, the over-wrought—had to be bound and secured in the trucks, where they passed the night howling like kenneled dogs. What the column must have looked like to someone watching from the bush, Jill could only imagine—like a nightmare, an apparition some sorcerer had conjured up, a shambling caravan of demons and freaks. The rebels bought into the spirit of the thing, buzzing up and down the line in their junkheap technicals and yowling like angels of the apocalypse, singing songs, urging the walkers on, doing note-perfect imitations of the lunatics. Toward Jill and the others they assumed a pose of bluff camaraderie, shouting advice and officiously pointing out the stragglers.

The engulfing dark, the fragile beam-shafts of the trucks' headlights, made it seem as if she was walking down a tunnel or chute, a low, dust-choked space of jagged shadows and light. From time to time Sawhey would leave his jeep and drop back through the column to find her. He'd give her a drink from his canteen, and they would walk together, herding the people at the rear of the column along. The nuns and their staff were farther ahead, spaced at intervals to keep the column intact.

"They just keep going," Sawhey said during one visit.

"Yes," said Jill. Everything hurt, legs, lungs, feet. She welcomed the pain; she hoped it would fill all her interior space.

"Do you think they understand what's happening to them?"

"No."

"That's what I think too," he replied. "None of us does, not really. That's the conclusion I've come to lately." They walked in silence for a time. "Wouldn't you care to ride in the jeep?"

"No."

"You're planning to walk all the way to Guendu."

"Yes, that's what I'm planning to do."

"You know," he said after a moment, "you make me ashamed of myself. I don't think I'm a particularly bad man, but you make me ashamed of myself."

She wanted to hit him then. By now she was convinced that something was wrong with her, and that was what she planned to say to Starkey: I'm sick, I'm mentally disturbed. That's why I gave away your diamonds, I'm fucked up in the head. To the women of the co-op she couldn't imagine what she'd say—nothing, hopefully, if she could manage it. If she could resist the idiot urge to explain herself. At dawn a detachment of peacekeepers met them at the outskirts of Guendu, and as the column filed into the waking town Jill pulled the daypack out from under Pa Conteh's seat and threw it to the Fullah youth. Tossed it carelessly, like so much dirty laundry, glad that she couldn't do any more damage with it. After that things ran together in a blur—the walk into town, the peacekeepers herding them along, everyone collapsing finally in the dusty square. Pa Conteh found Jill propped against a concrete wall; he led her back to the Mazda, got her settled in the cab, and went to find them something to eat. She was still there, dozing with the door swung open, when she heard someone approach.

"Miss. Excuse me, Miss."

She opened her eyes. Sawhey was standing there with a group of officers. Jill let her head fall back against the seat. Smoke from a hundred cooking fires was rising over the town, spindly columns drifting past the thatch and sheet-metal roofs, delicately twisting into nothing as they rose past the palms. For several moments she followed the smoke with her eyes, trying to find the exact point where it dissolved into air—there, that's where she existed, where she'd lived her whole life. Turning back to the soldiers felt like the hardest thing she would ever do.

"Please, Miss," Sawhey said. "We need to know what to do with these people now."

Brief Encounters
with
Che Guevara

1. Love and the Revolution

When I was six my father became president of a college in Virginia, a small, well-endowed Episcopal school to which generations of wealthy Southern families had sent their sons, and which, though it had admitted women since the early fifties, still very much expressed that ripe, combustible blend of sentimentality and viciousness so vital to the traditions of the monied Southern male. We lived in the president's mansion on campus, a massive Greek Revival structure in the old plantation style, with columns towering along the broad front porch, a sweeping central staircase fit for royalty, and high-ceilinged formal rooms whose hardwood floors had the acoustic qualities of a bowling alley. School tradition required my parents to host receptions for the faculty several times a year, and it was at these gatherings—peeking with my sisters from the top of the stairs at first, then later as a fringe participant, serving punch with the help in my coat and tie—that I became aware of my attraction to Mona Broun. Mrs. Broun was a faculty wife, a trim, petite woman in her early thirties whom I confused for a time with the actress Natalie Wood. She had the same wholesome looks as the famous movie star, the same well-scrubbed, faintly exotic sex appeal, along with fawn-colored hair worn loose and soft, this at a time—the mid-sixties—when women's hairdos, in the South at least, resembled heavily shellacked constructions of meringue. But it was her eyes that got our attention from the top of the stairs, intense brown eyes with rich, lustrous tones like shots of bourbon or maple syrup, framed by sharp, exaggeratedly arched eyebrows like the spines of enraged or terrified cats.

"She looks surprised," said one of my sisters.

"She's holding her breath," said another sister.

"She hates her husband," said my oldest and wisest sister.

As the youngest, and the only boy, I was expected to say nothing, but an opera went off in my head whenever I saw Mrs. Broun. That opera, of course, was the sound of sex, and the news that she hated her husband gave me a secret thrill, though *hate* was probably too strong a word—by then the Brouns had likely burned through enough high drama to have exhausted all the more flamboyant emotions. Years before, in the very early sixties, they'd lived in Cuba as part of an academic exchange, one of the last before diplomatic relations were broken. Either inspired by the Revolution, or sick of her husband, or both—maybe she'd met the dashing Che and already become entangled—Mrs. Broun remained in Cuba when her husband left. Her defection was a news sensation for a couple of weeks, a Cold War scandal of the human interest sort and a public humiliation for Dr. Broun, who returned to campus more abstracted and aloof than ever. He took up his old position in the sociology department and refused to speak to the press; when Mrs. Broun abruptly rejoined him several years later, she, too, maintained a stone wall of silence, resuming the life of a conventional faculty wife with no more fuss than if she'd spent a long weekend at the beach. Given material like that, the community had no choice but to glut itself with gossip. She'd been brainwashed, people said, or she was a spy, or had been switched out in Havana for a surgically altered double, but the steamiest and most persistent rumors concerned the affair she'd allegedly had with Ernesto "Che" Guevara, the famous revolutionary.

According to the orthodoxy of the times, Che was high in our pantheon of national enemies, but for me he was a clue, a key player in some essential human mystery that linked us both to Mrs. Broun and therefore to one another. In any case, I was consumed; at faculty receptions I couldn't take my eyes off of her. I watched her eat, her graceful juggling of purse and plate, and how she'd tap her ears from time to time to make sure that her earrings were still in place. I studied her clothes, the high heels and snug-fitting suits, the sleek bulge of her bottom underneath her skirt. She rarely spoke, preferring instead to be a poised and careful listener, though even when she seemed at her most engaged there was an air of distraction or restlessness about her, as if she sensed someone standing too close to her shoulder, an intimate, vaguely hostile presence to whom she would momentarily turn. I know now that this was her tragic aura following her around, though at the time I had only the coarsest sense that she would never be happy again. Certainly *I* couldn't make her happy, and that, for me, was part of the tragedy.

The fact that she ended up exactly where she started, as a faculty wife at a small, conservative Southern college, strikes me now as the sort of peculiarly specific hell that life has a way of devising for us. I remember my alarm on hearing the news that Che had been killed—what were we going to say to Mrs. Broun? It didn't occur to me that people could act as if nothing had happened, but when I saw her at the Christmas party later that year, she looked absolutely the same. She moved about the room as she always did, saying little, eating less, seeming to blink about once every ten minutes. I kept trying to make passionate eye contact with her, to convey some urgent message of solidarity or love, but my best chance came when she approached the table for a cup of punch. I was trembling as I filled the cup and reverently passed it to her, and as the punch changed hands, her eyes met mine. She froze, staring at me as if I'd just that moment materialized, and the next instant she seemed to know everything—she understood, at the very least, what I wanted to say, because little lightning strikes started going off behind her eyes. I think she would have slapped me if I'd opened my mouth. She was that ruthless, that jealous of her epic shame and grief, and no brat was going to taint the great love of her life by talking of things he knew nothing about.

I was desperate to speak to her, but that look stopped me cold. She scared me so badly that I remember thinking that I didn't want to fall in love with anyone, ever, not if that's what it could do to you.

2. Death in Bolivia

When I was twenty I dropped out of college and got a minimum-wage job delivering office furniture. At the time I was living in the

Northeast, in a cold, dirty, technically bankrupt city where dozens of random murders occurred every night, but my main concern was finding work of the sort that would allow me to stop thinking for a while, which seemed advisable after a near-sleepless sophomore year in which I fell prey to certain compulsive behaviors, such as trying to read everything Ezra Pound had ever written. So I got a job with a discount-office furniture company, found a cheap apartment in a high-crime neighborhood, and started taking the bus to work every morning. It was a lonely, orbitless time in my life; I had few friends, and was too bottled-up to talk to women, but delivering furniture had its satisfactions. You could double-park all over the city, for one thing, and I liked lifting stuff and riding around in the truck, and the other guys in delivery didn't mind me too much. I think they knew instinctively what they had on their hands, a stressed-out white boy whose life had jumped the tracks, but my troubles must have looked pretty puny to them. My first day they sent me out with Clifton Weems, an older black man with a barrel chest and a mangled, arthritic way of walking. After a couple of hours of brooding he turned to me and said: "Hey kid, you know what?"

"No, what."

"You turn sideways when your woman's shooting at you, you cut her target more'n half."

They thought I was funny with my goofy formal manners, the way I automatically called the older guys "sir" until they yelled at me to stop. During the day I hauled furniture and took a fair amount of guff; at night I listened to gunfire barking up and down my street and had conflicted, homesick dreams about the South. I'd come to this place of my own free will, following a perfectly honorable sub-set of the Southern tradition by going north for school, but somehow I'd managed to make an exile of myself. "Good luck," my father said when I called to say I was dropping out. By then he was president of a bigger, even more prestigious college. "Come see us when you feel like getting serious again."

Life became very basic. Work, food, sleep—as long as I rolled my body out of bed in the morning, everything else just seemed to happen by itself. One day I was out on deliveries with Luis Batista and Clifton, sitting in the peon's middle seat while Luis surfed the truck through six lanes of traffic. Clifton relaxed on my other side with his arm out the window, humming into the early spring breeze. We heard something shift in the back of the truck, then glass shattering. Clifton reached over and turned up the radio.

"Hey," he said, leaning back in his seat, "you know Gustavo's the guy who killed Che Guevara?"

"You're kidding," I said, instantly reeling with nostalgia; it was like opening an old steamer trunk full of mothballs. "You mean Che Guevara the guerrilla?"

"No, man, Che Guevara the nightclub singer. Who the hell do you think I mean?"

"I—"

"You're surprised I know about Che? You think I'm just an ignorant *nee-gro*, doncha boy."

"No Clifton, I just—"

"Shit, man, I knew Malcolm X. I used to hang with Adam Clayton Powell Jr. all the time, you dig? I was right in the middle of all that sixties shit."

I couldn't tell if Clifton was razzing me or really mad, so I shut up. Luis glanced at us and casually shifted gears.

"Yeah," he said, "I heard that about Gus."

"You think it's true?" Clifton asked.

"Sure, why not. He was in the army down there. He's a pretty tough guy."

"You ever ask him?"

"Fuck no man, you don't talk about stuff that happened down there." Luis was Chilean, a former soldier himself; it seemed a vaguely sinister coincidence that all the Latins in delivery were ex–military men.

"Dude ought to write a book, make himself some money."

"No." Luis was adamant. "No books. He'd just bring a lot of grief down on himself."

They were talking about Gustavo Torres, a taciturn Bolivian whose flat Indian features and long mournful nose gave his face the moral authority of a death mask. Gus exhibited behaviors that were baffling to most North Americans—modesty, reserve, and courtesy, to name a few—and transmitted with every gesture an urbane self-assurance that made me think of the best class of movie gamblers. He had a wife and kids in Bolivia and a string of stylish lady friends here in the city, along with a Monte Carlo that he garaged at unimaginable expense. Nobody knew how he managed to live so well on a workingman's wages, which only added to the Gustavo mystique.

Of course I asked him about Che; the question burned inside me like a lit fuse. The next time we went out on deliveries together I gathered my nerve.

"Ah, Gus," I began, "I don't mean to bug you or anything, but there's these rumors going around about you, and I was just wondering—"

He brought his hand down on the dashboard, *slap*, then raised it as if taking an oath. "The rumors are true," he declared.

"We're talking about Che, right?"

He flinched like I'd thrown acid in his face. "Che Guevara, of course. The *revolucionario.*"

"I don't mean to pry," I said by way of invitation.

"That's good," he said curtly, eyes fixed on the street. "You shouldn't be too curious about these things."

"Okay," I agreed, and then I told him about Mrs. Broun and her alleged affair with Che, because it made me feel good—more authentic and grounded, and less homesick, I suppose—to talk about Che. Gus just grunted, but a couple of days later he came up to me in the stockroom.

"It is true," he said in a low voice. "About that lady you knew, and Che. There was an affair."

"Yeah?"

"*Yes.*" Gustavo's English was all tight corners and crisp edges. "She lived in *La Habana* for two years, he kept her in an apartment in the Old City. It's a miracle she got out with her life, you know."

"How did you—"

"Yes, well," he said with a tidy cough. "I just thought you'd want to know."

So that was the end of it, I thought, and I filed it away until a couple of weeks later, when a bunch of us went out drinking after work, to the sort of serious, no-frills neighborhood bar where the walls sweat tears of nicotine and the waitresses have the grizzled look of ex–child brides. I had three quick ones, drinking too fast as usual; I looked up halfway through beer number four to find Gustavo watching me with imploding eyes.

"It is like the Pietà," he intoned. When Gus drank his face planed off like weathered drywall, and his nose seemed more commanding and ancient than ever.

"Say what?"

"The portrait of Che in death, his body lying on the table. Have you seen it?"

Of course I'd seen it, the famous Freddy Trigo image of Che laid out on a stretcher after his slipshod execution—it's one of the iconic photographs of the twentieth century. Che's eyes are open in the picture, fixed on some distant point, and his lips are parted in a sleepy half-smile. The tousled hair and beard give him a Christlike look; his naked torso, pitted here and there with bulletholes, seems to emanate light. In the hushed, satin tones of that black-and-white image, Che's body has an aura of distilled transcendence.

"I've seen it," I answered, trying to match Gus's gravitas.

"The Pietà," he repeated, "it's so beautiful the way his eyes gaze past the camera, he seems so calm and forgiving, so much at peace. Yet for anyone who was there that day, that photo is like a curse."

"Hunh," I murmured, afraid of spooking him, but I didn't need to worry. Gustavo was speaking from some deep confessional booth within himself.

"Jesus could not have been the Christ without his Judas, correct? And someone had to play the Judas for Che, too, for Che the man to be transformed into Che the martyr. But that goddamn photo, man, it drives me crazy, we were only trying to prove that Che was dead. Those were our orders that day, send us proof that Che is dead! So we looked for the best light, we took off his shirt to show his wounds, we had the nurse trim his beard and comb back his hair. We only wanted to take a decent photo that day—who could have known we were making the new Pietà?"

While we drank he described the military operation for me, how his unit—most of them Indians—had harassed and tracked the guerrillas for weeks, finally cornering the survivors in the Churo Gorge. They captured Che after a firefight and marched him into the tiny village of La Higuera, where they locked him in the schoolhouse overnight. When the order came the next day to execute him, the junior officers drew lots to determine who would do the shooting. "I talked to him early that morning," Gus said. "I brought him a cup of coffee and we chatted for a minute, I told him I was the guy who'd tracked him all this time through the mountains. Che was a human wreck by then—he was starving and sick, his feet were a bloody mess, and his asthma was like a snake crawling up and down his throat. But still fighting—that son of a bitch was still fighting his war. He just stared at me for a minute, and then he said, 'Look around you, Lieutenant. Look at this village—what do you see? There's no doctor, no running water, no electricity, no decent road, they have nothing, the lives of these people are shit. So all that time you were trying to kill me, brother, did you ever stop to think what this war is about?' "

"It's a conversation I have sometimes in my dreams," Gus went on. "We're in the schoolhouse there in La Higuera, and he's sitting on the floor in his filthy clothes, his feet sticking out in their bloody rags. But he's already dead! His skin is a pale blue color, and his shirt is torn and bloody where the bullets went in. We talk for a while, and he says he's not angry with me. I ask him if it hurts very much to be dead, and he says, No, not very much. And then I get up the nerve to ask him about heaven and hell, whether they're real, and where exactly he is in all that. He always smiles a little when I ask him that, and then he says, 'You know, Gustavo, it's a very interesting thing I've learned here, I had no idea God and the Devil live so close to-gether. They're neighbors, in fact, their houses are right beside each other, and sometimes when they're sitting around with nothing to do they play cards, just as a way to pass the time. But they never wager money—what good is money to them? No, it's only souls they're interested in, the souls of all these sinners running around the Earth. It's us they bet on when they sit down to cards.'

" 'So what about me?' I ask him then. 'Have they ever bet on me?'

" 'Of course,' he says, but when I ask him who won, the Devil or God, he never answers. He just sits there staring at me."

3. Comrades-in-Arms

In my early thirties I began making trips to the beleaguered island nation of Haiti. With the recent fall of the Duvalier regime, it struck me as an interesting place to be, and I had credentialed, more or less credible reasons for going—to write articles and, hopefully, a book—but my true motives seemed to have more to do with being Southern, and white, and having a natural affinity for the quagmire of race. By this time I had a beautiful wife and two wonderful children, a loving family which I'd done nothing special to deserve, but I'd leave them for weeks at a time to go messing around a place that was perpetually on the verge of devouring itself. After several trips I met a young Haitian, a doctor, with whom I became friends; Ponce, incidentally, was rather Che-like himself, an intense, good-looking, often disheveled mulatto who practiced near one of the downtown slums and treated most of his patients for free. Because he made so little money, he had to live with his wife and their two sons in a cramped, buggy apartment in the middle of Port-au-Prince, a few rooms carved out of an ancient gingerbread mansion that must have been quite grand in its time, but now looked more like a pile of moldering elephant bones. He insisted that I stay there when I came to Port-au-Prince, and often I did, though with some misgivings. The apartment had no running water, for one thing, and for another it was always crammed with friends and poor relations and mysterious strangers whose connection I never could figure out. They just arrived, hung around for a couple of days, and moved on; I got the impression this was how a lot of them lived.

It was by staying at Ponce's apartment that I met an elderly Haitian who claimed to have been comrades-in-arms with Che. Laurent was a tall, spry, ebullient old man with jaundice-yellow eyes and ebony skin that glistened in the heat of the small apartment, and I suppose there's no point in withholding the fact that he was quite insane. He'd turn up several times a week, usually in the mornings for a cup of coffee; in his guayabera and slacks and white patent-leather loafers, carrying his zippered portfolio under one arm, he looked every inch the tropical man of affairs, but as soon as he opened his mouth you wanted to run for the doors.

"I have an appointment with Mandela this morning," he might say, shrewdly tapping the portfolio he was never without. Another day it might be Thatcher or Mitterand, or he might be going to the palace to confer with President Aristide. The thing is, if you listened to him long enough, his delusions began to take on a plausible air. For most of his life he'd flirted around the edges of power, ever since he'd been a captain in the Haitian Army and launched an early, failed coup against Papa Doc. He could talk quite rationally about politics and history, and there was a gamesmanship to his madness, a playful self-aware quality, that kept us guessing as to how seriously he took himself.

He liked taunting the *blans*, the foreigners, best of all. If there were journalists at the apartment, and often there were since Ponce spoke English and lived near the Holiday Inn, Laurent would shake their hands and solemnly declare, "I am the lidder of the Haitian pipple!" Which was absurd, of course, but with time I found myself adjusting to the notion that, madness aside, Laurent would have made as decent a president as anyone could hope for. He spoke five languages, held degrees in business and economics, and boasted a distinguished if brief military career, and over the course of his harrowing thirty-year exile he'd kept body and soul together on four different continents. But Cuba had been his first stop, where he had offered his protean talents to the freshly anointed Minister of Industry, El Che. "We recognized at once that we were brothers," Laurent told anyone who would listen. "He put me in charge of the office of Bureau of Statistics, and often I would accompany him as he traveled about the country inspecting projects of industrialization. We talked about so many things in our time together—about his life, about philosophy, about my dream of liberating Haiti, which he fully supported. 'Laurent,' he asked me on one occasion, 'what is the first priority of government? What is the first thing you would do if you were President of Haiti?'

" 'Education,' I said at once, 'I would build schools, Comandante Guevara. To raise the awareness of the people.'

" 'Good answer,' he said, 'but wrong. Before schools, before medicine, before anything, there must be security. Security is the pre-condition for all other advances.' Therefore," Laurent continued, raising his voice to an imaginary crowd of thousands, "when I am elected president, the security of the nation will be my number one priority!"

"Don't laugh when he talks like that," Ponce told me later. "Don't ever laugh when a Haitian tells you he's going to be president, because it might happen. And if it does he won't forget that you laughed at him."

Ponce was right, of course—as proof we had the elections of several years before, when only a fluke of history kept Laurent from high office. After thirty years in exile, he had returned shortly after Baby Doc's fall and declared himself a candidate for the senate, one of a pack of hopefuls vying for the three senate seats from Port-au-Prince. He ran a lucid if little-noticed campaign until the final week, when Duvalierist diehards launched a terrorist blitz that threatened to doom the elections. Amid the all-too-familiar scenario of lies, international hand-wringing, and a rising body count, Laurent caused a sensation by appearing on TV and announcing that he was going to dance for peace. "All Haitians should dance!" he cried wherever he went, breaking into a hot, hip-swiveling shuffle that brought cheers from an instantly smitten electorate. "Let's dance instead of fight, all Haitians should dance!" Election day turned out to be a disaster, with death squads running wild all over the country, but before voting was canceled observers in Port-au-Prince reported that huge numbers of people were marking their ballots for "the guy who danced."

It was scary to think how close he'd come to real power, though the idea was good for some vengeful laughs too, because the sane politicians had made such a mess of things. But as for poor Laurent, he'd missed his chance; now he spent his days dropping in on friends and battering them with stories about his time with Che. At the Bay of Pigs he'd commanded a detachment of militia, putting his life on the line for the Revolution; he'd also been at Che's side in the humiliating aftermath of the missile crisis, when angry Cuban crowds had chanted "Khrushchev you faggot!" There in the small, sweltering apartment without running water, Laurent would describe Che's brilliant mind, his Herculean work habits, his love of practical jokes, and the curse of his asthma, the stories piling one on top of another until we lapsed into a sort of historical trance. Then the old man would catch himself and glance at his watch.

"*Bon,*" he'd say, taking a last slurp of coffee, "please excuse me, I'm due for my appointment now," and off he'd go to meet Carter or Yeltsin or whoever was on the agenda that day, dismissing us with a wave of his empty portfolio.

4. The Consoling Voice

Throughout my thirties I kept going to Haiti, convinced that I'd found ground zero for all the stupidity, waste, and horror inflicted on the hemisphere since Columbus and the Spaniards set up shop.

Meanwhile Ponce, as part of his duties for a national medical commission, made several trips to Cuba, returning with tapes of Che's speeches that he'd play in the evenings on a cheap boom box, Che's voice ringing through the old gingerbread mansion with the propulsive resonance of hammered sheet metal. As he rose in prestige and prominence, Ponce began to neglect his wife, a beautiful woman with piercing anthracite eyes and skin the color of brandied chocolate. She came from a poor family, but she was direct and strongwilled, and had a quick, intuitive mind that put my college degree to shame. She and Ponce had met shortly after the Aristide coup, when a ruthless military regime took control of the country; their romance had flourished amid the heady atmosphere of brutal repression and messianic resistance, but the adrenaline rush of those days was long gone. Now they spent most of their time together arguing about money. There was never enough, of course, and they spent too much, and the debts were piling up and so forth, and watching them fight I began to think that Marx, who was so wrong about so many things, had been right about money's relentless genius for invading every aspect of human life.

Ponce, not the most practical man when it came to finance, dealt with the problem by running around on his wife, and he described his erotic adventures to me in an urgent, hissing whisper that sounded like the air leaking out of their love. He told me everything; to her he denied everything, though what he was doing was pretty obvious. "I'm going out to get some Cokes!" he'd yell, and then be gone for three hours. So she and I would sit in the dark at the kitchen table, drinking rum without Coke and talking into the night while her family snored on mattresses scattered around the room.

"Je suis une femme déçue," she told me, *I'm a disappointed woman.* She knew her position was tenuous; even though Ponce introduced her around as his wife, they'd never actually married, and along

with her lack of legal standing she had no money, no family means, no education to speak of. Things lacked clarity, she said. I don't know what I'm doing anymore. She kept returning to a dreamlike story about a resistance group that she and some friends had formed shortly after the coup. At first it was all *blòf*, just meetings and talk, but then a *blan* turned up and started teaching them things. How to use a gun, how to make a bomb. How to plan an ambush. How to disappear.

Who was this guy? I asked.

She shrugged. Just a man, a *blan*. An American.

Was he military? CIA?

Another shrug.

Where did you meet?

In Carrefour, she said vaguely, at a friend's house. At night.

It sounded like a fantasy to me, a crude form of wish fulfillment; on the other hand there was the .38 she always carried in her purse, with which she seemed as casually proficient as your average American housewife with her cell phone. So maybe I was the one dreaming, living the fantasy. When I asked what happened to the group, she said, I quit. I got scared. One night the *blan* gave them a stack of Aristide posters and told them to blanket the neighborhood. They split into teams of two and slipped out the door with their sheaves of posters and pots of wallpaper glue, and within minutes she and her partner were picked up by attachés. She would have been shot if this boy hadn't convinced the attachés that she was a stranger, just a girl who happened along and stopped to talk. So the attachés told her to go, get lost; the next morning her partner's body was found in a sewer on Grande Rue. A few days later she met Ponce and moved in with him, in a different part of town where she wasn't known.

"He saved my life," she said. "He got me out of there." When I was alone with either of them, they spoke tenderly of one another; when they were together they couldn't stop arguing, and eventually Ponce threw some clothes in a suitcase and moved out. He gave her some money now and then, but it was never enough, and whenever I was in Haiti I'd go by to see her and bring a little cash if I was able. Sometimes when I arrived for one of my visits, Che's speeches would be playing on the boom box. It surprised me at first, because she didn't understand the words any more than I did, but then I realized that the sound alone was enough, that the tense, florid arabesques of Che's Spanish served her much the same way as a torch song. This was the record she chose to play in her solitude, the music that spoke all the longing and truth and hurt that we couldn't talk about in ordinary conversation. Those secrets we keep, even when they aren't so secret. When I asked, half-joking, if she was learning Spanish, she just laughed and turned away.

5. *Seremos Como El Che!*

"Be like Che!" Fidel urged his countrymen on the day that he announced *El Comandante*'s death. Thirty years later Che's unmarked grave was discovered at last, bringing an end to one of the Cold War's more potent mysteries. For eighteen months a team of forensics experts had poked holes in the airstrip near Vallegrande, Bolivia, searching for the famous revolutionary's remains; I followed the story with guarded interest from three thousand miles away, wary of attaching yet more personal baggage to the subject. For decades Che's enemies had kept his shameful grave a secret, fearful of creating a shrine and rallying point for the militant left, but once he was found it seemed that everyone wanted him for themselves. The Bolivian government lobbied to keep him in Vallegrande, where he was sure to generate millions in tourist dollars. The Argentines, their savage "dirty war" safely in the past, laid claim to him as a native son. The Cubans, who had ignored Che's pleas for help in his last desperate days, insisted on their rights as his adopted countrymen and spiritual brothers.

The Cubans got him, though not without some ugly bickering. I continued to follow the story in the newspapers, goaded by the notion that I had some sort of stake in the outcome. In any event, the discovery and subsequent reinterment of Che's remains inspired a spasm of worldwide reflection on the Guevara legacy. Dozens of new books were published, and old ones reissued. Thousands of sordid CIA documents came to light. Fidel made a lot of interminable speeches, while tidal waves of Che merchandise swamped the world's free markets. The global revolution prophesied by Che had yet to come to pass, though he would surely find the reasons just as compelling as ever. Poverty, injustice, oppression, suffering, these remain the basic conditions of life on most of the planet—whatever else has changed since his death, this hasn't, but as life becomes more pleasurable and affluent for the rest of us, the poor seem more remote than ever, their appeal to our humanity even fainter.

I'm in my forties now, halfway to heaven, as they say—the years are going faster, gathering speed. Recently it occurred to me that I've spent a lot of energy and many years trying to learn a very few basic things, which may turn out to be mostly crude opinions anyway. There's so little in the world we can be sure of, and maybe it's that lack, that flaw or deficiency, if you will, that drives our strongest compulsions. The last time I visited Haiti, Ponce was harried and overworked as usual, embittered by the terrible working conditions. "I'm like a jet pilot without a plane!" he cried. There were more sick people than ever, and fewer doctors to cure them; what was left of the Haitian professional class was bailing out, liquidating their assets and heading for the U.S.

"Not me," Ponce declared. "I'm staying. Everybody says I'm crazy, but I'm staying." I told him I wanted to see Laurent, to get his thoughts on the final chapter in the Che story—it might be an interesting historical exercise, I said, though secretly I was hoping for some sign or clue that always seemed to be hovering just beyond my reach. Because his health had declined considerably, Laurent rarely left his home these days, but Ponce knew where he lived, and so one hot, sleepy Sunday afternoon we bought some sweets and rum to present as gifts and drove over to his house. Laurent lived in the old Salomon quarter near the center of town, close enough to the palace that he could still, if proximity counted for anything, sustain his dream of ruling the country some day. Ponce got lost in the tangle of eighteenth-century streets, made some random turns, swore, seemed to find his way again. Bands of sunlight and shadow tiger-striped the narrow streets; the old houses had the slumped, encrusted look of shipwrecks lying at the bottom of the sea. After some more addled swearing and driving around, Ponce pulled up in front of a crumbling wood-frame cottage. The sorry state of the house, the piles of trash in the yard, seemed to belie the fundamental human wish to cope. Two teams of wild-looking boys were playing soccer in the street, the match swirling around us as we climbed from the car.

"I'm sure he's home," Ponce said as we crossed the street. "He hardly ever leaves his house anymore."

The afternoon light had a coppery, brackish tint. The dry weeds seemed to explode at the touch of our feet. "He might not recognize us," Ponce warned as we crossed the yard. "He's pretty senile, but maybe the rum will get us in." We stepped from the sun into the cavelike shadows of the porch, careful to edge around the rotten floorboards. We knocked on the door, waited, and knocked again. I turned and watched the street for a minute, the shrieking boys absorbed in their game of soccer, the slow procession of Sunday passersby. The wall of sunlight tracking the porch's shadow-line seemed as smooth and final as marble slab.

"Is he sick?" Ponce wondered out loud. "My God, has he died?" We knocked again, and we called, then we walked along the porch tapping all the windows, trying to rouse some sign of life from the house. He could be sleeping, we told each other, or maybe his hearing was gone, or maybe he was confused and couldn't find the door. So we kept knocking, though after a while it was useless, we knew. And yet we stayed, we knocked and called until we made fools of ourselves, but no one ever answered within.

Fantasy for
Eleven Fingers

So little is known about the pianist Anton Visser that he
belongs more to myth than anything so random as historical fact.
He was born in 1800 or 1801, thus preceding by half a generation
the Romantic virtuosos who would transform forever our notions of
music and performer. Liszt, more charitable than most, called him
"our spiritual elder brother," though he rather less kindly described
his elder brother's playing as "affectation of the first rank." Visser
himself seems to have been the source of much confusion about his
origins, saying sometimes that he was from Brno, at other times
from Graz, still others from Telc or Iglau. "The French call me a

German," he is reported to have told the countess Koeniggratz, "and the Germans call me a Jew, but in truth, dear lady, I belong solely to the realm of music."

He was fluent in German, Slovak, Magyar, French, English, and Italian, and he could just as fluently forget them all when the situation obliged. He was successful enough at cards to be rumored a cheat; he liked women, and had a number of vivid affairs with the wives and mistresses of his patrons; he played the piano like a human thunderbolt, crisscrossing Europe with his demonic extra finger and leaving a trail of lavender gloves as souvenirs. Toward the end, when Visser-mania was at its height, the mere display of his naked right hand could rouse an audience to hysterics; his concerts degenerated into shrieking bacchanals, with women alternately fainting and rushing the stage, flinging flowers and jewels at the great man. But in the early 1820s Visser was merely one of the legion of virtuosos who wandered Europe peddling their grab bags of pianistic stunts. He was, first and foremost, a *salonist*, a master of the *morceaux* and flashy potpourri that so easily enthralled his wealthy audiences. He seems to have been something of a super-cocktail pianist to the aristocracy—much of what we know of him derives from diaries and memoirs of the nobility—although he wasn't above indulging the lower sort of taste. His specialty, apparently, was speed-playing, and he once accepted a bet to play six million notes in twelve hours. A riding school was rented out, fliers printed and subscriptions sold, and for eight hours and twenty minutes Visser incinerated the keyboard of a sturdy Érard while the audience made themselves at home, talking, laughing, eating, playing cards, and roaming about, so thoroughly enjoying the performance that they called for an encore after the six-millionth note. Visser shrugged and airily waved a hand as if to say, Why not? and continued playing for another hour.

No likeness of the virtuoso has survived, but contemporaries describe a tall man of good figure with black, penetrating eyes, a severe, handsome face, and a prominent though elegantly shaped nose. That he was a Jew was widely accepted, and loudly published by his rivals; there is no evidence that Visser bothered to deny the consensus. His hands, of course, were his most distinguishing feature. The first edition of *Grove's Dictionary* states that Visser had the hands of a natural pianist: broad, elastic palms, spatulate fingers, and exceptionally long little fingers. He could stretch a twelfth and play left-hand chords such as A flat, E flat, A flat, and C, but it was the hypnotically abnormal right hand that ultimately set him apart. "The two ring fingers of his right hand," the critic Blundren wrote, "are perfect twins, each so exact a mirror image of the other as to give the effect of an optical illusion, and in action possessed of a disturbing crablike agility. Difficult it is, indeed, to repress a shudder when presented with Visser's singular hand."

Difficult, indeed, and as is so often the case with deformity, a sight that both compelled and repelled. Visser seems not to have emphasized his singular hand during the early stages of his career, but the speed with which he played, to such cataclysmic effect, in time gave rise to unsettling stories. It was his peculiar gift to establish the melody of a piece with his thumbs in the middle register of the piano, then surround the melody with arpeggios, tremolos, double notes, and other devices, moving up and down the keyboard with such insane rapidity that it seemed as if four hands rather than two were at work. His sound was so uncanny that a certain kind of story—tentative, half-jesting at first—began to shadow the pianist: Satan himself was playing with Visser, some said, while others ventured that he'd sold the devil his soul in exchange for the extra finger, which enabled him to play with such hectoring speed.

That Visser had emerged from the mysterium of backward eastern Europe gave the stories an aura of plausibility. "There is something dark, elusive, and unhealthy in Visser," remarked Field, while Moscheles said that his rival's playing "does not encourage respectable thoughts." His few surviving compositions show a troublingly oblique harmonic stance, a cracked Pandora's box of dissonance and atonal sparks, along with the mournful echoes of gypsy songs and the derailed melodies of Galician folk tunes. He became known as the Bohemian Faust, and was much in demand; neither the sinister flavor of his stage persona nor his string of love affairs seemed to diminish his welcome in fashionable salons.

In 1829, however, there was a break. Some say it was due to an incident at the comte de Gobet's, where Visser was accused of cheating at cards; his legendary success and extra finger had long made him an object of suspicion, though others said that he was discovered making free with the fifteen-year-old daughter of a baron. Visser was, whatever the cause, refused by society, forced out into *le grand public* to make his living, this at a time when there were few adequate venues for touring virtuosos, and concert managers tended to have the scruples of slave traders. Visser billed himself as The Man with Eleven Fingers, the freakshow aspect of virtuosity made explicit for once, and over the next two years of playing in rowdy beer gardens and firetrap opera houses he perfected his florid stagecraft: the regal entrance, the lavender gloves portentously removed, then the excruciating pause before his hands fell on the keyboard like an avalanche. It was early noted that his audiences were disproportionately female; more remarkable was the delirium that his performances induced, a feature that grew even more pronounced with the addition of the *Fantaisie pour Onze Doigts* to his repertoire. Hummel, who heard it played in a ballroom in Stuttgart, called it "a most strange and affecting piece, with glints of dissonance issuing from the right hand like the whip of a lash, or very keen razor cuts."

Kalkbrenner, who happened on it at a brewery in Mainz, compared the chill of the strained harmonies of the loaded right hand to "a trickle of ice-cold water down the back," and added: "I believe that Visser has captured the very sound of Limbo."

The effect on audiences was astonishing. From the first reported performance, in October 1831, there were accounts of seizures, faintings, and fits of epilepsy among the spectators; though some accused Visser of paying actors to mimic and encourage such convulsions, the phenomenon appears to have been accepted as genuine. Mass motor hysteria would most likely be the diagnosis today, though a physician from Gossl who witnessed one performance proposed theories having to do with electrical contagion; others linked the *Fantasy* to the Sistine Chapel Syndrome, the hysterics to which certain foreign women—English spinsters, chiefly—sometimes fell prey while viewing the artistic treasures of Italy. In any event, the *Fantasy* was a short-lived sensation. From its debut in the fall of 1831 until his death the following January, Visser performed the piece perhaps thirty times. He was said to be traveling to Paris to play for the princess Tversky's salon—the fame of the *Fantasy* had, conveniently, paroled his reputation—when he was killed stupidly, needlessly, in a tavern in Cologne, knifed in a dispute over cards, so the story goes.

People naturally believed that the *Fantasy* died with him; even the stupendously gifted Liszt refused to attempt it, rather defensively dismissing the piece as "a waste of time, an oddity based on an alien formation of the hand." One might study the score as scholars study the texts of a dead language, but the living sound was thought to be lost forever, until that day in 1891 when Leo and Hermine Kuhl brought their six-year-old daughter to the Vienna studio of Herr Moritz Puchel. Herr Puchel listened to the girl play Chopin's "Aeolian Harp" Étude; he gave her a portion of Beethoven's

A-flat Sonata to sight-read, which she did without stress; he confirmed, as her current teacher Frau Holzer had told him, that the child did indeed have perfect pitch. Finally he asked Anna Kuhl to stand before him and place her hands on his upturned palms.

"Yes," he said gravely, much in the manner of a doctor giving an unhappy diagnosis, "someday she will play Visser's *Fantasy*."

Herr Puchel himself had been a prodigy, a student of Czerny's, who in turn had been a student of Beethoven's; though he was an undeniably brilliant musician, Puchel's own career as a virtuoso had been thwarted by the misfortune of thin, bony hands. He had, instead, made his reputation as a teacher, and by the age of sixty had achieved such a degree of eminence that he accepted only those students who could answer in the affirmative the following three questions:

Are you a prodigy?

Are you of Slavic descent?

Are you Jewish?

This, the Catholic Puchel believed, was the formula for greatness, and Anna Kuhl qualified on all counts. The Kuhls came from Olomouc, in Moravia—a town, as would often be noted, that has some claim as Visser's birthplace—where Anna's grandfather founded the textile factory on which the family fortune was based; by the time of Anna's birth, Leo and his brothers had built a textile empire substantial enough to be headquartered in the Austrian capital. The Kuhls were typical of Vienna's upper-class Jewry: politically liberal, culturally and linguistically German, their Judaism little more than a pious family memory, they devoted themselves to artistic and intellectual attainment as a substitute for the social rank which would always be denied them. And yet the desire to assimilate, to be viewed as complete citizens, was strong; theirs was a world in which any departure from convention provoked intense, if grimly decorous, fear, and the Kuhls were so horrified by Anna's deformity that they considered amputation in the hours after her birth. When the doctor could not ensure them that the infant would survive the shock, the parents relented, though one may reasonably wonder if they were ever completely rid of their instinctive revulsion, or of the more rarefied, if no less desperate, fear that Anna's condition threatened their tenuous standing in society.

Great pianists manifest the musical impulse early, usually around age four; for Anna Kuhl the decisive moment came at two, when Frau Holzer, giving a lesson to Anna's older brother, discovered that the little girl had perfect pitch. On further examination the child revealed astonishing powers of memory and muscular control, as well as profound sensitivity to aural stimulus—she wept on hearing Chopin for the first time, burst into fierce, agonal sobs as if mourning some inchoate yet powerfully sensed memory. Frau Holzer undertook to form the child's talent; by age four Anna had composed her first song, "Good Morning," and by age six had mastered the *Versuch, The Well-Tempered Clavier,* and most of Chopin's *Études.* That year she performed at an exhibition of the city's young pianists, playing with such artistry that Grunfeld, the notoriously saccharine Court pianist, was seen shaking his head and mumbling to himself as he left the hall.

"A prodigy," Frau Holzer wrote in her recommendation to Herr Puchel. "Memorizes instantly; staggering technique and maturity of expression; receptive to hard work, instruction, challenge." Regarding what Frau Holzer chose to call the child's "unique anatomy," Puchel was matter-of-fact to the point of brusqueness, devising technical drills suited to Anna's conformation but otherwise focusing, for the present, on the traditional repertoire. Herr Puchel— stout, bushy-bearded, with a huge strawberry of a nose and endearingly tiny feet—had concluded after forty years of teaching that his students would never be truly happy unless coaxed and cudgeled to that peak of performance in which nervous breakdown is a constant risk. Students, by definition, could not reach Parnassus alone; they were too weak of will, too dreamy and easily distracted, they had to be cultivated into that taut, tension-filled state without which pure and lasting art is impossible. Thus it was that visitors to Herr Puchel's studio could hear "Falsch!" regularly screamed from the teaching room. "Falsch!" *der Meister* would shriek at the first missed note, "Start over!"—his screams punctuated in summer by the *swack* of the flyswatter with which he defended his territory against Vienna's plague of flies. In moments of extreme aesthetic crisis he would push aside his student and sit at the piano, hike up his legs and pound the keyboard with his dainty feet, legs churning like a beetle stuck on its back. "You sound like this!" he would howl at the offender, though his gruff tenderness could be equally effective. "Don't be afraid to stick your neck out," he is said to have told one student after a risky, rubato-laced *Polonaise*. "You might find that it gets stroked instead of chopped off."

A dangerous man, yet prodigious in his results, and apparently Anna responded to this sort of treatment. By all accounts she was a preternaturally serious little girl, self-assured, disposed to silence but precise in speech, with an aura of unapproachability that discouraged all but the very determined or very frivolous. A photographic portrait made at the time shows a girl as slender and graceful as a tulip stem, with long, ringletted masses of black hair, deep-set dark eyes, high Slavic cheekbones, and skin as pale as January snow. At this age she seems unconscious of her unique right hand, or perhaps trusting is a better word; she has allowed herself to be posed with her fingers draped to full effect across the back of a Roentgen chair.

"A perfect breeze of a girl," is how the *Salonblatt,* Vienna's snob-society newspaper, described the young Anna. "A perfect breeze who turns into an exquisite storm when seated before the 88 black and white keys." Puchel believed that the loftiest musical heights could be reached only through the ordeal of performance; he wanted Anna to start playing in public immediately, and arranged through court connections her society debut at a soirée of the princess Montenuovo. *Salonblatt* rhapsodized over the playing of this "mystical" child whose arpeggios "flashed and shimmered like champagne," while the baroness Flotow left an account in her diary of a charmingly poised little girl who devastated the company with Chopin's nocturnes, ate cakes and drank Turkish coffee with the ladies, and complained about the quality of the piano.

She continued awing the impressionable aristocracy for several years, until Puchel judged that she was seasoned enough for her concert debut. In October 1895, the Berlin Philharmonic was scheduled to perform in Vienna; when Julius Epstein, the featured pianist, fell ill, Puchel arranged for Anna to take his place, and after the monumental program of Beethoven's C major Concerto, a set of Rameau variations, the Weber-Liszt *Pollacca*, and a Chopin group consisting of the *Berceuse*, the E-flat Nocturne, and the E minor Waltz, the girl prodigy left Vienna gasping for air. Brahms toasted her in absentia that night, at a banquet intended to honor the suddenly forgotten Epstein. Mahler enthused over her sonorities and golden tone, while both traditional and Secessionist critics marveled at her luminously refined technique, her uncalculated emotion and spontaneity. Agents and concert managers came seething; after interviewing numerous candidates, Leo and Hermine settled on the well-known agent Sigi Kornblau, who appears to have been the kind of dry, hustling administrator that every genius needs, although Anna reportedly told her cousins that visits with Herr Kornblau were "not much fun," and "rather like going to the dentist." Within weeks the young virtuoso and her entourage—her mother, her French governess, a servant girl named Bertha, and Herr Puchel, who carried along a dummy keyboard for practice on the train—had embarked on her first European tour, and for the next three years she alternated between prolonged seasons of close-packed concert dates, and equally demanding, if more solitary, periods of study and practice.

Many have speculated as to the brutalizing effect of such a life on someone who was, after all, a mere child. Regulating Anna's program would seem to have been within the power of her parents, but it appears that Leo and Hermine were no less susceptible than their fellow bourgeois to validation by the aristocracy. Through Anna they might cross, for brief moments at least, the glacis separating them from the remote nobility. Their daughter's labors brought them acceptance, and whatever the cost to Anna in personal terms, the strain seemed not to diminish—perhaps even enhanced?—the remarkable message of her playing. Like all virtuosos, she had exemplary technique: critics wrote of her fluent, almost chaste clarity, the pinpoint accuracy of her wide skips and galloping chords, the instinctive integrity of her rubato, and her broad dynamic range, from shadowlike pianissimo to artillery-grade forte. But more than that there was the singularity of her sound, the "golden sound" that the critics never tired of describing, along with a tenderness of expression that ravished her listeners. This was not yet another robotic prodigy pumping out notes like a power sewing machine; there was, rather, a quality of innocence in her playing, an effusion of trust and vulnerability all the more remarkable for being conveyed through supreme artistry.

"The child," wrote Othmar Wieck, a critic not known for charity, "is a veritable angel come down to Earth." And in Vienna, a city that more than cherished art, that craved it as an escape from the gloom and pessimism that had settled over the Empire in the century's final years, it was perhaps only natural that people would project their fears and longings onto the young virtuoso. Haut bourgeois concertgoers openly wept at her performances, while for others she became an object of obsession, her name turning up with arcane frequency in suicide notes or the vertiginous ramblings of the mentally disturbed. But even those of sturdier, less enervated natures would lapse into deep melancholy after one of her concerts, as if they had sensed within their grasp some piece of information crucial to existence, only to feel it slip away as the last note was played.

Her first "phase," as the family neatly termed such episodes, seems to have occurred in the autumn of her thirteenth year. Engagements in Brussels, Paris, and Berlin were abruptly canceled, due to "temporary illness," according to the notice released by Herr Kornblau's office, though even then there were rumors of a nervous attack. Some said that Anna was under the care of the famous Professor Meynert; others, that she was in residence at the luxurious psychiatric retreat of Professor Leidesdorf, where doctors in white gloves and silk top hats administered the latest in electric and water-immersion therapies. In any event, the young virtuoso's reemergence several weeks later marks the first known instance in which she kept her right hand purposely concealed. Anna, along with her parents and a number of family friends, attended the opening of the Kunstlerhaus exhibition in late October; she was observed wearing a tailored suit of steel gray bengaline, the long sleeves that grazed her palms even further extended by a ruffed trim of Irish lace. She carried in addition an embroidered silk kerchief wrapped as if casually about her right hand, and from that time forward the young pianist never showed her hand in public until the instant she sat before the keyboard.

Commentators have noted in this eccentricity all the character-
istics of a neurotic symptom. Without doubt, the compulsively veiled
hand, as well as the "phases" during which she retreated from the
outside world, indicate significant stress in the girl's life. Some have
portrayed these symptoms as a response to her treatment by the
pan-German press, which, in the course of advocating the union of
Austria's German-speaking regions with the Reich, had begun to
review her performances in the manner of anti-Semitic diatribes.
Others surmise that these were a sensitive girl's reactions to the
more general malaise hanging over the city, although the pursuit of
art, with its constant, debilitating risk of failure, not to mention the
solitude and unwholesome narcissism that sustained concentration
necessarily entails, is, even in the best of circumstances, enough to
induce the entire range of psychopathy. That Anna was merciless
with herself, and suffered accordingly, is evident from her cousin
Hugo's diaries. For instance, in the entry dated 11 November 1898,
we find Anna telling Hugo:

> "It's only when I'm with you that I'm allowed not to work."

And on 5 December, in response to Hugo's entreaties not to strain
herself:

> She looked down at her shoes and smiled to herself, as if I
> were a rather dense little boy who'd asked her to make the river
> stand still.
> "To play well — I suppose I've always assumed that it's a
> matter of life and death."

It was Hugo to whom the family turned when Anna lapsed into
one of her phases. Hugo Kuhl was destined to become a minor ce-

lebrity of the age, an ironic, deliciously blasé feuilletonist for the liberal press and the author of a number of drawing-room plays, of which *The Escape Artist* and *Dinner with Strangers* are still known to scholars. But at the time in question, Hugo was merely a literary-minded student at the University, known to his circle as a stylish, handsome wit of no defined vocational goal, also an accomplished amateur pianist with a *sec* touch. It seems that he alone, out of all of Anna's siblings and numerous cousins, could give some organizing principle to the drift of her phases, during which Anna managed to dress and feed herself, but little else.

21 MARCH

To Uncle Leo's flat in the p.m.

Anna listless, almost catatonic, Hermine tearing around like a fishwife, railing at her to practice—

"Shame on you Anna, for shame! Herr Puchel will be so furious!"

Anna silent, tears in her eyes; I could have cheerfully throttled dear Aunt at that moment. Chose instead to move A into the afternoon sun, onto the cut-velvet sofa by the window. Sat for a peaceful hour while I read *Tantchen Rosmarin* aloud, A's head on my shoulder. For me, a perfect hour. For her, I imagine that existence was almost tolerable.

In fact Hugo was basically helpless when confronted with a phase, and admitted as much in his diaries. His therapy seemed to consist of taking her out for long walks on the Ringstrasse, or among the earthier amusements and shops of the Prater. The two cousins were often seen strolling arm in arm, a strikingly handsome, fashionably dressed young couple, and yet mismatched for all their good looks and evident wealth: Hugo obviously too old to be Anna's suitor, Anna clearly too young to be Hugo's wife. Even so, some have suggested that their devotion to one another surpassed the usual bond of sympathetic cousins, and, indeed, there are aspects of the diaries that imply infatuation. Hugo notes even their most casual physical contact, as when Anna places her arm on his, or their legs happen to brush while riding in a carriage. He remarks frequently on her beauty, variously describing it as "radiant," "precocious," and "disabling," and once comparing her, without his usual irony, to Rembrandt's sublime portraits of Jewish women. And then there are the insights which come of close observation, as when he tries to make sense of Anna's stern artistic will:

> When one is sickened by ugliness, tedium, stupidity, false
> feeling—by daily life, in other words—one must construct
> rigorous barriers of tact and taste in order to survive.

They walked in all weathers, at all times of day, sometimes covering the entire four kilometers of the Ringstrasse. After one such outing Hugo made this terse entry:

> Walking with A today on the Ring.
> Insolent thugs holding a meeting in the park opposite the
> Reichsrat, chanting, singing vile Reform Union songs.
> Cries of *Ostjuden*—they actually threatened us!
> I have never been so furious in my life. Still trembling six
> hours later, as I write this.
> A in a state of collapse.

Witnesses gave a decidedly sharper account of the incident, which arose not in connection with a Reform Union "meeting," but rather with a demonstration by some Christian Social toughs over the language rights bill currently paralyzing Parliament. These witnesses—including a *Dienstmann* on break and the note-bearer to the emperor's First Lord Chamberlain—said that perhaps thirty demonstrators strutted out of the park and approached the young couple, chanting "Jew, where is your patch? Jew, where is your patch?"—an obvious reference to the triangular yellow patch that Jews were required to wear before emancipation. It was unknown whether the mob specifically recognized the Kuhls, or simply assumed they were Jewish on the basis of looks; in any event, they continued chanting as they surrounded the couple, crowding in so closely that there was, as a nearby coachman put it, "a good deal of mushing about, not blows exactly." With one arm around Anna, the other fending off the mob, Hugo maintained a slow but determined progress past the park. Eventually the mob broke into laughter and fell away, manifesting a mood that was, on that day at least, more sportive than resolutely bloody.

Months later Hugo was still brooding in his diary, his humiliation evident; as for the young virtuoso, if the incident put her in a state of collapse, she recovered quickly. Within the week she traveled to Budapest and performed a program of Beethoven's C minor Concerto and Brahms's *Paganini Variations*. Her novel handling of Brahms's octave glissandos was especially stunning, the way she took them prestissimo, staccato, and pianissimo all in one, producing a feverish, nearly unbearable nervous effect which electrified the critics no less than the crowd.

"The child," Heuberger wrote in the *Neue Freie Presse*, "does not play like a child, but with the mastery of genius powered by long and serious study." The pan-German press reviewed the performance in typically viperish tones. "Like glass shattering," the *Deutsche Zeitung* said of the sounds she produced. "Her hair is almost as beautiful as Paderewski's," the *Deutsches Volksblatt* sarcastically remarked, adding, "the position of her fingers on the keys reminded one of spiders." Her fingers: though Puchel's technical exercises ensured that all fingers developed equally, the teacher had not, to this point, chosen to emphasize her sixth finger in performance, though it could be heard, or perhaps more accurately, *felt*, in the cascades of her arpeggios and brass-tinged double notes, the dizzying helium lift of her accelerando. But at some point during the spring or summer of 1899, Herr Puchel sat Anna before the *Fantasy*. Even from the beginning, practice sessions devoted to that work took place in the privacy of the Kuhls' comfortable Salesianergasse apartment, rather than in Puchel's more accessible Rathaus studio. In the interest of maximizing box-office receipts, Kornblau had decreed to Anna's inner circle that the dormant and presumed-lost *Fantasy* would be presented to the public with all the drama and mystery of a Strauss debut.

"Such an odd piece," Hugo recorded after hearing it for the first time. "And needlessly difficult; Visser's rolled chords seem impossible even for Anna's hands." Several days later he makes this entry:

> Lunch at Sacher Garden w/Anna, Hermine, Mother.
>
> When I brought up the Fantasy, the weirdness of it, A simply smiled. "Visser was enjoying himself when he wrote that," she said. "He was *being* himself, perhaps for the first time in his life. I suppose it felt like taking a deep breath after holding it in for all those years."
>
> "But do you like it?" I asked her. "The sound of the thing, I mean."
>
> Answer: "I like *him*. I like him in that particular piece, though he scares me."
>
> "Scares you?"

She laughed. "Yes, because he's flaunting it. The thing that made him different. Which seems dangerous, in a way."

Engagements throughout Europe were scheduled for the fall, among them a series in London in which she would play twenty-two Beethoven sonatas. In the midst of her preparations, Anna was approached by officials from the Ministry of Culture, requesting her, as the child prodigy and pride of Vienna, to take part in a special Wagner program. In an attempt to defuse rising political tensions, the government was promoting those aspects of culture that all of the Empire's competing factions shared. Thus it was no coincidence that Anna, a Jew, was being asked to perform Wagner, the champion of pagan vigor and Teutonic mysticism so beloved by the pan-German zealots.

And beloved, incidentally, by Anna as well; she agreed. The evening approached with much fanfare; even the emperor Franz-Josef would attend, emerging from high mourning for the late empress, stabbed to death in Geneva the previous year by the anarchist Luccheni. The program began well enough. Winkelmann roused the audience with "Der Augen leuchtendes Paar"; Schmedes and Lehman lifted them further with the "Heil dir, Sonne!" from *Siegfried*. Anna took the stage and was fairly into the Prelude from *Tristan* when jeers of "Hep! Hep!" rang out from the audience. Within moments everyone understood: a contingent of pan-Germans had taken a block of seats near the stage, and on prearranged signal they began braying the classic anti-Semitic insult. Others in the audience tried to shout them down while a phalanx of policemen came scurrying down the aisle; in the meantime Anna set her jaw and played on, furnishing heady background music for the impending riot. At the last moment, just as the police were poised to wade into the seats, the pan-Germans rose and marched out in ranks, singing "Deutschland über Alles" at the tops of their lungs.

Until now the pan-German press had, however thinly, veiled its attacks in the rhetoric of musical criticism, but now they savaged Anna with unrestrained glee. "No Jew," declared one reviewer, "can ever hope to understand Wagner," and to the list of Jew bankers, Northern Railway Jews, Jew peddlers, Jew thieves, and subversive press Jews, they now added "this Jew-girl, this performing metronome with her witch's hand and freakish improvising." And when word leaked of her intention to perform the *Fantasy* the following January, her enemies were livid. "A perversion," the *Kyffhäuser* shrieked of the *Fantasy*, seizing at once on Visser's putative Jewish origins, "an immoral composition born of the ghetto's foetid mewlings and melancholies," while the *Deutsches Volksblatt* called it "degenerate, antisocial music, full of contempt for all great ideals and aspirations." The liberal press counterattacked with accusations of revanchism and demagoguery, the pan-Germans fired back in shrill paranoid-racist style, and the battle was joined.

Herr Kornblau, of course, could not have been more pleased. The contract had already been signed for Anna's performance at the Royal Opera House on the twentieth of January; she would present the *Fantasy* in a program that, calculated for balancing effect, would include such standards as Liszt's *Love Dreams* and Beethoven's "Moonlight" Sonata, along with works by Mozart, Schumann, and Chopin. Meanwhile Anna continued her rigorous schedule of practice and performance. She played in Berlin's Kroll Hall, battling the poor acoustics, then Leipzig, Paris, and London, which brought her back to fractious Vienna in mid-November with a scathing cough and bruiselike discs beneath her eyes. Hugo was clearly worried for his cousin; *"elle travaille comme une negresse,"* he confided to his diary, and then there is this entry for November 29: "I feel as if Anna is being slowly ground up." Her name figured in the Parliamentary debates over the new, allegedly decadent, art; *Deutsches Volksblatt*, the paper of the ascendent Christian Socials, warned that "fists will have to go into action on January 20," while the writers of the Young Vienna movement published a pro-Kuhl manifesto, vowing to meet the "barbarization" of public life with an equal strength of purpose.

She gave her final concert of the century in December, at the Royal German Theater in Prague. It was, at her insistence and over her managers' objections, a program consisting entirely of Chopin. Those present said that she looked pale and strained; critics noted a fragile, almost glassine quality in her playing, which seemed to heighten rather than diminish the emotional effect. "She was dreaming," the countess Lara von Pergler recorded in her memoirs, "and she allowed us to dream with her. It is a dream which, after all these years, haunts me still." And indeed, it appears that Anna captured the rare essence of Chopin that night. Romantic and expressive, yet aristocratic and restrained, it is difficult even for masters to convey the spirit of Chopin, which is, ultimately, sadness. Not the sadness of great tragedy, but the irredeemable sadness of time itself: days pass, the world changes, and that which we most treasure must inevitably be lost.

WEDNESDAY 20 DECEMBER

To Uncle's; pretended to read while Anna practiced, then got her bundled in her cloak and out the door before Hermine et al. could come along, thank God.

Gray skies, bitter cold; plane trees along the Ring limned in snow. Walked in contented silence for a kilometer, her arm on mine. Blessed moments! We understand silence, cousin and I.

"How do you do it?" I finally asked. "What you create on the piano, how do you do it?"

A: "I concentrate, and I hear it. But I must concentrate very hard—that's the value of practice, really, learning to concentrate properly, but in a way it's not me, it's something coming through me. If I concentrate very hard it comes through me.

"Then there's this." She pulled her right hand out of her muff, shot back her sleeve, and held up her hand, examining it as one might judge a piece of fruit.

"You see this." She was smiling! Smiling as she waggled her extra finger, and blushing, her breath rapid. I was excited too. "This isn't mine either."

"Nonsense," I said. "It's yours and it's wonderful, just as everything about you is wonderful." But she only shrugged and slipped her hand back inside the muff.

At the time she was trying to master the nearly impossible fingering of the *Fantasy*, a task made harder by the fact that her hands were much smaller than Visser's—she could stretch somewhat past an octave with her left, and marginally better than that with her right. In the midst of her efforts Christmas came and went, followed by the turning of the century. Hugo duly noted the fireworks and balls in his diary, along with the latest crises in Parliament, new ideas for plays, and his obsessive running count of the city's suicides, a not unusual preoccupation in Vienna—to the mystification and endless fascination of its citizens, the Austrian capital led Europe in the self-murder statistic. He rather drily records as well his engagement to Flora Lanner, the blond, beautiful, magnificently wealthy daughter of Oskar Lanner, manufacturer of fruit conserves. By all appearances it would be a brilliant match, not least for the families' smooth pragmatism regarding matters of faith; though Jewish, the Lanners were so fully assimilated that two of Flora's brothers had been baptized in order to join the Imperial officer corps. Whether Hugo's engagement had any bearing on his cousin's fate—whether, bluntly put, he and Anna were in love, and the engagement a source of despair to her—is impossible, at this late date, to say; the chaos of two world wars, not to mention a highly efficient program of genocide, have erased much evidence that we otherwise might have had, and Hugo demonstrates in his surviving diaries a sure talent for glossing over his own emotional turbulence.

In any case, his famous cousin soon found herself the object of a nerve-shredding public hysteria. The pan-Germans continued their threats to disrupt the concert, citing as justification the "occult" fits and seizures which the *Fantasy* had induced seventy years before. The Secessionist and Young Vienna movements appropriated the young pianist as their champion, while a congeries of beards from the Conservatory accused Anna and her managers of sensationalism, fomenting needless conflict for publicity purposes. An obsessed fan worked out a dizzying mathematical correlation between the date of Visser's death and Anna's birthday, which the *Abendpost* featured in a front-page story. Professors of neurology and musicology were invited to propose theories explaining the *Fantasy*'s violent effect on listeners, while Sigmund Freud—obscure, struggling, no longer young, shunned by the medical establishment and passed over for professorship—followed the controversy from his office on the Berggasse, where he read the newspapers and wrote the *Interpretation of Dreams* in the long stretches between patient appointments.

"You don't have to do this, you know," Hugo told Anna on January 11. "Nobody would blame you for backing out." "Nor you," is the curt answer that he recorded—apropos of Flora? Mayor Lueger of the Christian Social Party said that he could not guarantee security outside the Royal Opera on the evening of the twentieth, citing "forces beyond all but the Almighty's control." But the young vir-

tuoso was nevertheless resolved. Those with access to the Kuhl
household at this time reported that Anna was the very essence of
composure. Though it seems that a phase was widely feared, and
perhaps secretly desired, among her inner circle, she practiced un-
stintingly each day, the Beethoven, the Liszt, her beloved Chopin,
and the *Fantasy* over which her fingers were gradually gaining control. Pianists will tell you that they practice in order to reduce the
risk of catastrophe, but they know that to play with complete safety
is an insult to their art. Music demands risk, a condition that Anna
seems to have embraced with near-manic devotion, as if by engaging the demons inherent in her art she might destroy all claims they
might have on her.

Overwrought fans, and on several occasions journalists, were
caught infiltrating the Kuhls' apartment house in hopes of overhear-
ing Anna practice. An old man, one Zolmar Magg of Lvov, a tanner,
was discovered to have heard Visser perform the *Fantasy* in 1831,
and the local music society appealed for funds to send him to Vienna
for the revival. And on January 16 Hugo makes this entry:

> To Uncle's in the p.m. I can hardly bear to listen to the
> thing now, this "Fantasy," this nightmare—it's like a dream in
> which you're trying to flee some hideous creature, yet for all
> your terror your legs refuse to move.

The following day the Ministry of Culture announced that it
was unilaterally canceling Anna's engagement at the Royal Opera
House, citing security concerns and the previous autumn's Wagner
debacle, for which, the Ministry's communiqué suggested, Fraulein
Kuhl was in part responsible. Even as shock resolved into shrill
outcry, a second announcement was made, this time issuing from
the Theater an der Wien, one of Vienna's oldest theaters and its

leading operetta house. The impresario Alexandrine von Schonerer, owner and director of the theater and, incidentally, estranged sister of the notorious anti-Semite George von Schonerer, had offered to suspend her current production of *Die Fledermaus* so that Anna might perform the *Fantasy* as scheduled. Kornblau publicly conveyed the Kuhls' acceptance of the offer, noting that the Theater an der Wien had generously chosen to honor all tickets for the Royal Opera venue; the following day, the eighteenth, the pan-German press went into convulsions, calling for vengeance on "the Semitic vampires and their insipid hangers-on" and once again vowing to enjoin the concert. That afternoon the Adjutant General announced that the Emperor's own First Hussars would be deployed in the streets around the theater, with orders to ensure the strictest security.

THURSDAY 18 JANUARY

Anna detached, quite removed from the outer chaos. What Kornblau, Leo, everyone fears most is a phase — Puchel looks to be on the verge of a stroke, so great is his anxiety — but it doesn't occur to any of them that a phase might be the most normal response to all of this.

And yet she carries on — meals, lessons, study, practice, all in the coolest way imaginable. A method of storing up energy, I suppose. Tonight I played Soirées de Vienne for her after dinner, then read Goethe aloud, *Italian Journey.*

"I will be at your side, every step," I told her, which she acknowledged with a grave nod. "God bless you, Hugo."

"God bless you" — the truly blessed would get her out of here, had he the slightest scrap of courage.

For the performance she chose a black, full-skirted gown with dark brocade roses, a shirred waist, and a high collar of mousseline

de soie. A light snow was falling that evening as she and her entourage departed the Salesianergasse, the flakes fine and dry as ash,
forming brilliant silver aureoles around the street lamps. Approach-
ing the theater they began to pass mounted Hussars at the street
corners, the soldiers magnificent in their blue capes with sable trim,
their crested helmets and gold-edged riding boots. Soon the streets
were filled with carriages all moving in a thick yet peaceable flow
toward the theater. As the pan-Germans had vowed, the virtuoso
experienced difficulty in reaching her destination, but it was this
mass of coaches, rather than virile nationalism, which proved to
be her sole hindrance—Anna was delayed by her own traffic jam,
in effect.

Frau von Schonerer received her at an obscure side entrance to
the theater, along with a captain of the Hussars, six uniformed police, the theater superintendent, and three muscular assistants, as
well as two plainclothes agents from the Emperor's secret police.
Anna was escorted first to her dressing room to remove her cloak,
then to a basement rehearsal space where a Bösendorfer grand
stood waiting for her final warmup. Puchel entered with Anna and
shut the door, leaving the others to endure the chilly hall while Anna
ran through fragments of her repertoire, the glorious bursts of notes
and supple noodlings followed by Puchel's muffled voice as he delivered last-minute instructions.

"So small," the Hussar captain later remarked, describing Anna
as she left the rehearsal room. "So frail and small, it seemed impossible that this delicate girl could be the cause of so much furor."
With the theater superintendent and police in the lead, Puchel and
Frau von Schonerer on either side, Anna walked amid a vast entourage back to her dressing room, thirty or more people snaking with
her through the backstage labyrinth. The captain was close at her
heels, then her parents, her uncles, Hugo and several other cousins,

Kornblau and his mistress, then a trailing flotsam of stagehands and well-connected journalists. For twenty minutes Anna sat in a corner of the dressing room while this crowd was allowed to mingle about, sampling the sumptuous buffet of meats and cheeses and admiring the flowers and telegrams sent by well-wishers. Hermine and Kornblau, still in mortal dread of a phase, sought to distract the young pianist with trivial chatter. Hugo positioned himself nearby, saying nothing, while Frau von Schonerer furnished periodic updates on the size and eminence of the audience.

"She seemed to withdraw into herself," Hugo wrote later, "to seek some deep, unfathomable place within her soul, a refuge from this ridiculous melee." Finally, at ten minutes to eight, Anna announced that she wished to be alone. Her parents and managers protested, fearing a collapse, but the girl was firm.

"I must have these last few minutes to myself."

"But at least Herr Puchel—" Hermine began.

"No one."

"Then Hugo, dear Hugo—"

"No one," Anna insisted. "I won't set foot on that stage unless I have this time alone." With difficulty, amid pleas and anxious protestations, the room was cleared and the door shut. For several minutes the entourage was forced to stare at itself out in the hall; presently the stage manager arrived to inform Frau von Schonerer that the audience was seated, the scheduled hour had come. Kornblau relayed this information through the closed door. Some said that what followed came within moments, others, that at least a minute had passed—in any event everyone heard it, a crack, a sharp report within the dressing room.

"Like a small-caliber pistol," one of the policemen said later; the captain compared it to the bark of a smartly snapped whip, while Hugo described it as the sound of a block of ice spontaneously splitting in two. For a moment no one moved, then several of the men leaped for the door, piling into an absurd heap when it refused to yield. The superintendent was pushing forward with his ball of keys when Anna spoke from within.

"I'm fine," she called in a flat, faintly disgusted voice. "I just fell, that's all. I'm fine."

The superintendent hesitated. He was still standing there, frozen, when Anna unlocked the door and stepped into the hall, her eyes firm, her carriage irreproachably straight, her face pale and fixed as a carnival mask. She proceeded down the hall with the measured walk of a bride; Hugo, who happened to be standing near the superintendent, fell into step beside her, taking her arm and guiding her through the crowd, which closed ranks behind them in a flurry of whispers. He later recounted how he spoke to her several times as they made their way to the backstage area, asking if she was well, if she'd injured herself; so great was her concentration that she seemed not to hear. He stood with her in the wings as Frau von Schonerer, with all the force of her dramatic training, gave a prolonged and eloquent introduction in which the significance of the performance was justly noted. When she concluded, as previously agreed, Anna did not appear at once; rather, she waited until Frau von Schonerer had left the stage, then stepped onto a platform empty of all save the piano and bench.

To those standing in the wings, the ovation that greeted Anna swept over the stage like a shock wave. The audience rose to its feet as if physically impelled, the thunder of hands rippling with cries of "Brave girl!" "Beautiful girl!" Anna walked toward the piano, then unaccountably veered toward the front of the stage, proceeding to the apron's far edge as if to acknowledge, even encourage the volcanic applause. Slowly, almost shyly, she removed the kerchief with which her right hand was concealed, then extended her hand toward

the audience. Witnesses said later that the effect was one of inde-
scribable horror, how the applause of those who failed to understand mixed with the gasps and shrieks of those who did, until, at
the very last, a kind of groan, a mass, despairing sigh seemed to rise
from the audience.

For, in the end, they all saw and understood: a glistening rose of
blood had taken root on Anna's hand, shining from the stump of her
severed extra finger. This was, in effect, her final performance, the
last instance on record in which she appeared in public; indeed,
from that point forward Anna Kuhl disappears so thoroughly from
history that she might have been plucked from the face of the Earth.
No explanation for her self-mutilation was ever forthcoming, neither from Anna, nor her family, nor the concert-making industry
which had so stringently run the better part of her life. Some have
surmised that heartbreak was the primary cause; others, the strain
of performing in such a charged and poisonous atmosphere, of finding herself the prey of a new, peculiarly intoxicating politics of hate.
Or perhaps she sensed, through the harrowing susceptivity of her
art, where these forces would lead us in the new century? But we
remain as pitifully ignorant as her audience, which for many moments could do no more than stare at her ruined hand. They were
in shock; many sank as if numbed to their chairs, while others staggered in a daze toward the exits, and only later, much later, would
it occur to them that the *Fantasy* was now lost forever, its score as
useless as a mute artifact, or the vaporous relic of a forgotten
dream.

Insights,
Interviews
& More . . .

Meet Ben Fountain

© Liliana Castillo

BEN FOUNTAIN is the recipient of the PEN/
Hemingway Award, the Barnes & Noble
Discover Award, an O. Henry Prize, and two
Pushcart Prizes, among other honors and
awards. He is the former fiction editor of the
Southwest Review and his fiction has been
published in *Harper's, The Paris Review,
Zoetrope: All-Story*, and *Stories from the
South: The Year's Best, 2006*. He lives with
his family in Dallas. ∾

A Conversation with Ben Fountain

Have you spent time in the places of the stories in Brief Encounters with Che Guevara?

I'VE SPENT A LOT OF TIME in Haiti, at least thirty trips since I started going in 1991. My impulse for initially going there is still a bit of a mystery to me; I'd been following the situation for a couple of years, intrigued but with no real project in mind, but it gradually dawned on me that things were happening there that I needed to explore, things having to do with power and money and history and race and the most brutal sort of blood-politics. I decided I'd try to write a novel about all that, and after a couple of months of telling myself that I could do this novel without actually having to go there—I was scared— I finally admitted to myself that, yeah, if I wanted to do the kind of book I had in mind, I really had to go. So I went; didn't know a soul, just showed up one day. It's amazing what happens when you stick yourself in a place and let things take their more or less natural course. I kept going back while I was writing the novel—which never sold, may it rest in peace—and by the time it was finished I had too many connections to Haiti to walk away. Didn't want to walk away; couldn't imagine it.

So that's the rational, speakable explanation. On another level, I think I was half-consciously looking for a shock to my system, and Haiti seemed to offer plenty of opportunities for that. But ultimately, I don't think I've ever really satisfied myself as to ▶

> ❝ My impulse for initially going [to Haiti] is still a bit of a mystery to me. ❞

how or why all this got going. Maybe these kinds of things pick you more than you pick them; in retrospect there seems to be a certain kind of inevitability to it.

When I conceived the stories set in Colombia and Burma, I very much wanted to go to these places, but my wife drew the line at that point. Can't say that I blame her; nobody was paying me to do this traveling, and we had two small kids at home, and there was the issue of whether I'd get myself in a situation that would, in retrospect, look incredibly careless and stupid. I didn't even bother mentioning to her that I wanted to go to Sierra Leone. So to write these stories I did what any writer would do—read a lot, mind-tripped a lot, and relied on imagination. Which I think are all acceptable things for a writer to do.

How do you research your writing? What kind of collaboration goes on between real life, news and politics for instance, and your own imagination?

Research is done by the saturation method; I try to get my hands on whatever is out there, and by the end of the process I'll usually have a big thick file and half a shelf full of books. I almost always reach a point where the thing seems unmanageable—I've got too much information and too little ability to handle it, but I've learned over time that this too is part of the process, the despair that comes of "oversaturation" if you will, where you think you're paralyzed. So the method, basically, is I research myself into a corner, then try to work my way out of it with the help of the

66 When I conceived the stories set in Colombia and Burma, I very much wanted to go to these places, but my wife drew the line at that point. 99

story that got me going in the first place. A number of these stories started with something in the news. "Near-Extinct Birds" began with the story of the New York Stock Exchange chairman's visit to Colombia— I had this image of the rebels collapsing in laughter at his offer to walk the floor of the exchange with them, and I started working from there. For "Asian Tiger," a blurb in the sports page about some obscure tournament in Malaysia, I think; for Sierra Leone, the sheer horror of what went on there, and the confluence of that with the diamond trade. Maybe what I'm trying to do in all this is get a handle on how things work, the human mechanics of it—how does the money or the cocaine or the golf pro start at point A and end up at point B, the daily life of what's involved in that.

These stories have a wonderful and seamless blend of plot, adventure, mystery, and important ideas. Is it ever difficult for you not to let the ideas take the upper hand?

Now that I think about it, not really. I guess I'm much more interested in what people do with ideas, or what the ideas do to them, than in the ideas themselves. I'm not much of an abstract thinker.

There is an inseparable weave in your narratives between global politics and a more dream-like personal reality. Are there other writers who have inspired you in this particular vein? ▶

66 'Near-Extinct Birds' began with the story of the New York Stock Exchange chairman's visit to Colombia— I had this image of the rebels collapsing in laughter at his offer to walk the floor of the exchange with them. 99

A Conversation with Ben Fountain
(continued)

Yes, absolutely. Robert Stone, Joan Didion, Norman Mailer, Gore Vidal. The Latin American writers, especially García Márquez and Vargas Llosa. In a rather different vein, Walker Percy.

How would you answer Alberto's statement about beauty and pleasure vs. "useful things"? ("Near-Extinct Birds of the Central Cordillera.")

Well, I guess I'd say that a person deprived of beauty and pleasure would have a lot in common with the Haitian notion of a zombie—a person disconnected from his or her soul, a person who works for others' profit but never his own, a person who mindlessly does the bidding of the boss and exists in an emotional and mental fog. So I'd say that if a person wants to be of any use to himself, he better insist on getting his fair share of beauty and pleasure. ❧

From Dixie to Haiti— The Origin of *Brief Encounters*

SOMETIMES A THING CHOOSES YOU rather than you choosing it—this is the only reasonable explanation I can offer for the origins of this book, which began with a stack of material I'd accumulated about the Caribbean country of Haiti. Or maybe it began earlier than that, much earlier, with my first awareness of the racial divide and what I seem to recall were my primary childhood responses to that: confusion, deference, shame, fear. I came to consciousness in the tidewater South of the early 1960s, where for all of that culture's cruel and rigorous insistence on segregation, blacks and whites engaged in a constant daily traffic that can only be described as intimate. We lived side by side, certainly, as well as with, around, underfoot, and on top of one another; there was no escaping the fundamental mystery that the other represented, though I think many tried, and by their denial made that mystery the maddening central fact of their lives. I remember lots of crazed, embarrassing racists from my childhood, on TV, on the radio, in proximate life. The veneers were thinner in the South, in those days. The poor side of town— that is, black—was never more than three or four blocks distant, and out in the country the evidence of a general breakdown, of some broad moral failure that by virtue of money and whiteness somehow included me, could be even rawer and more direct.

That, at any rate, is how I've come to ▶

From Dixie to Haiti—The Origin of
Brief Encounters (continued)

interpret those remembered sensations of confusion and shame. I remember as well a kind of compulsion, a near-constant mental tic of trying to imagine myself into that other world, the reality on the other side of the divide. To me it was normal, this staring and brooding, this interior acting out of a different life; in hindsight I think it was a protective device, a child's private talisman for warding off the threat that I must have felt. People carried on as if nothing extraordinary was happening, but something in my nature would not let it rest, some profound unease, a sense of artificiality, maybe. A sense of disorder beneath the evident order. Though soon enough events would show anyone with eyes to see that we'd been living on assumptions that could not be sustained.

Some twenty years later I started going to Haiti. Tropical, alien, exotic, African, with an overlay of French from the antique *colons* and loud, random slices of American pop culture, the place always stunned me sufficiently on arrival that I'd walk around with a fever for the first couple of days. I had no journalistic credentials, no corporate or government affiliation, nor any of the technical or medical skills that normally served to validate foreigners in that place. I had a vague idea for a novel, which is no validation at all. That stack of material at home had led me to conceive that Haiti might be the New World paradigm, ground zero for the confluence of forces that exploded with the coming of the Europeans. Empire, politics, power, economics, race, plus the more recent catalyst of environmental degradation—all of it, the sum total of five

> ❝ The sum total of five hundred years of complex history seemed to be coming to a boil in Haiti. ❞

hundred years of complex history, seemed to be coming to a boil in Haiti, and if I was ever going to know anything worth knowing then I had to go and see for myself.

An undertaking that might well strike others as abstract or academic, but for me it was intensely personal. I believed that I would never understand my own life, much less the lives of others, without some grasp, some dim appreciation at least, for the powers and structures that mean to control us. I spent the better part of five years on that novel, reading and writing at home between trips to Haiti, and what seems counterintuitive to me, in retrospect, is that I spent most of my time in Haiti down at street level, among those against whom power is usually applied. Every once in a while I'd snake my way into an embassy party or someone's carpeted office, and I made the best use I could of the Freedom of Information Act option, but otherwise I was on the outside looking in, and not expending much energy to change that. I suppose the more regular approach to the study of power is to examine the apparatus from the top, but Haitians have a saying: *Bay coup, blié; poté mak, sonjé.* The one who delivers the blow forgets; the one who carries the scar remembers. Remembers, which implies a further tendency to brood, reflect, study, question, analyze. In extreme situations these are tools of survival. I've found that the opinions of the screwed and abused of this world have a great deal to recommend themselves.

The novel, incidentally, got rejected all around. Some measure of painful though ▶

“ The novel, incidentally, got rejected all around. ”

From Dixie to Haiti—The Origin of
Brief Encounters (continued)

probably necessary illumination resulted
from that failure, along with a brand new set
of drastically lowered expectations. All of
this took a year or two to unfold, and in the
meantime I continued going to Haiti. I'd
always assumed that once the novel was
done I'd be excused from going again, but
the compulsion was as strong as ever. "Rêve
Haitien" was the first story to come out of this
new round of travels, and the others in the
book followed by fits and starts, with not
much more on my mind during the writing
beyond trying to get them right and hoping
to please myself. I suppose you could look at
this book as a record of my initiation into
that other world, that other reality that I kept
running into as a boy in Jim Crow's Carolina.
That's the rational explanation, anyway, the
one you tack on after the fact, though in this
case I think there's some truth in it. ❧

The Way Back

The following "Lives" column appeared in
The New York Times Magazine, *July 16, 2006.*

My great-aunt was the last survivor among
my paternal grandfather's many brothers
and sisters, and so her death, when I was
in my early twenties, marked the passing
of a generation—a more special death than
most, the implications a bit more urgent for
those who cared to notice. By this time our
extended family was thoroughly urbanized,
but on the day of her funeral a hundred of
us gathered at the small church in lowland
tobacco country which had been home
ground for two hundred years, and we did
the old drill: hymns, prayers, eulogies, a stiff
Presbyterian sermon, all without the benefit
of air-conditioning, which seemed apt, given
the retrograde nature of the day. After the
service I stepped out onto the church's tiny
portico and looked off past the shade trees
and the small, neat cemetery, out to the rows
of tobacco and the deckle-edged woods hazed
in the distance, sealing off the horizon like the
rim of a bowl. I suppose the emotion of the
day had something to do with it, the sudden
compression of past and present, but at that
moment the place seemed so beautiful to me,
so resonant, so truly and completely home
that I thought my heart would break, and
then it hit me: I've got to get out of here.

This wasn't as clean a revelation as it might
seem. First college and now law school were
already drawing me away, but that moment
on the church steps clinched it: if I stuck
around, the cumulative weight of family ▶

> **❝** On the day
> of [my great-
> aunt's] funeral
> a hundred of us
> gathered at the
> small church in
> lowland tobacco
> country. **❞**

11

and history and place, a kind of endlessly repeating nostalgic fog, would keep me from something that seemed important. I wasn't sure what that other thing was, but shortly after graduation I left the state. I ended up making my home 1,400 miles away, and I've kept going ever since, at times finding myself in places that have seemed only slightly less foreign than the moon.

To leave the place where you grew up, and that you love very much—I expect there's some sort of avoidance strategy working there, ambivalence expressed as a compulsion, but along the way a strange inversion occurred: although I didn't stay home, home stayed with me, and in many respects that's the only place it still exists. When I was growing up in the sixties and seventies, the South was still overwhelmingly rural, poor, arcane, antique—past-haunted, to put it in romantic terms. For a dreamy kid preoccupied with textures of time and place, seeing things as they'd been seventy or eighty or one hundred years ago was often as simple as walking a few steps or turning your head, framing the view in such a way that got rid of the odd power line or asphalt strip. Given terrain this complicit with imagination, it was easy to make that other, older place appear right before your eyes.

All that, or most of it, has changed, of course. So much of the South has been transformed that when I go back to visit my parents, I usually find myself floundering around some new section of superhighway or the latest eruption of suburban sprawl. Sure, you can go home again, but you'll probably get lost a lot.

66 Sure, you can go home again, but you'll probably get lost a lot. 99

Several summers ago, a trip to the beach took us through home ground again. By going a few miles out of our way, we would pass the house where my mother grew up, a two-story wood-frame built in the 1840s by my great-great-grandfather. Some time ago my mother sold the house, and I hadn't seen it in more than twenty years. By now I'd learned that to return to a remembered place is to risk ruining the thing archived in your mind; you'd better have good reasons for running that risk, something more to be gained than the vague playing out of aimless sentiment. But my kids were with me; I wanted them to see. There was a new highway to negotiate, and what landmarks remained barely matched up with my memory, but in the end we found our way to it, the dirt lane that teed into the old paved road like an oxbow to the side of the new highway. I parked on the shoulder and we climbed out, and I pointed to the white farmhouse a half-mile away across the hedgerows and groomed fields. We're stopping here, I told my kids, because we don't know the people who live there—the sort of explanation that explains nothing at all.

The house seemed so sharp and clear in the afternoon light that I might have been looking through binoculars: distance temporarily bridged, but not negated; the object clarified, but no closer. Some kind of compaction, reduction, confirmed the distance, and maybe that's where the ache came from, all that empty space. You would never mistake this nearer view for proximity, but from where I stood that day, a half-mile distant and across twenty years, the house looked the same, and that was almost enough. ❧

Author's Picks
Works That Cross the Divide

THE RAINY SEASON by Amy Wilentz

Part memoir, part reportage from Wilentz's years in Haiti following the fall of the Duvalier regime.

"BEYOND THE MOUNTAINS" by Mark Danner

This three-part series on Haiti was published in *The New Yorker* in the issues of November 27, December 4, and December 11, 1989, and won the National Magazine Award for Reporting in 1990. "Beyond the Mountains" is the best primer I've found on Haitian history, culture, and politics; www.markdanner.com delivers the full text. Danner's *Massacre at El Mozote*, which deals with the events and aftermath of the massacre of an entire Salvadoran village by an "elite" U.S.-trained Salvadoran army unit, is a masterful study of ideology, blood-politics, and systematic deception.

SAMBA; THE HEART THAT BLEEDS; LOOKING FOR HISTORY by Alma Guillermoprieto

Three explorations of Latin America by one of the best writers working today.

THE IMMACULATE INVASION by Bob Shacochis

Recounts 1994's "soft" American invasion of Haiti which restored Aristide to power.

66 'Beyond the Mountains' is the best primer I've found on Haitian history, culture, and politics. 99

NOTES FROM THE LAST TESTAMENT: THE STRUGGLE FOR HAITI by Michael Deibert

This unflinching book continues the story of post-Duvalier Haiti that began with Wilentz's *Rainy Season* and continued with Shacochis's *Immaculate Invasion*.

SALVADOR; MIAMI; THE LAST THING HE WANTED by Joan Didion

The extraordinary reportage of *Salvador* and *Miami* is distilled into powerful fictional form in *The Last Thing He Wanted*.

BEST NIGHTMARE ON EARTH by Herbert Gold

A lively memoir of one American's forty-year love affair with Haiti.

DIVINE HORSEMEN: THE LIVING GODS OF HAITI by Maya Deren

In the course of explicating Haitian voodoo, Deren produced a masterful study of human nature and experience.

CHASING CHE by Patrick Symmes

Symmes ships his motorcycle to Argentina and replicates the journey made famous by *The Motorcycle Diaries*.

A FLAG FOR SUNRISE by Robert Stone

Stone's depiction of Americans in the fictional Central American country of Tecan is one of the seminal novels of the twentieth century.

> " [Robert] Stone's depiction of Americans in the fictional Central American country of Tecan is one of the seminal novels of the twentieth century. "

Author's Picks *(continued)*

**ALL SOULS' RISING; MASTER OF THE
CROSSROADS; THE STONE THAT THE
BUILDER REFUSED by Madison Smartt Bell**

Bell's splendid trilogy of historical
novels recounts the Haitian revolution
of 1791–1804. ∽

Don't miss the next
book by your favorite
author. Sign up now for
AuthorTracker by visiting
www.AuthorTracker.com.